1 St Ed

400
Brattle Street

400
Brattle Street

GEORGE WOLK

Wyden Books

FIRST EDITION

Trade distribution by Simon and Schuster
A Division of Gulf + Western Corporation
New York, New York 10020

Designed by Tere LoPrete

Library of Congress Cataloging in Publication Data

Wolk, George.
  400 Brattle Street.

    I. Title.
PZ4.W8597Fo   [PS3573.0565]   813'.5'4   78–13423
ISBN   0–88326–154–5

To Susan

400
Brattle Street

Chapter One

The night before it began, there were two men in a parked car in Detroit—one black, the other white. The white man was behind the wheel. He wasn't tall, but he was broad shouldered, barrel-chested, and heavy. He took up more than his share of the front seat.

The black man would have been prettier if he'd had a chin. He had a cold or a cocaine habit, swiped at his nose periodically with a white Kleenex, and sniffed. He had small eyes that kept darting from side to side as if he were afraid he was about to be attacked. His name was Harvey.

"He'll come out any time now; you'll see, Mr. McGraw," Harvey said. "He's been in there, in the back room, every night this week, testing the men."

"With the polygraph?"

"Yes, sir. With the polygraph." Harvey swiped at his nose with the Kleenex. "The men get the polygraph test to make sure they aren't planning a double cross." After a time Harvey added, "I don't know why no one ever thought of it before."

"Neither do I," McGraw said.

"Maybe they have. Maybe you have to pass a lie-detector

test to get in the Mafia." Harvey sniffed; he left the Kleenex against his nose a moment longer than usual.

"You think the man with the polygraph is from the Mafia?" McGraw asked.

"I don't know."

McGraw cleared his throat—it was a habit he had—and slipped four fingers of his right hand into the side pocket of his sport coat. It was the position in which he was most comfortable during a stakeout. He'd been doing this sort of thing for over thirty years, sitting in parked cars, watching doorways, waiting. He had done it first for the House Un-American Activities Committee. After that he'd done it for the FBI. If this time the people he was doing it for were left wing, the same kind of people he had once done it to, he could live with that. It wasn't that he'd changed his politics; he'd always put work first.

"Tell me about Mr. Johnson," he said to Harvey.

"I already told you. No one does anything in this neighborhood without Mr. Johnson getting a cut or knowing about it or making him sorry he did it."

"Has Johnson had the polygraph test?"

Harvey sniffed and showed his teeth. Obviously the idea amused him. He opened his mouth wide, then shrugged and closed it.

The car in which the men were talking was parked down the street from a single-story rectangular stucco building with a red neon sign in the high front window: Jack's. It was almost midnight, and there was a handful of mixed stars against the summer sky. The men had been waiting behind a row of parked cars for almost an hour. A new Lincoln Continental went slowly past. Then for some time there was no traffic at all.

"Does he leave the polygraph there, or does he take it with him every night?" McGraw asked.

"He takes it," Harvey said. "Look, when he comes out, you put the money in my hand, and I'll be gone." He wiped his nose again. "I have seen some dangerous men, but this one is the worst."

"How do you mean worst?" McGraw asked.

"He smiles too much," Harvey said.

"Do you know what he's planning, Harvey?"

Harvey shook his head. "I already told you what I know."

McGraw reached further into his pocket. He was still watching the doorway steadily through the windshield of the automobile. He felt for the hundred-dollar bill he had stashed, found it, and held it out.

Harvey shook his head again. "Just that there's talk about guns. Military guns. Rapid-fire. M-16's. Nothing I didn't already tell you."

McGraw put the money back in his pocket. He hadn't said anything to Harvey when he'd offered it to him, and he hadn't said anything when he'd withdrawn the offer. Nothing had to be said. McGraw and Harvey understood each other. It sometimes seemed to McGraw that he'd spent half his life in close quarters with informers and small-time hoods. He cleared his throat again. Two men, both black, left the bar and walked the other way. After awhile two others went in. A small truck went by, then a Volvo that needed a valve job.

Suddenly a white man left the bar carrying a large suitcase.

"Look, that's him!" Harvey said. "Give me the money."

"Jesus, he's big," McGraw said.

"That's right; he's big."

The man was about six foot six and two eighty. He put the suitcase in the trunk of a Chevrolet, closed it, and started toward the door on the driver's side.

"Give me the money," Harvey said again.

Without taking his eyes away from the big man, McGraw handed over the hundred-dollar bill. At once Harvey let himself out of the car and was gone.

The big man got behind the wheel of the Chevrolet and

pulled away from the curb. McGraw started his engine and went after him.

It was possible, at first, for McGraw to stay well back, but soon the Chevrolet turned into a side street. McGraw had to take a chance. He stepped on the accelerator and turned into the street only a few seconds later. The Chevrolet was there. McGraw slowed down.

The big man turned several times. Each time McGraw stayed with him. On a street lined with warehouses, the man finally pulled over to the curb. A half block away, McGraw pulled his automobile behind a truck and turned off the lights.

McGraw got out quietly. Ahead, he saw the big man bent over the trunk of the Chevrolet. He saw him lift the suitcase, shut the trunk, and walk into an alley.

When McGraw got to the alley, he put his hand on the butt of his .38 and withdrew it. It was too dark to see more than a few feet ahead. For a moment McGraw waited for a sound or a light to give him some idea what the big man was doing or where he had gone, and for his eyes to grow used to the dark. When no light and no sound came, he moved forward again, softly, slowly.

Twenty yards in, the alley turned ninety degrees, and McGraw made out the shape of several large cardboard cartons, stacked as high as he was. Further on there were more of the same. Then the alley became narrower. McGraw could just make out a low fence on his right and the rear wall of one of the warehouses on his left. When he had gone three more steps, he stumbled against the suitcase the big man had been carrying.

McGraw swung around too late. The big man had already vaulted from behind the low fence and was coming at McGraw like a shadow. In a continuing motion, he kicked the automatic out of McGraw's hand. McGraw put all his force into his left fist and his fist into the big man's stomach. Nothing happened. That close, McGraw could see the man's face. His expression had been benign. It remained benign as he backslapped McGraw and shoved him back, staggering, against the warehouse wall.

McGraw hit the brick with the flat of his back and came off it. He spread his arms wide as he attacked and brought his right foot up, with as much speed and force as a fifty-two-year-old man can be expected to muster, directly into the big man's groin.

The man's expression never changed.

"What are you, a machine?" McGraw whispered. "Or a castrato?"

The big man's eyes were wide and happy; his smile was so serene, his expression so angelic, McGraw almost let down his guard.

"My name is David," he said softly. His voice was so sweet, he might have been talking to a woman he planned to proposition.

"You fool them; that's it, isn't it? You let them use the machine on you, and you fool them with it. That's how the hell you penetrate in the first place. You're a goddamn robot."

David backslapped McGraw again, too fast for McGraw to see it coming. McGraw went down. Then David moved in for the kill. He took a revolver from underneath his jacket. McGraw knew he was going to use it.

Far away, inside one of the warehouses, a telephone rang. There was a several-second interval, then it rang again.

David straightened and turned toward the sound. The revolver in his hand was aimed at McGraw, but his attention was momentarily distracted.

For a split second McGraw was dumbfounded that a ringing phone had provided him with an opportunity to save his life. Then he acted. He slashed violently at the big man's wrist with the side of his right hand, making him drop the revolver. He scrambled quickly over the low fence. He found an alley and ran down it about as fast as he had run when he had played football for Notre Dame in 1947. He ran very fast.

/ 2 /

Dawn rose over New Jersey, and a soft, spare light spread over Camden, Collingswood, Gloucester City, and Merchantville. It spread over West Depford, where the refinery was. Just enough light leaked from the ridge of the eastern sky to bring up the dark form of the forty-thousand-ton tanker that had been anchored in the Delaware River off the refinery shore, in position to unload since sundown the night before.

Standing on the foredeck in the darkness above the boatswain's stores and the forepeak tank, a man known as Lawrence Douglas watched a rose-colored finger of cloud for a moment, then looked carefully along the shoreline between the river and the refinery. At first he could see nothing more than he had been able to see for the last hour. Then from a point about a half mile away, where the rows of storage tanks rose like black fists against the sky, came a needlepoint of light. Then it was gone.

It was what he had been waiting for. He had a flashlight. Using his body as a shield, he depressed the button once. He put the flashlight back in his pocket.

He had a rangy, athletic build, an oblong, equine face, and an angelic expression exactly like that of David in Detroit. He was standing in the bow of the tanker as if he owned it, the land, the river, the entire universe.

Lawrence sensed something behind him and turned. He heard footsteps approaching from the direction of the house amidships, about a half a football field away. Soon he saw the outline of a man.

"You been out here long?" a voice asked.

"Who's there?"

"It's your chief, Lawrence. What're you doing?"

"Nothing, Chief."

"The watch told me he thought he saw someone out here.

I figured it'd be you. You're a spooky son of a bitch, you know that?"

"If you say so."

"If I say so. If I say so," the chief said sarcastically.

He came closer to Lawrence along the deck. His posture was as rigid as his voice. For a few moments he stood looking out at the refinery, where the shadows of the square mile of pumping and converting plants, processors, and holding tanks were becoming clearer against the bleak sky.

There was absolute silence. To the south the house amidships was a black mass against a black background. The unloading hose and boom, in place since the night before, were entirely invisible. Only the two derricks for the dry stores could be seen clearly. They loomed like giant insects behind Lawrence's head as he stood watching the chief.

"I swear, I never knew a man like you," the chief said. "You on dope or—what the—"

There had been a second pinpoint of light, this one in the river about twenty yards offshore.

The chief turned, stared at Lawrence and at the flashlight in his pocket. "There's something going on out there! You're part of it, aren't you? All right Lawrence, are you going to tell me what's happening?"

"Of course," Lawrence said. "If you ask politely."

The chief took a .22-caliber pistol from his jacket pocket and came forward.

"I'll ask you politely," the chief said. *"Please* tell me what's going on out there; *please* tell me very quickly, or I'll put a hole in you. Understood?"

"Of course, Chief."

"Tell it!"

"All right, Chief. Seven men in two rubber rafts drifted down from a side street just this side of West Depford and entered the refinery grounds at three A.M. Timed charges have been placed on all refinery installations, except those immediately against the fence to the highway and immediately against the checkpoint at the entrance. There are three night watchmen who walk the shoreline and the roads. They will all be dead."

The chief had grown wide-eyed. His mouth had opened and his breath had become quick. Despite Lawrence's constant smile, the chief believed him. Abruptly he raised his revolver and fired once into the air.

Lawrence sprang forward as the shot resounded, but the chief was fast, too. He brought the pistol down quickly and fired again. A bullet ripped into Lawrence to the left and below his collarbone.

Despite his wound, Lawrence took hold of the revolver with his left hand and put his right elbow and the full force of his body against the chief's face. The chief went sprawling against the ship's rail. The pistol came loose.

Lawrence stood over the chief. He wore precisely the same smile he had been wearing before he was shot. Blood was pouring heavily from the bullet hole, dark against his light shirt.

Someone, perhaps several men, were coming from amidships at a run.

"Say good-bye, Chief," Lawrence said.

Lawrence leaped to the rail. He raised both arms over his head smoothly and dived. His body fell evenly toward the water; there was a splash, and he was gone.

The chief got to his feet. He held on tightly to the rail and peered at the river, but he could see nothing. He looked out to the spot where he had seen the light, but if there were anyone there, it was still too dark to make them out.

Two men arrived.

"It was Douglas. I shot him," the chief told them.

"What?"

"There was a signal light from the river. He said he was a saboteur." The chief didn't seem to believe his own words. He repeated, "A saboteur! He said the plant is set to go up.

Get to the radio! Get back to the radio! Warn the plant! Call the Coast Guard!"

"Go!" one of the men shouted.

The second man turned and ran back toward the house amidships as the chief strained to make out what was happening below.

"I put a bullet into him, and he came at me as if it hadn't touched him! He dived like an athlete."

There was still no sign of Lawrence or of any rafts.

"Spook!" the chief said. "I tell you I put a bullet into him!"

A mile away, near the extreme land edge of the refinery, one of the big, round storage tanks exploded. There was a flare of red that shamed the dawn.

"Oh my God," the chief said.

A second went up, then a third. One after another the holding tanks on the far perimeter exploded into fire. The far edge of the refinery, over a mile long, became a fence of fire. Over the brilliant red, orange, and yellow flames, black smoke poured toward the gray heavens.

"Jesus God!" the other man yelled. He stared at the chief wide-eyed. The two men held each other's gaze for several seconds.

Together they leaped for the rail. Just as they went over, the ship burst at its center. The sound of the explosion broke against them like a tidal wave. The force of it hurled them, turning them over and over, toward the shore.

First the chief saw the refinery, the far perimeter ablaze, then he saw the ship, burst and on fire, then the refinery, then the ship again.

The oil from the ship poured into the Delaware. On shore tank after tank and plant after plant went up. The explosions went on for some time.

/ 3 /

One hundred miles south by southwest, a private jet touched the tarmac at Dulles International Airport and screamed down the runway between the rows of lights. When it had taxied to the terminal and had stopped, the pilot got out of his seat and went to see to the single passenger: a robust man who wore a full, gray, neatly trimmed beard without moustache, like a Pennsylvania Dutchman's, and who had prematurely gray hair, medium length, neatly combed. The passenger seemed cheerful, comfortable, and in charge. His face, framed by the farmer's beard, was interesting and easy to look at, the face of a favorite uncle. His name was Thomas Pauling.

"Did you have a pleasant flight, sir?"

"Yes, thank you, Ahmed."

"Then I will be pleased to tell that to Mohammed Ibn Saud Imani. He asked that I give you this." The pilot handed him an envelope.

Disentangling himself from his safety belt, Pauling got to his feet. When the pilot opened the cabin door for him, he descended and walked to the terminal. He was six feet tall and had an easy, loping gait. As he had done a thousand times before, he handed his passport to the uniformed official in the customs box.

"You've come on a private flight from London, Mr. Pauling?"

"Yes."

"No luggage."

"No."

"I'll take you through the baggage check then, sir. This way."

"Thank you."

"Go right on ahead, sir."

Pauling walked from the building under a sky in which a

few stars were discernible despite the increasing light. He went toward the lot where he had left his car. If he was tired, he didn't show it. When he had found his Porsche, he paused for a moment with one hand on the roof of the automobile to stare at the dawn. Then he let himself into the car. As the oil pressure came up, he took the envelope the pilot had given him, carefully opened it, and flipped on the overhead light.

Please do not allow anything to provoke you to un-usual action for us—check with me first. There may be more to any situation than might be revealed by even a careful examination. My fondest regards to your new wife, and again, congratulations to you both.

Mo

"Awfully cryptic, Mohammed," Pauling muttered to him-self.

He reached into his jacket pocket and withdrew a palm which held a scattering of yellowish pebbles, their value ap-proximately a thousand dollars a carat.

Pauling put the diamonds back in his pocket, turned off the light, and put the car in gear. He paid the young man at the gate of the parking lot and drove toward his house in George-town.

He looked like a farmer, but Thomas Pauling ran, and had run for several years, a firm of Washington-based consultants whose real work was covert intelligence and private investiga-tion. For twenty years, until U.S. policy in Southeast Asia—Pauling had been stationed there—temporarily soured him on government service, Pauling had been employed by the CIA. Because that was well known in certain circles, and be-cause it was suspected Pauling maintained working contact with the agency, he had done very well; he had become financially independent very quickly.

Pauling had, for instance, just finished laundering a sum

of money for the Saudis. He had also been the Saudis' un-official lobbyist in Washington. The diamonds were unofficial payment for the unofficial work.

Pauling turned onto the highway for Georgetown. As the sky to the east grew lighter, he realized he felt tired but remarkably good, as if he had spent the last six hours chopping wood in open country instead of crossing the Atlantic in a small jet. That knack he had, that ability to experience a sense of well-being in almost any circumstance, was what Marcia gave as the reason she had married him. Maybe it was true.

When he arrived, he parked in front of the garage and walked across the lawn to the front door. It was a large brick house on a double lot between a similar one owned by a man who worked for the State Department and a white clapboard structure lived in by someone in the Department of the Army. He let himself in, turned quickly to shut off the automatic alarm—otherwise it would have alerted both Marcia and the police—and bent down to rub the black Labrador bitch who had turned over on her back and was whining and wagging her tail as if he had been away a year, not less than twenty-four hours.

"Come on," he said. "Come on, Miss Margo."

The dog followed him to his study where Pauling turned on the light, put the diamonds on his desk, and his jacket over his desk chair. Then he hit a button on the tape machine on the bookshelf behind him and listened while Marcia's recorded, husky voice spoke to him.

"Nothing very important at the office or on the news tonight. But I taped the NBC version while I watched it, in case you wanted to keep up before you went to bed. They gave Grace Argent a minute."

There was a pause. "Tom, Michael's here. I told him he could sleep in his old room. He's been having a hard time with his mother, I assume." After another pause she added, "When you're ready, come up and see me."

Pauling smiled. He turned off the tape machine and went to the TV recorder to hit the appropriate button.

While John Chancellor talked to him about a killing in Chicago and promised to tell him about rising oil prices and their effect on inflation, he loosened his tie and went to work on the combination safe in the top of his desk. He placed the diamonds in the safe, closed it, spun the lock, and replaced the piece of teak that hid it.

Chancellor had been interrupted by a shot of an offshore oil installation, which wasn't news but a commercial. Pauling took the envelope and the note the pilot had handed him and fed it into the shredder beside his waste basket.

He watched the program for a few minutes more, enduring several features of no immediate interest, waiting for Grace Argent to make her appearance. He petted Miss Margo, who had come over and put her head on his thigh.

Pauling was a man whose life had turned. When he had been recruited for government service in his senior year at Loyola, he had been a conservative Republican, a rabid patriot, and a Catholic. Now, he was none of the above. Like some men whose politics change one hundred eighty degrees in later life, Pauling had been completely shaken out of the mold he had once accepted.

The CIA had been partially responsible. Most of the men Pauling had worked with in the agency were staunchly anti-totalitarian but liberal. Almost all were atheists. If they had not won Pauling over to their position, they had certainly helped him to lose his own. So had his experiences abroad.

Once he had changed, he changed his life. He went into business for himself. He asked a woman eighteen years his junior to marry him, and she had done it.

If contradictions remained, if he worked for people like the Saudis whose politics he did not love, he could live with it. He put the work first. He did what he enjoyed doing and what he did well.

Finally the segment Marcia had referred to came on the

TV. Grace Argent, a congresswoman from New York and once Pauling's client, was shown outside a congressional committee room. Her committee was investigating possible links between the Mafia and the CIA. Argent said that there was a rat in the pantry, and that she intended to go in with a broom and kill it. The implication was that the rat was the CIA, and the pantry was the country. She said there was a cover-up. She was going to do her best to expose it. Then John Chancellor came back on to talk about crops, and the screen showed acres of half-grown corn.

Pauling shut off the machine. With his jacket over his shoulder, he left his study, petted the dog again, and went to the kitchen to give her a Milk Bone. He took his blood-pressure pill with a half glass of milk—as long as he took the pills, he had no symptoms—and went up the stairs. The dog stayed below.

Michael's old room was under the eaves. When Pauling's eyes became accustomed to the dark, he went over to stare down at his son.

Michael was seventeen, seventeen and a half September ninth. His face was like Pauling's but heavier, his hair light blond. He lacked his father's general good cheer, but he might someday get some.

Michael's mother—and Asher's and Robert's—had left him ten years before, when Pauling was still in the agency. She said she couldn't stand her life. She said being legally alone, raising the children alone, in some other house, in some other town, would allow her to keep her sanity. If it had, Pauling never noticed. He was not unaware that the changes in himself had aggravated her problems. He left Michael and went to his own bedroom, where he hung away his jacket and began to undress.

"I hope that's you," Marcia said.

"And I hope it's you."

"What happened?"

"Nothing unexpected, until the pilot handed me a note.

Mohammed seems to think we'll be provoked to look into something for him without checking with him first."

"That's ominous." She turned on the low light beside her on the table.

"Yes. Anyway, he warned us off. What's with Mikey? Why is he here?"

"He wouldn't say. He doesn't like me well enough to tell me his troubles."

"Good."

Marcia laughed. It was an enticing sound.

"Mohammed sends his congratulations to you for winning me, by the way, and about forty carats in uncut diamonds."

"Nice. About the diamonds."

"Yes."

"Are you coming to bed?"

"I'm tired as hell."

"And getting old too."

He snorted. He went to the bedroom door and locked it, just as he had done when there had been children in that house every night. Then he returned to Marcia.

She had long, bright yellow hair, large brown eyes, and a sunshine smile. Her pleasant features gave her an open, earthy look. Pauling would not have argued with anyone who wanted to call her beautiful, but he didn't think of her as a beauty. She was too real for that, too present.

It also helped that she was without question the one best agent—male or female—Pauling had worked with since he'd been in the business, that she had a particular knack he relied on. It enabled her to penetrate complicated situations and complicated people.

Not that he had asked her to marry him because she had yellow hair and was a good spy. He'd asked her, he supposed, for the same reason she gave for having said yes. She was centered. She emitted well-being and good cheer.

The digital clock on her side of the bed read six twenty-three before he finally fell asleep.

/ 4 /

In Cambridge that morning, it was raining too fast and too hard for the drains; on Brattle Street, about a half mile down from Harvard Square, the water was almost as high as the curbs. Lightning rent the sky, followed immediately by a terrific redoubling thunder. The torrent of water hit the roofs of the cars and the trees and houses and pavements. There was a sudden easing of the downpour as the storm moved away. The thunder sounded further off, separated from the lightning that had preceded it by almost a full second. The level of water above the asphalt of Brattle Street went down a half inch, and the woman at the window of the top floor of number 400, who wasn't quite as beautiful as Botticelli's *Primavera,* and not nearly as white, pulled her summer robe more tightly around her and turned away from the weather to face her bedroom.

Her name was Rita Facett, she was twenty-nine, and she had jet black hair and dark chocolate skin with highlights of reddish brown. She was lucky not to have been even more beautiful; it was difficult to make people believe she had an M.D. and a Ph.D. as it was. She was lucky to be a quarter inch short of dazzling.

She was a psychiatrist, an expert in narcosynthesis—the induction of revelations of trauma from drug-induced deep hypnotic states—and had been with the Weldmore Institute as one of the resident psychiatrists for over three years. But Dr. Facett's first-line responsibility was to act as the institute's liaison with its sponsor, the Central Intelligence Agency.

Facett walked to the sink—all the rooms on the upper floor except the dormitory had plumbing—and was about to wash, when the intercom on her bureau sounded. She depressed the tab, which was like the tab on a pop-up toaster.

"Yes."

It was Harold Berger, the institute's director. He was a baritone, his accent Bostonian, his attitude professorial. "Rita, did I wake you?"

"No."

"Good. Good. I didn't think you'd be able to sleep through this. I hope the power doesn't go out. I don't want to have to fool with the generator."

Outside there was another peal of thunder.

"Why should the power go out?"

"You're right, of course. Nevertheless, I seem to be worried about the power. I seem to worry about a lot of unnecessary things lately; I don't really understand it. Rita, could you come to my office before you have your breakfast?"

"All right."

The intercom clicked; it was unlike Berger to break off a conversation abruptly. Shrugging, Facett went back to what she'd been doing.

A few minutes later, Dr. Facett left her room. She walked down the narrow carpeted corridor past the rooms for the staff and the graduated trainees. Instead of waiting for the small elevator, she took the stairs.

She went to one of the several soundproofed programming chambers on the second floor. She thought Berger wanted to ask her about her work, and she had left her notes there the day before. With the help of a trainee assistant, she had been listing results in a biofeedback experiment in which a guinea pig—human—was made to consciously re-create a childhood trauma discovered through hypnotherapy. Eventually the re-creation would no longer produce changes in his pulse rate, blood pressure, or body temperature.

Berger's office was on the main floor. Facett knocked, entered, and smiling to Berger, took a chair in front of his desk. Mark Harriman was standing behind the director. She had less than a smile for him. He was the other Weldmore psychiatrist, and his techniques of inducing permanent trance and deeper states of willed trance had proved superior to

Facett's. Harriman relied upon what he called "a yogic ladder of personal transformation" to turn the trainees into superior intelligence agents, and he kept certain aspects of his technique secret. All the experiments and procedures on which she had been working recently were his.

"Good morning, Reets," Harriman said.

Harriman was in his late thirties, but he looked younger. He was slender, his face was pale—he'd been too long indoors—and he had a heavy lower lip. His lip had once made Facett guess that he'd been overmothered. He was almost Hollywood handsome, dark haired, dark eyed. He had so well mastered self-hypnosis, he could put knitting needles through his upper arm without pain and without excessive bleeding. Facett had seen him do it; it was quite a trick. There were other things he could do that made him awesome—and hateful. He was fluent in French, German, and several dialects of Chinese. He showed off in restaurants. He always had money, all he wanted; and he disdained what he considered small amounts of it. Facett had once found him washing his sports car with a new Brooks Brothers' shirt. He had perfect pitch, a great talent for music; he had surprised her once by sitting down at a piano and composing a song for her. He had called it *Sweet Rita*.

Harriman was usually placid or running one of his acts: fury, disdain, mad scientist, or uninhibited lover. Facett had seen and loathed all of them. At the moment he was placid. He reached up, touched his nose, ran his fingers along an imaginary moustache, and dropped his hand. Facett must have seen him do that a thousand times.

"I asked you not to call me Reets," she said. "If you can't call me Rita, you can call me Dr. Facett."

"Oh, I'm sorry, *Rita,*" Harriman said. He smiled.

Berger said, "Good morning, Rita. I'm sorry to have made you come down quite so early. Mark wanted to talk to you."

Berger was in his late fifties, thin, and completely bald. He was divorced and, Facett believed, unhappy. Lately he would stare straight into her eyes until she was convinced he had lost all track of what they were talking about. When this happened, it always came as a complete shock when he picked up the conversation where it had left off.

"Then why didn't Mark—"

"Because I have to say this," Berger's tone became unusually distant. "Mark wants to take you to his operations room. I want you to go with him. I want you to cooperate with him in every way you can."

"Is that an order, Harold?"

"Short of sex, of course," Harriman put in jocularly.

"Of course," Berger said. "Yes, it's an order. Please go."

Berger shut his eyes and Harriman came forward. He had been standing in front of the open curtains on the Harvard side of the building. Although it was almost seven thirty in the morning, it was still dark, the thunderstorm still heavy in the sky above.

"Come on, Reets, it won't be so bad," Harriman said.

"Damn it," she said. She looked to Berger for help, but his eyes were still closed. When he opened them, he reached for a file at the back of his desk. He was immediately concentrated on its contents.

"This way," Harriman said.

Grudgingly, Facett followed him out of the office.

He insisted they take the elevator down because it was small, made them almost touch. In the basement he showed her past the glass doors to the room containing the Rand computer— he nodded to Levine, the machine operator; then he used his key to the door of his inner sanctum.

She had not been allowed in that room for over a year, not since Harriman had learned how to control her as easily as he controlled the trainees who graduated from his yogic ladder.

She didn't know what small thing to complain of first. She could have started anywhere. The nickname he had used for her when they had been lovers. The appropriation of half the basement for his secret games.

"This way," he said. "In here." He used another key to switch on the lights.

A motion-picture screen was set up on the far side of the room. On the wall behind it, and almost entirely hidden by it, was an enormous photograph. Berger? She could see the top of a bald head. About a dozen folding chairs were set up facing the screen.

"Sit down, Dr. Facett," Harriman said softly.

When she was seated, he turned off the lights and hit the switch on the projector.

"I thought you'd want to know how things are in the country."

"Damn you," she said. "God take you to hell."

Harriman chuckled. "God," he said.

The film had been taken at the farm. She recognized the red house and the weathered barn from photographs he had shown her. Harriman loved farms. He had an acquaintance of theirs, a physicist, working on some secret project on still another one.

There was a sound track to the film, but as yet there had been nothing but a low hum and the slamming of a car door.

The scene shifted toward tall, late-summer growth in a field—sumac, she thought—then showed a ten-year-old black boy lying still in the grass. Suddenly the boy jumped up and stuck out his tongue at the camera.

She sighed deeply.

"Yes, quite healthy," Harriman said.

"I hate you," she told him. "I hate you so very much."

"I appreciate that," he said.

The camera moved back, and Lawrence Douglas, the agent with the equine face who had been on the tanker that morning, appeared. He called to the boy, who turned, startled, and backed away.

"If he hurts him," she breathed.

"What?" Harriman said.

Lawrence withdrew a gun from the rear pocket of his blue jeans and pointed it at the boy who continued to look frightened and to back away.

Lawrence called, "Hey you." The boy stopped moving. They were closer to the brush, and now Facett was sure it was sumac, tall sumac.

Lawrence went up to the boy and put the gun to his head. The boy shouted, "No! No!" Lawrence fired. Blood appeared in a sudden gush on the far side of the boy's head as he fell over into the tall grass.

Facett screamed. She stood up, her breath coming faster and faster. She could not believe what she had seen. She could not believe it.

At once the boy appeared on camera again, laughed, waved, and showed off the false wound. It had been an act. It had all been an act.

Harriman switched off the projector and turned on the lights. Facett regained her seat. She was still breathing too quickly. There was a pain deep in the center of her chest. When she looked up at the screen, it was white. She stared at the slice of bald head behind it.

"You see what it could be like," Harriman said.

Facett said nothing.

"Right now he's still all right. He's even made a friend."

"Lawrence," she said with difficulty.

"That's right."

She nodded weakly.

"Let's go back upstairs. I just wanted you to know, to really know, to *experience,* what I will do if you don't cooperate. Really *cooperate.* There's too much at stake, Reets, for me to take any chances. We've started the operation. We're full out this morning, Reets."

She said nothing.

"So you will cooperate?" Harriman said a moment later.

"Yes."

"Oh good. Good. Soon, tomorrow or the next day, I'll be able to give you an even better reason to be on my side in this, entirely on my side. Frankly I think you may even come around entirely, come to trust me again."

"This way," he said.

Chapter Two

/ 1 /

Pauling came out of a deep sleep to find Marcia sitting beside him. He had been dreaming he was in Mohammed's jet, staring down from thirty thousand feet.

"What is it?" he asked.

"Something's happened in West Depford."

Marcia smiled and stood up to give him room to move. She was wearing a light blue skirt and a white, man-tailored shirt open at the throat. Her long blond hair was held at her neck with a large copper clip he had bought her in Ireland. It was supposed to be Celtic. The digital clock said it was eight thirty-five. Sunlight was pushing through the spaces left by the shades and curtains on the far side of the bedroom.

"West Depford?"

"It's across the river from Philadelphia. Texaco has a big refinery there. *Had* a big refinery there."

He moved the bedclothes off his legs and put his feet on the floor. His pajamas were a red plaid.

"I've never seen anything like it. They're broadcasting it live. The whole country must be watching."

She wasn't smiling any longer.

"Someone has very carefully blown it up," she said. "They

must have planted charges on every oil storage tank and every refining installation. There was a tanker, too. It was going to unload this morning. Before it got blown in half. The cargo is burning or floating downriver."

Pauling found his robe, got into it, felt his beard—he wanted to wash—and started toward the door. Marcia preceded him.

Miss Margo, the Labrador, was waiting at the foot of the stairs, her swinging tail threatening a potted dracaena. She followed the Paulings into the living room and through it toward the sound of the television on the sun porch.

"Have you got the tape—"

"The one in your office, yes," Marcia said.

She meant she was recording this television coverage of the fire as she had the news the night before.

"Jesus," Pauling said.

He had walked onto the porch and seen the television picture. There was no voice-over at the moment. The newsmen were just letting the public watch. It looked as though a small civilization had been destroyed. The flames leaped hundreds of feet in the air; above the flames black smoke billowed into the morning sky.

"They've got the cameras set up on the shoulder of a highway above the plant," Marcia said.

The cameras panned back and forth. Very little was not burning: what must have been the main office building, a smaller building at the refinery gate, and a few installations along the fence. Everything else was blazing; there may have been as many as a thousand separate fires.

"Remember Mohammed's note?" Marcia said.

Pauling grunted. Miss Margo was flat at his feet, her tail still swiping the empty air, her eyes focused on his knees.

An announcer asked, "Marvin? Marvin, are you still there?"

Marvin must have been a Philadelphia newsman. He cleared his throat and said, "Bob, no one here, no one on the police or fire departments has any idea who is responsible for this. As yet we've been unable to get an estimate of the total dollar damage. It's all a complete shock to everyone. Someone has compared it to Pearl Harbor. The governor may have called out the National Guard. We've got an unconfirmed report that he was considering that, but just what the guard would do isn't clear. Whoever did this didn't wait around to have their pictures taken. There's simply been nothing like this, ever, on this scale in this country."

Bob's voice put in, "No, you're right, Marvin. There hasn't been. Not to my knowledge. There still doesn't seem to be any effort to put out the fires, and they've been blazing now, some of them, for what, two hours?"

"Yes. As we've already said, the fire departments and the refinery crews have moved most of their equipment back out of the way. In some cases back into Philadelphia. There isn't anything to do except let it burn out. There is also fear that the departments may be caught off guard or shorthanded, that whoever did this may strike elsewhere in the area. Bob, there just hasn't been anything like this, I don't think, since the Hindenburg disaster. At least that's the only thing that comes to mind."

"If I can interrupt, Marvin, we've received word that our man at the Coast Guard station has a report. Dick, are you there?"

The screen showed a reporter with a mike in his hand standing outside a white building on the river's edge.

"Go ahead, Dick," Bob said.

"On the ship itself the loss of life is now estimated to have been fifty-five lives. That's almost the entire crew, the captain, everyone. No one knows if anyone was in the refinery itself. We know there were night watchmen, guards, and it's suspected they're all dead too. The Coast Guard has tried to get close to the refinery from the riverside, but the heat is intense there. Apparently the oil in the ship's unloading hose caught too, even though it was unrefined. There's fire in spots up and down the shoreline."

Pauling seated himself on a hassock. He rubbed his face again.

He said, "Mohammed said not to move unilaterally. Hell, that was his Saudi way of saying if we decided to move, it would be dangerous."

"It would be a good first stop for someone, Tom."

"I understand. I'm beginning to wake up."

He stood up to turn down the volume on the TV. As he turned to face his wife, Michael walked into the room and took his hand. He had just enough fuzz on his face to need a shave, which, Pauling supposed, was an accomplishment for a kid his age. He had pajamas, a robe, and slippers on, so he had obviously come prepared to stay for some time.

"Hello," Pauling said.

"Hello, Dad. What's going on?" Michael nodded toward the screen. They were televising the fire again.

"It seems someone's declared war on Texaco," Pauling said.

"Is that a *live* picture?"

"They don't know who did it, not yet," Marcia said.

"I bet some of your government friends know."

Pauling frowned.

"Dad! Geez, I was just joking. Look, is it all right if I stay here awhile? I . . . I wasn't too comfortable at home."

"I'll call your mother; I'll talk her into it. It's all right with us."

Michael looked toward Marcia.

"Sure it is," she said.

"You need a shave," Pauling said.

"So do you."

Pauling grunted and started back toward the door to the living room.

"Tom?" Marcia said.

He answered her unasked question. "Yes. I'm going to wash up."

He stopped a few feet from the door to the living room. The Labrador had run on ahead, hoping Pauling was going to the kitchen to get her a dog biscuit. She put her head back through the doorway.

"Maybe we'd better get clearance from London to go as industry reps," Marcia said.

"Good." Pauling turned back to look at the TV again.

"The ship might belong to an independent. I'll have the office see to it," Marcia said.

"Ship?" Michael said. "Are you going . . . ?"

"Classified," Pauling told him.

Pauling went toward the kitchen. When the retriever was happy, Pauling started up the stairs.

He heard Michael ask, "What were you and Dad talking about?"

"Classified," Marcia replied. "I've got a couple of calls to put through. Can you make your own breakfast?"

Pauling was already halfway up the stairs. He went into the bathroom, and as he turned the water on in the sink, he remembered he'd once had second thoughts about asking her to marry him. It was possible, obviously, even for a supposedly mature and intelligent man to be a horse's ass.

He also remembered how, in the early seventies, when Nixon's antidrug policies had turned the CIA into an international narc squad, Marcia had conned a gang of Algerians who were smuggling Turkish opium. She had pulled them into a buying operation Interpol had set up in Marseilles.

He didn't like remembering that part of it. She had been in constant danger during the operation. He worried about it every minute. In those days he hadn't even known her very well. He hadn't even liked her very much.

While he was dressing, he realized he didn't believe for a moment that West Depford was going to be an isolated incident.

/ 2 /

Grace Argent was not unattractive. She was in her forties, wore her black hair shoulder length and had a pale, freckled complexion. Controversy was her business and her hobby. Because of her outspoken stance on women's rights and the publicity it had earned her, her seat from a liberal New York district was considered secure. If she cared whom she offended, in or out of government, she kept it secret. She was wearing her favorite earrings, gold and as big as the loops in a pair of shears.

One of the black, cylindrical TV network mikes—it looked like a cross between a World War II bazooka and a small telescope—was in front of the dais and pointed at her. Another was pointed at the chairman, Razwell of North Carolina: wavy, gray hair, horn-rimmed glasses, very handsome. The cameras were on risers in the back of the room.

Razwell was saying, "Because of that refinery fire this morning, none of this hearing is being televised live as had originally been planned. But we are being taped." He shuffled some papers in front of him. "We're going to go about our business and clear up this matter as quickly as possible. As you know, we've been at these hearings for three weeks. We have not uncovered any evidence that the Central Intelligence Agency, or the FBI, or anyone involved with these agencies established any actual working relationship or made any deals with members of organized crime. I know that not everyone here agrees with what I believe now will be the majority report.—However, each representative will have the chance to speak."

He paused, then said, "We have taken the testimony of the director of the CIA and of the head of the FBI. We have interviewed almost fifty witnesses outside of committee and a dozen here, in front of the cameras. In the interest of fairness, before I will accept any motions to the effect that we begin to close down the work of these public hearings, I will give the floor over . . ."

The chairman leaned back to speak to the committee counsel, then leaned forward again and spoke into his microphone, "The distinguished representative from Texas, Helen Reed."

"I yield my time to Congressperson Argent," Reed declared loudly.

It was no surprise.

"Four minutes please," Razwell said.

Grace Argent glowered at the television cameras. She glowered at the chairman.

"This is a farce!" she declared.

There was some commotion during which Razwell pounded his gavel but remained silent.

Argent went on, "The chairman knows we haven't had a chance to hear the one report that may have a crucial bearing on these questions."

There was more commotion, some of it among the representatives.

"A committee investigator named McGraw, *Frank* Mc-Graw."

Someone near Grace Argent laughed for no apparent reason.

"Called Stub," she said.

There was general laughter. Argent overlooked it. She continued in a louder voice. "Mr. McGraw has not been available to the full committee! Mr. McGraw has been fired by the committee counsel! Luckily, not before some of us were told of the allegations he was prepared to make. I want to know, I want the committee counsel to tell me, why Mr. McGraw was fired, what his allegations were, and why none of the members of this committee other than the chairman and the cochairman had any opportunity to question McGraw."

There was a silence during which Razwell, frowning heavily, allowed the man sitting behind him to reach the microphone. This was a bald man with a small, dark moustache. He was Henry Duane, the committee counsel.

"If you like, Representative Argent, I'll try to answer those questions."

"Four minutes," Razwell repeated into the counsel's microphone.

There was a louder disturbance from the spectators; Razwell had to use his gavel again.

The counsel said, "It doesn't have to take very long. I'm sure I can satisfy the representative from New York and any other committee member on this. It's news to me, frankly, that Mr. McGraw had any information pertinent to this investigation, or that anyone thought he did. But he did have certain classified—"

"How are we to know this classified information isn't *central* to our pursuit?" Argent said sternly.

"Yes. Well, Mr. McGraw submitted his full report to us, and that report has been—"

"I have information that the copy we received was cut in half!" Argent shouted.

"Look," the counsel said, "if you want to make—"

"Just a minute! Just a minute!" Razwell said. "Go and take the witness seat."

The committee counsel got up and moved behind about a dozen representatives to get clear of the dais. While he got into the chair in which the committee witnesses had testified, the television mike turned his way.

"Shall I take the oath?" the counsel asked sarcastically.

"That won't be necessary, Mr. Duane," Razwell said. "Unless of course Representative Argent thinks it is. Miss Argent, I want you to be fully satisfied. I've just been told that three other representatives, other than the distinguished representative from Texas, have volunteered their time to you, so if you wish to—"

"Thank you," she said. "Yes, I would prefer it if Mr. Duane were sworn in. Not on my time."

There was some laughter. The committee counsel, shaking his head, was sworn in. He was laughing too, but he stopped when Grace Argent began to question him.

"Is the report that we have been issued supposedly by McGraw the full report, Mr. Duane?"

Duane said, "No. The classified material was not included."

"Where is Mr. McGraw now, Mr. Duane?"

"That's one of the things I was trying to explain," Duane said. He sounded weary and had the look, suddenly, of a man ill understood and ill used. "We've lost touch with McGraw for the moment, but it's misinformation that he was fired. I never fired him. To my knowledge no one on the committee except myself, one member of my staff, the chairman, and the cochairman even spoke with him. We're not exactly sure where he is, but we could call him to appear, of course, if the committee voted to do it. But there was nothing in his report to indicate it would be in our interest."

"You're not exactly sure where he is?" Grace Argent's voice was heavy with sarcasm.

For a long time there was no answer. Finally, sighing deeply, Duane said, "Yes."

"And we are expected to let this matter drop?" Argent yelled.

"Please!" Razwell said.

"For the moment," Argent said, "I have no more questions. But I insist that the work of this committee will not be ended until Mr. McGraw is questioned by the full subcommittee."

There was a louder commotion than the one that had accompanied Duane's swearing in. Once again the chairman had to resort to his gavel. Meanwhile Representative Argent was handed a note by a staff member.

She rose, left her seat, made her way past the press into the corridor, where she reread the note, then proceeded down the hall toward the bank of telephones.

"Grace?"

It was her assistant, a fortyish, short woman in a brown suit.

"Did you send me this note?" Argent asked.

"No. What is it?"

"I'm to call this number from a public phone if . . ." She showed her assistant the note.

"To get in touch with Stub McGraw," the assistant said. She looked worried.

"Go watch for me."

The assistant nodded and returned to the committee room, while Argent continued down the hall.

There was only a small crowd at the telephones. Argent lifted the receiver of one and began to dial. With her free hand, she dug her notebook out of the pocket of her skirt. She thought she might have to write something down.

Suddenly there was a tough-looking, heavy, middle-aged man leaning into her booth.

"Don't say anything. The note's a ruse, of sorts."

"What?"

"I'm McGraw," the man said.

"What? You're going to come with me then! Right into that committee room. God, that will get the chairman's goat if—"

"Quiet!" McGraw said. "I'm not going anywhere except precisely where I decide to go. Listen carefully: there's a revolver in my pocket. I have reason to think I can trust you, that we're on the same side in this. Until I can be sure, you're to do just as I say. First hang up that phone. Then come with me quietly. Lady, if you give me trouble, I'll kill you."

He had the face, Argent thought, of a man who would do what he said. She nodded very carefully. When he moved back from the front of the booth to let her out, she went in the direction he indicated.

/ 3 /

Mark Harriman's special bodyguard—two clean-cut young men with hair as short as MPs', both dressed n chino slacks and red polo shirts—got out of the front of the Chevy van behind the mansion at 400 Brattle Street and went to slide back the side door. Lying on a mattress inside the van, Lawrence Bachelder, a/k/a Lawrence Douglas, was wan and motionless.

"Okay, we're going to carry you in," one of the men said softly. "Better go into total, Lawrence."

The two men climbed in, lifted Lawrence between them, and, using a chair carry, brought him out. The ground under their feet was still soggy from the morning's storm. They carried him through the rear door of the mansion, past the guard at the door and the television cameras in the back hall.

When the elevator came, they squeezed in carefully and took Lawrence down to the basement. The glass doors to the computer room were closed, the room empty. Harriman, a doctor, and a nurse were waiting for them in the operations room.

An examination table was set up in the center of the room. The motion-picture screen was down and folded out of the way. The wall behind it had curtains drawn in front of it.

"Put him on the table," the doctor said.

He was a dark man with a hooked nose and brown curls. The nurse was also dark, with bright, dark eyes, perhaps twenty years his junior.

Harriman spoke to the two young men who had carried Lawrence in. "Park the van in the garage and go up to the dormitory and sleep. Ted is assisting Dr. Facett. On your way up ask him to come down and guard the door at the end of the corridor. I don't want the doctor disturbed while he works on Lawrence."

The men nodded, turned, and went away.

Harriman closed the door after them and turned to the doctor and the nurse.

The doctor was cutting open Lawrence's shirt. A wide bandage had been taped over the patient's chest.

"Nurse, get this bandage off," the doctor said.

"I understand the bullet is still in him, Doctor. Is the bullet still in you, Lawrence?" Harriman asked.

"The bullet is still in me, Mark," Lawrence said.

The nurse's eyes widened, and the doctor said, "I still don't think we ought to do this here. I still think our clinic would be better. We could have him transported. Secrecy could—"

"This will do," Harriman said. "Won't it, Lawrence?"

"This will do," Lawrence said.

The nurse had begun to cut away Lawrence's bandage.

"He's lucky it was so high," the doctor said. "There probably won't be any permanent damage." Then he said, "This man ought to be in a great deal of pain."

"The doctor says you ought to be in a great deal of pain, Lawrence."

"He must know, Mark."

"I really don't like working under these conditions," the doctor said.

"Do it anyway," Harriman said.

The doctor wet his lips with his tongue. He forced Lawrence's shoulder toward him and seemed surprised when Lawrence did not complain.

"All right, bring the plasma," the doctor said.

The nurse opened a large metallic cooler and removed a glass bottle. She placed the bottle alongside another—one with a clear glucose solution—on an IV rack that had been set up near the examination table.

"Absurd conditions, when you have facilities upstairs and the clinic in Wellesley," the doctor said. "And you know it's empty! I don't see why this man was not just—"

"You'll just have to do your best, won't you?" Harriman said, cutting him off.

"You'll just have to do your best, won't you?" Lawrence said.

"Every premature connection between my people and the clinic," Harriman said, "endangers this project. You will do precisely as you're told. Both of you."

The nurse looked at the doctor anxiously. Lawrence, who had never seen them before, examined their faces carefully, understood that they were husband and wife, or lovers, and smiled.

"This is going to hurt," the doctor said.

"He says it's going to hurt," Harriman repeated.

"The least I can do is give him some morphine."

"All right," Harriman said.

"Actually—" Lawrence began.

"Take the morphine, Lawrence."

"I don't know why I should, Mark," Lawrence said.

"Harold asks that you cooperate fully. Harold would want you to take the morphine, Lawrence."

Lawrence smiled. His face, wan before, now appeared even whiter.

"If that's what Harold would want," he said.

The nurse went to a satchel and removed a number of small bottles. She prepared a hypodermic needle.

"I'm going upstairs to talk with Harold, Lawrence. You will cooperate with the doctor, won't you?"

"Of course, Mark," Lawrence said.

"It went very well, Lawrence. You were right, once wounded, to cut away from your group and return to base."

"I know, Mark."

"Harold said to tell you so. He's quite pleased."

Lawrence smiled.

The nurse, still wide-eyed, looked at Harriman and drew a deep breath. She approached Lawrence with the hypodermic and put it in his arm.

"It's extremely nice to work with people you can trust," Harriman said.

He went to the door and used it. Another young man with a disarming smile—this one stocky with a bushy red moustache —was standing at the end of the corridor.

"No one goes in or comes out, Ted," Harriman said.

"Yes, Mark."

"Under any circumstances. If anything is needed, call me on the intercom from the computer room."

"Yes, Mark."

Inside the room Lawrence was looking at the wall against which the curtains had been drawn. He was still smiling.

/ 4 /

The man in the hospital bed had a bandage over his eyes, the hair on his head had been partially burned, a heavy gelatinous substance was spread on his face. He was connected to an IV glucose bottle and plasma, and there were more bandages around his arms and chest.

Pauling waited at the door of the room for a few moments before walking in. The Paulings had been given security passes by the FBI and had split up to question the survivors as quickly as possible. This one, Chief Stevens, had regained consciousness only a few minutes before.

Pauling pulled a steel chair over. He leaned forward to speak into the patient's ear. "Stevens?"

"Uh."

"My name is Pauling. I've got to speak to you. Do you know who Arnold Leidner is?"

"Chairman of the board," Stevens said slowly.

"That's right. Leidner wants you to cooperate with me."

"You work for the company?"

"In a way. I work for someone who does business with the company."

"I know who did it."

Pauling leaned closer to the injured man. The burn ointment made him look as though he were perspiring heavily.

"I know who planted the charge, the one that blew up the boat. I may be blind. Pauling? Did you say your name was Pauling?"

"That's right."

"I may be blind. The doctor just told me. The police haven't come. Is the doctor here? Is the nurse?"

For a moment Pauling was reminded of a child asking if his parents were close. The impression vanished quickly.

"No. We're alone. If you can tell me what you can . . ." Pauling left the sentence unfinished.

"His name was Lawrence Douglas," Stevens said. "Strange. Spooky. His eyes were too wide, as if he were retarded. He signed on in New Orleans."

"Was he retarded?"

"No."

"How do you know he planted the bomb?"

"You won't find him among the injured. Or among the dead. He'll have swum to his people on the raft; they'll have picked him up. The ones who destroyed the refinery. I don't think he had help aboard. The bullet didn't slow him down."

"What?"

"I shot him," Stevens said, "but he kept coming, and he handled me as if I were weak."

"Did you see him plant the blast?"

"He all but told me," Stevens said more loudly. "I asked him what he was doing on the peak deck at dawn . . . there was a light from upriver . . . and he told me."

Pauling drew a deep breath. "What did he tell you?"

"Men in rubber rafts drifted down from a side street in West Depford. They planted charges. I had my revolver pointed at him, and after I saw the light, I asked him what was going on. He told me. I fired a signal shot. He tried to jump me, so I shot him. He kept coming. Before the mate got there, he jumped . . . dived off the rail. The refinery started to go. It started near the far edge. The mate and I looked at each other. Then we did what he had done."

"Jumped into the river?"

"We jumped. He dived."

"What's the mate's name?" Pauling asked.

"Porter," Stevens said. "But don't look for him; he didn't make it. He was ahead of me, coming out of the water, when . . ."

Stevens didn't finish, and Pauling said nothing. There was a powerful odor in the room from the burn medicine.

"I got him high in the chest, you could see the blood," the chief added after a moment. "Like I said, it didn't slow him down."

"Wide-eyed?" Pauling said.

"That's right. Who the hell was he? Why did he do it?"

"I don't know," Pauling said. "But why did he tell you so much?"

The chief moved his head slightly to the side. "He'd have told me anything. I could have asked him anything. Maybe because he thought I was going to die, but I don't think so. You just ask, he tells you."

"You're going to make it," Pauling said.

"Sure."

"Is there anything else about him you can tell me? Something that might help us find him."

"No," the chief said. He had lowered his voice. Perhaps it hurt him to speak. "The main charge was midships, but there must have been one in the boatswain's stores. I was thrown a couple of hundred feet. Does that sound possible?"

"I don't know," Pauling said.

"The doctor said they hadn't caught them. Is that true?"

"Yes. So far."

"Did anything else happen? I mean there haven't been other things—airports, factories?"

"No," Pauling said. "No, there hasn't been anything else."

"I never knew anyone like him. His eyes were empty. He could sit for hours just staring straight ahead. Smiling like an angel. I wish I knew something about him. I wish I did."

After a moment Pauling said, "I'll tell the Special Agent what you've told me. They'll be by to confirm it."

"Special Agent?"

"The FBI," Pauling said. "They're the ones running the investigations. There'll be army intelligence sitting in."

"CIA?" the chief asked.

"I wouldn't know."

"I hope they get that son of a bitch. I hope they get him, especially him."

Pauling got up and moved the steel chair back against the wall. "If anything else comes to mind, let your employers in on it, all right? I'll have my office call you to make sure. Anything I can get you? Any messages you want sent?"

"The doctor took care of that," the chief said.

"You're going to be all right," Pauling said. "You're lucky. Some of us pull through when the people next to us get it. Don't kick it."

"You're talking about combat."

"Something like that," Pauling said. "Be seeing you."

"Yeah," the chief said.

Pauling went out of the room and thanked the nurse for her cooperation. He walked down the wide hospital corridor and found Marcia waiting for him at the desk.

"Anything?" Pauling asked.

She shook her head. "No. None of them knew anything. How about you?"

"Yes. I think so."

Pauling nodded to the nurse at the desk, and he and Marcia went toward the elevator. They went down in silence. The Porsche was in the back lot.

It was a bright summer afternoon; the winds had shifted the smoke from the last of the refinery fires to the east, so it wasn't possible to smell it any longer. They had heard from a journalist that early that morning Philadelphia had smelled like "Nam" when they burned off the latrines with kerosene.

They got into the car.

"Well?" Marcia asked.

For a moment, Pauling just sat there. Then he said, "The chief, Stevens, said a man named Lawrence Douglas set the bombs, that he was waiting for men who drifted down the river in rubber rafts. The chief said Douglas would have told him anything he wanted to know. 'You just ask, he tells,' the chief said. Douglas had a retarded look, wide-eyed; again, that's the chief's words. When the chief shot him and hit him, he kept on coming."

Marcia stared at him. "Was Stevens delirious?"

"No."

"What do you think?"

"I don't know. What do you think?"

"Maybe Douglas is a junkie; maybe that's all there is to it."

"I doubt it," Pauling said.

"Maybe Stevens missed."

"He bled," Pauling said. "It was stupid. He would have told Stevens anything. Of course he didn't know the chief was going to survive, but he couldn't be sure the blast would kill him either."

"Then you're thinking the worst?"

"Aren't you?"

The Paulings had quickly formed the habit of letting silence fall between them. It meant they were thinking, usually along the same lines.

Finally Marcia said, "I'll call the office and have Harriet get Douglas's employment file. As soon as we get back to Washington, I'll study it. There might be something in it, some hint or connection."

Pauling nodded. Because he had not spoken, Marcia waited

before reaching for the phone. She understood Pauling felt there might be something left undone. But there wasn't; it was the possible ramifications of what they had just found out that had him temporarily inert.

She said, "We've checked with the survivors. We've checked with the FBI. We've got everything here there is to get. More than we could have expected."

Pauling suddenly wanted a cigarette. He rarely smoked, but sometimes he would buy a pack and smoke until it was empty. Sometimes he would buy two or three. He decided to stifle the urge for the moment. He started the automobile and took it out of the lot.

Marcia reached for the phone. She raised the office in Washington while Pauling maneuvered into the street past three unmarked bureau cars and a cruiser. He saw a man he recognized from the FBI, waved to him, then turned at the corner and headed toward the Franklin Bridge.

"Go on," Marcia said.

"Hold on," she said a minute later.

She put her hand over the mouthpiece.

To Pauling she said, "Grace Argent telephoned. She said it was important. Do you want to handle it?"

"All right."

Marcia spoke into the phone. "All right, Harriet. Look, get the employment file for a man named Lawrence Douglas, yes, a tanker-company employee, yes. And anything else you can get on him. Have you got Grace Argent's number?"

A moment later she used her index finger to break the connection with the office.

"Are you going to call her now?"

"In a minute," Pauling said. "First I'd like you to convince me we haven't walked into something neither of us is going to like at all."

He was already on the bridge. When it was time, he turned for the highway south.

Chapter Three

The Porsche slid into a parking space easily, and Pauling got out and slammed the door.

The Paulings had eaten west of Baltimore, and Thomas had dropped Marcia at the office. They would meet at home. Grace Argent had said it was urgent that he come to her apartment. She had sounded distraught.

The last time the Paulings had done business with her, Argent had wanted them to prevent a newspaper columnist from revealing information about her private life that would have endangered her political career. Grace Argent had once made the mistake of having an affair with a man later implicated in a scheme in which a number of senators and representatives received substantial sums of money. Argent had nothing to do with the scheme, but the columnist could prove that the affair had taken place. Thanks to Pauling, the story had never appeared. On the phone, Argent had led him to believe the problem had surfaced again. Pauling felt he might be able to calm her down just by talking with her.

Argent lived in a crescent-shaped six-story apartment building with potted plants in the foyer and a reception desk with a matronly woman behind it in the sunken lobby. Pauling told the woman whom he was going to see and hit the button between the aluminum doors to the elevators.

Argent's place was on the top floor. When he'd been there before, he'd been surprised by her eclectic taste: a reproduction of a Titian—Christ bearing the cross—greeted you when you walked into the narrow hall; there was Chinese statuary on Victorian tables, potted plants like those the management kept downstairs, fine oriental rugs—a Bokhara in the living room and two narrow Kazakhs in the hall—and a case filled with tiny figurines like the one in *The Glass Menagerie*.

Bracing himself for the view of Jesus—it reminded him of the churches of his childhood—Pauling rang the apartment bell.

"Come in."

He opened the door and stepped in front of the Titian.

"In here, Tom."

He went toward the living room. Argent was on a plush vermilion couch next to an end table with a green T'ang horse on it. Standing in front of Argent's curtained windows was a man holding a snub-nose .38.

"Sorry," Argent said. "Sorry, Tom."

"Your jacket, Mr. Pauling," the man said.

Pauling did not immediately remove his jacket.

"Please," the man said.

"Tom," Argent said. "This is Frank McGraw, an investigator for our committee. He—obviously—made me bring you here. It has nothing to do with that other matter. That was just something he told me to say. He claims someone is trying to kill him."

At first Pauling did not reply. Finally he said, "I can see why."

"Your jacket," McGraw repeated.

Pauling removed his jacket; he tossed it over the back of an overstuffed wing chair the same color as the overstuffed couch.

"Turn around, please," McGraw said.

Pauling did it.

"Why aren't you carrying a gun?"

"Why should I be?" Pauling said.

"All right, let's go and lock the apartment door."

He went, and McGraw followed him. When the apartment door had been secured, McGraw motioned him to return to the living room. Pauling took a seat on the couch about a yard from Argent. McGraw sat in another matching chair, and for a little while the two men, the one with the gray, Pennsylvania Dutchman's beard and the stocky one with one hand in his jacket pocket and one holding the gun, stared at each other.

"He's held his revolver on me for hours," Argent said. "Figuratively."

"All right, McGraw, what is it?" Pauling asked.

"The CIA or someone in it is after me or ought to be. I don't think I'll stick my head up just to see if someone puts a bullet through it. Believe me, someone has reason to want me dead."

"What are you talking about?"

"I'm talking about knowing too much about something very sensitive. I got back to Washington this morning to find CIA men on watch at my apartment. There are agents at the congressional committee staff rooms. My life is in danger," McGraw said. "First the agency had my report squelched. Now that I have more—"

"Look, McGraw, I—"

"Relax, all right? This is going to take a little time."

"What has Grace to do with this? What have I to do with it?"

"That's what I'd like to know," Argent said. "What have I got to do with this?"

"It's not too hard to explain," McGraw said, "if you'll give me a chance, Miss Argent."

"You're an extremely stupid man," Argent said.

McGraw grimaced. Then he sighed and put his revolver away in his shoulder holster.

"That's much more comfortable," Pauling said.

McGraw cleared his throat. "If you don't mind, I'd like a drink."

Argent took the glass McGraw was holding out to her. Frowning severely, she went to the bar near her case of glass figurines. Obviously she knew what he wanted.

"Tom?" she asked.

Pauling was still watching McGraw closely, as if he might bring his .38 back out. "Nothing for me," he said.

"First of all, I know about you," McGraw told him. "And you may have heard of me. I worked for Roy Cohn in the fifties, before I—"

There was a crash at the bar as Argent set McGraw's glass down violently. "Redneck."

"Let him talk!" Pauling told her.

"I'll be damned if I'll make another drink for a man who has held a gun on me all day and now turns out to be a McCarthyite!"

She returned from the bar empty-handed and sat down on the couch.

McGraw got up. Keeping an eye on Pauling as he spoke, he finished what Grace Argent had started.

"I'm a dead man unless I go down deep. Is that part of it clear? Have you some reason to doubt that? Men like you and I learn to trust the feeling that someone wants them dead. I don't think the men at my apartment house are there to ask me to a dance."

"Go on," Pauling said.

"All right. Look, I've uncovered something so rotten the stench will knock the CIA right out of the government."

Pauling didn't respond. He leaned back in the couch and drew a deep breath.

McGraw took the drink back to his chair. "As Miss Argent said, I've been working for her committee, investigating CIA-Mafia connections. "

"I'm listening," Pauling said.

McGraw made a fist of his left hand, looked at it, then slipped four fingers back into his jacket pocket. "I need you, whether I like it or not. Whether you like it or not. I may know who blew up that refinery this morning."

"Who?"

"You're investigating that, aren't you? I tried to get hold of you all day, through her," he looked at Argent. "I knew she was one of your clients. Finally you returned her call from your car. You were up there, weren't you? Because of your connection with OPEC."

Pauling said nothing.

"And you were in London yesterday. My guess is you were meeting with Ibn Saud. You don't have to confirm it. It doesn't matter. What matters is there are some very strange and very dangerous people running around this country." McGraw took his hand out of his pocket and looked at his fist again. "They're our people—not someone else's. For one, they've infiltrated the black Mafia in Detroit, and my guess is they blew up that refinery or saw to it that it got blown up. That last part is a guess. The first part isn't."

Grace Argent was mesmerized. She leaned toward him with her mouth open and her eyes bright.

"You know I'm right, don't you, Miss Argent? Your instincts tell you I am. Now you're glad I chose you to tell it to because you're going to see to it that something's done about it soon enough for it to make a difference."

"Why didn't you tell me any of this before?"

Pauling said, "Come on. Come on. You've got more."

McGraw cleared his throat again. "I was in Detroit. I was put onto a man who matched the description of an agent connected to a CIA operation around Boston. I was told this man was setting up something very special with the black Mafia. Whatever it is, it hasn't come off yet, as far as I know. I think I'd know. I think we'd all know. Let's call this man David since that's what he called himself. David has been using a polygraph to test the people who want a part of the Mafia operation."

McGraw sipped from his drink. "My money says he's used that polygraph before, that he let the black Mafia use it on him, and that he fooled it. He went in saying hey, let's get the police agents out of your inner core with this, and pointed to his machine. Pretty soon, he was in the inner core himself. My money says there are others just like him."

"Go on," Pauling said very slowly.

"Pauling, I kicked that SOB in the groin hard enough to make an elephant bleed, and he just smiled—like an angel. My life was on the line. I went in with everything I had. *He just smiled.*"

Pauling said nothing.

"Then a phone rang behind him," McGraw said. "He turned. Suddenly he was more interested in the phone than in me. Or I'd be dead now."

"Tom?" Argent said. "Tom, is there a link to the refinery fire? Was there a man like that involved at the refinery? Is there anything to what this man is saying?"

"I have a better question," McGraw said. "Is there a CIA operation so damn quiet maybe only two or three men know of it outside the project itself, a project to make—"

"You're jumping to conclusions," Pauling said.

"She's got to know it all, Pauling. Programmed agents! Like yogis, Miss Argent, they can walk on hot coals. They can't feel, or they don't care what they feel. But they could take orders. They could kill. Probably the CIA figured to use them as assassins."

"If we could produce agents like that, anyone could," Pauling said. "If there's an agent like that in Detroit—"

"There's a woman," McGraw cut in. "Named Rita Facett. She's a psychiatrist, an expert in narcosynthesis and a CIA asset. She's hard to miss. A friend of mine in the bureau saw her having lunch in Cambridge with two men, one of the men was named Laamb. He's a physicist. The other man was Mark Harriman, another agency psychiatrist. After the meal some-one followed Laamb. That was my man David. He's hard to miss too. My friend knew I was interested in Facett. When he noticed David a second time, getting on a plane for Detroit at Logan, he called me. All that was in my committee report."

"And you went after him?" Pauling asked.

"No, I was already in Detroit. Detroit has a lot going for it. The agency is thought to have connections in Detroit."

"Gangster connections," Argent said.

McGraw went on, "You see, five years ago I worked on Dr. Facett's clearance for a federal project. I was with the bureau then. I got the job of checking into her background. Deep into it. That was before she was recruited by the CIA." Mc-Graw took another sip from his drink. "I found out something I never passed on to the bureau because it didn't seem like it was anyone's business but Facett's. The job wasn't that important."

Grace Argent leaned back, just as bright-eyed as when she had leaned forward a moment before.

"Facett has a son," McGraw went on. "Apparently the agency never found that out. I only did because I was lucky enough to be tailing her one day. There was no way to find out without getting really lucky. She drove to a school yard and stopped to watch the kids. The boy never knew who she was or why she was there. But it wasn't too hard to figure out. I called her on it. She asked me to keep the lid on it if I could, and I did. I liked her. The trouble is now I'm the only one who knows who the kid really is."

"All right," Pauling said.

"All right. So I checked on Facett when I got back from Detroit a few days ago, to talk to her. I couldn't find her. That's unusual. She must be on a sensitive project. So I thought to check on the son. I knew the name of the people who had adopted him. Strange coincidence," McGraw said, "the kid disappeared about a year ago; his adoptive parents have all but given him up for dead. They think he's the victim of a sex maniac, but they won't admit it. And if you go to get the kid's adoption file you'll find it says his mother's name was Carol something."

After some time Pauling said, "Rita Facett."

McGraw nodded. "Most of this is circumstantial, hearsay, and dependent on my word. Some of it, the link to Texaco, is pure conjecture."

Now Pauling took a cigarette from a Persian box on Argent's coffee table and used her silver lighter. He blew smoke through his nostrils.

"I think you see where this puts me," McGraw went on. "If I'm adding things up right, I've stumbled onto the truth that someone is making a move against this country from inside a CIA operation, an operation that uses hypnotized, robotized, agents—"

"You can't go to the agency to prove it," Pauling said. "You can't trust anyone, especially the project's control. And you can't blow a project like that if you're wrong."

"That's right! And there's no *me* about it. *I've* been marked. I'm a dead man because I talked to the committee. I thought the committee would protect me, but it worked the other way. All I can do is get out of this town and try to work from hiding."

"Unless it's not the agency that's trying to kill you," Pauling said. "Then, with care, you could show yourself. How would you work?"

"Find out what they're up to in Detroit for one thing. Look, I've got no reason to love you, Pauling, any more than you've got reason to love me. I would guess we stand on different sides of any fence you can name, but I think we've got to work together on this. These robot agents have been turned around. There isn't any other reason for the agency to squelch my report and to want me dead."

"I'm damned," Grace Argent said.

"Pauling, you've got to get to someone. You've got to

penetrate from inside the CIA, from someone you can trust absolutely or someone you can blackmail, preferably both. Find out where their base operation is. There must be something in the reports to clue us to what's really happening. Get proof the operation or the agency has been subverted, get the name of the control."

Pauling didn't move. He didn't even nod.

McGraw said, "Get it fast, Pauling. What do you suppose they'll hit next?"

Finally Pauling said, "If you're right. You may not be."

"Yes. If," McGraw said.

"Now wait a minute, this doesn't make sense. . . . Why . . . ?" Argent said.

"It's called undeclared or nonadmitted war," Pauling told her. "Someone may go to war with us, and we may never find out who they are."

"To what advantage?" Argent yelled. *"Why?"*

Pauling said, "We wouldn't be able to retaliate. They could move into our spheres of influence, to take over our political structure."

"They could weaken us badly," McGraw said.

A moment later McGraw said, "Well, I never knew what the agency called it, but I'll bet it comes right out of their own think tanks. A nonadmitted war, I like that."

There was silence in Grace Argent's apartment.

"Rita Facett?" Pauling said again.

"That'll be the way to go. Whichever operation she's with, it'll be a cover for a program to make these yogis."

"Nonsense!" Argent said suddenly.

Neither McGraw nor Pauling said anything.

"Isn't it?" she asked. "Thomas, excuse me but you're taking Mr. McGraw's conclusions at face value without—"

Pauling shook his head. "No," he said. "It fits."

"You know something too," McGraw said.

Pauling told him. "There may have been one of these robots at West Depford."

"Damn!" McGraw exclaimed. "I hoped to God I picked the right man to come to with this! I did, didn't I?"

Pauling said, "There will be some kind of group, as you said. There will be a splinter group of SDS . . . terrorists . . . ," he shrugged, "something for the agent to subvert."

"As I said!" McGraw was still excited. "That's the polygraph angle! They infiltrate subversive groups. That's probably the original idea of the project! Look, find Facett. Get me the names of the yogis. We'll put it together. We'll tie them in with West Depford. You get your hair combed."

"What?" Argent said.

"To go to the White House," Pauling guessed.

"That's right," McGraw said. "You and Miss Argent here."

"I'm damned," Grace Argent said again.

"If I agree to take this seriously," Pauling said, "you have to go along with my way of doing things."

McGraw nodded. "You already take it seriously."

A moment later McGraw handed his revolver to Pauling.

"What's this?" Pauling said.

"I'm not much interested in wasting any more time. If I've blown it, if I read the whole thing wrong and you're with them, if the CIA is up to something I don't understand, a coup maybe," he shrugged, "then screw it. Blow me away now. I'd rather have it happen now than next week, when I can't watch my back. I can't watch my back out there." He motioned toward the street. "Go ahead, kill me," McGraw said.

Pauling looked at the .38 in his hand. He handed it back to McGraw and stood up to make himself a drink.

/ 2 /

There was a picture window in the living room of the farmhouse, and through it the man in the blue jeans and starched white shirt saw the lights turn at the bottom of the hill and come up the long dirt road. He began to pace back and forth as the van approached. Then he went into the kitchen and lifted a yellow legal pad from the round oak table and read what he had written on it. When he heard the van in the dooryard and the truck's horn, he put the pad back.

Tall, with a high forehead and a long, pinched nose, he was Victor Laamb, once famous for his work in high-energy physics. Laamb had been the first man to measure the captive cross section of beryllium, but that was a long time ago when he was working on his dissertation. The past fifteen years had been less auspicious. Since then, he had worked in California for the TRW Corporation and at the Brookhaven cyclotron, but he was no longer famous and no longer happy.

Laamb walked to the door to the yard and opened it. Mark Harriman was standing beside the van. Harriman had brought the black woman with him, the expert in narcosynthesis Laamb had met at lunch six weeks before. This left him with mixed emotions. He was glad to see her because he found her remarkably beautiful, but he didn't want her to know about the work he and the machinist, Carter, were doing for Harriman. It was like Harriman to keep a woman that beautiful around him.

She was just getting out of the van. Two tall young men wearing red polo shirts, both with angelic smiles, got out to take in the New England night, cloudless and still. There was a view across a mowing to a beaver pond and a wooded hill illuminated by the moon. Three other people remained in the van, an attractive, pale woman in her thirties with an Orphan Annie hairdo named Caroline, a man with a red moustache, Ted, and another, a very thin man with an acne-scarred complexion known as John Harcourt. At one time or another, Laamb had met each of them.

Mark Harriman took Facett's arm and brought her forward.

"Hello, Victor," Harriman said.

"Hello, Mark, Rita."

"Hello, Victor," Facett said softly.

"I didn't know you were coming," Laamb said to her.

"It was Mark's idea." She did not sound particularly happy about it.

"Well, come in," Laamb said. "Your people will wait outside?"

"Yes," Harriman said. "Come on, Reets."

Laamb showed them through the hall to the kitchen.

"I have coffee up. Would you both like some?"

Harriman nodded. He looked around cautiously, then sat at the round oak table and fingered Laamb's yellow pad.

"You might as well read it," Laamb said. He frowned at Facett again; he was still sorry she had to be there.

"What is this, Victor?" Harriman asked. "Lecture notes?"

"Yes. In a way." Laamb was not offended by Harriman's sarcasm; he was used to it. Laamb moved the coffeepot from the stove and set it on a hot tray on the worktable. As he reached for cups he said, "I've organized my thoughts. I try to be methodical. There are some things I want to say."

"I thought everything had been said. You told me on the phone yesterday that they were ready." Harriman put the pad down in front of him.

"Yes, they're ready. All five vans. They're in the barn. After we talk, and after . . . well, after we talk, you can have your friends in the truck drive them away. Carter is with them— they're his babies as much as mine. Are we going to conduct our business in front of Rita?" he added.

Harriman nodded. "That's right, Victor." He touched his hand to his face.

"Oh," Laamb said. "Now look, you won't be able to make them work; you might make a terrible mistake."

Harriman smiled.

Laamb was still uncomfortable to have Facett present, with the knowledge that she was part of all this. He could imagine what would happen if a black militant organization got hold of his work. He poured the coffee and brought it over.

"What's the matter, Victor?" Harriman asked.

"It's all right."

He put a yellow-and-white milk container, spoons, and a sugar bowl on the table. Some of the sugar was crusted on the edge of the bowl.

"If you hand me the pad, I'll read it aloud," Laamb said.

Harriman smiled and handed Laamb his notes.

"First," Laamb said, "I want you to know anyone could have done this. I mean this is not an important point, this first point, it's just something I want you to know. With the materials you provided, anyone, a graduate student, even a bright undergraduate, could have done the work I did."

"Dear God!" Facett said.

"You see, Reets, I promised you I had something that'd help you to experience things differently. Now please be quiet and let Victor continue. Drink your coffee."

Facett looked at Harriman as if he were insane.

"All right, Victor," Harriman said. "Go on."

"Yes. All right. Anyone could have made them. I know that. But I'm the one who did, and so, in effect, I'm partially responsible for what happens with them. Partially. Aren't I?"

"Yes," Harriman agreed.

Laamb was surprised. "All right, yes," he said. "So first I'm to be paid what we agreed. That's point two on my notes."

"Yes. All right."

"All right. Now, I have a schedule here of how I want it done. So you can't double-cross me, Mark."

"All right," Harriman said smiling.

"Because if you pay me in cash, then you could kill me and take it back, so—"

"We've been over this. I'll make the call, and then you'll make the call. All right?"

"Yes, all right. You'll make the call and then I'll make the call and then, if the money is in the Swiss account, I'll ask Carter to activate them, and I'll show you how they work. Now, point three. I want to know how you're going to use them."

"What?"

"Yes. I want to know. It's down here on the pad. I want to know how you're going to use them."

"Now? You want to know now? I didn't think you wanted to know that."

Facett had not touched her coffee. She was staring at Laamb the way, a moment before, she had been staring at Harriman.

"I've changed my mind. I have a right to change my mind. It's one of the conditions. I want to know."

Harriman was silent for some time. Finally he took a sip of his coffee, replaced his mug on the table, and smiled.

"I can't tell you."

"It'll be a good thing," Laamb said very quickly. "Actually, it's necessary. It will show them what big ones could do to have little ones like these go off. It'll make them more careful about the raw materials. It will put them on their guard. There will be restrictive measures. It's the only way, the best way, to make them all aware. Nothing else has done it."

"Awareness is important," Harriman conceded.

"Dear God," Facett said again. She seemed out of breath.

"It is," Laamb said to her. He recognized a certain shrillness in his tone. "It's important." He was no longer sure what he wanted to say. He looked down at his notes. "I must be sure it won't be a populous area."

Harriman smiled. "That, my friend, is the last thing I want. I'm an extortionist, Victor, not a mass murderer."

"No," Facett said, "you're not an extortionist."

Laamb was nodding. He continued to do so. He said, "Make your call."

The phone was on the wall near the door to the living room. Harriman got up and lifted the receiver.

"You have to dial 'one' before the area code," Laamb said.

Harriman dialed. A moment later he said, "Do it." He replaced the receiver.

They waited. Facett still had not touched her coffee. Laamb smiled at her. He was sorry she had to know.

She said, "Don't do this, Victor."

Laamb paid no attention to her. After a few moments, he got up and called the operator. It took very little time to get through to Switzerland and the man he had spoken to before. Laamb could speak some French, but he preferred English. He said, "Monsieur Landis, this is Victor Laamb. Did you get the call?"

"Thank you," Laamb said. He replaced the receiver.

"The money is in our account," he told Harriman and Facett. "In mine and Carter's." He sighed very deeply. He was quite relieved.

"We can go out to the barn now," he said.

"Victor," Facett said.

He turned away from her.

Harriman looked at Facett until she got to her feet. The three of them went out to the dooryard. The two men in red shirts were waiting near the house. Out at the van the three people who had been in the back seat had stepped out to stare toward the beaver pond.

"All right, Victor," Harriman said.

Laamb led the way around back. It wasn't the old gray barn which was near the road, but a newer one behind the house and approached by a dirt drive. It had three bays of double garage doors on the downhill side.

Laamb walked to the entrance to the main part of the structure, up along a path wide enough for a tractor or a car. Everyone followed him, Harriman, Facett, and Harriman's other people. Laamb looked at the attractive, pale woman in the Orphan Annie hairdo. She was staring straight at him in a disarming way. They went inside.

"Where's Carter?" Harriman asked.

"Carter!" Laamb yelled.

A man with a full reddish brown beard and twinkling blue eyes emerged from a bay with a light over it. In the bay was a new chocolate brown Ford van. Unlike the Chevrolet van in which Harriman and his people had arrived, this van had a square protruding nose and only one rear seat. Under that seat was a boxlike structure; it appeared to be part of the original design. It was covered with the same material with which Carter had carpeted the floor. Like the four others in the garages below, the van had heavy-duty springs to accommodate the heavy lead shielding of which the box was constructed.

"It's all right. We have the money," Laamb said to Carter.

Carter smiled and bowed slightly. Laamb thought the gesture remarkable.

"If you'll stand clear," Carter said.

He got into the driver's seat of the van.

"He's going to back it out," Laamb told everyone.

They all stood away so Carter could bring the van out into the center of the barn where there was plenty of light and room.

"It worked well, having five exactly the same," Laamb said to Harriman. "It always seemed that we only had the three vehicles here, mine, Carter's, and the one van." He laughed shortly and noticed when Facett looked away.

Carter got out from behind the wheel and looked at Laamb.

"Take out the stop," Laamb said.

Carter nodded. He went to the side door, and as everyone peered through windows or over Carter's body, he removed a slice of steel from the rear center of the bottom of the seat and left it on the carpeted floor.

"That steel would have prevented it from going off," Laamb explained. "There's one like it in each of the vans below. Of course. You can put it back if you like. Open the side, please," Laamb said to Carter.

Carter turned a crank in the front of the rear seat and showed them how the side of the box opened, revealing an empty rectangular compartment.

"Each of the five suitcases you'll find with the vans downstairs contains a detonation charge," Laamb said, "the amount of fissionable material that has to be introduced at just the right speed to the cavity of the bomb. Just slide one of the cases in. They fit exactly. You can drive with it in. Come with me, please."

"Which end of the case goes in?" Harriman asked.

"Either end, Mark," Laamb said. "The charge is symmetric. Now here."

Laamb was at the back of the van. He opened the double doors and lifted the rug. Below the rug the metal floor of the van had been cut out with a welding gun. A slice of steel had been put over the weld. Laamb showed them this by lifting off the steel. Three knobs, like the knobs of a combination safe, were revealed, each numbered from zero to sixty and set at fifty-five.

"Turn each of these to zero then back to fifty-five, then to zero. Begin counterclockwise, each back to zero. Then this middle knob, turn it counterclockwise to the number of minutes. If you don't turn it, you have a full sixty maximum— I really recommend the maximum—before it goes off. If you turn the middle knob manually all the way to zero, you will go off too," Laamb said softly.

Harriman sighed deeply. No one else, with the exception of Facett, lifted an eyebrow. She seemed horror-stuck.

Laamb said, "If you have to stop it, turn the left one and the right one all the way around, clockwise, in either order, left or right one first. *Clockwise.* Else it will explode."

Laamb laughed and nodded. He felt remarkably good, remarkably in control. He knew his devices would work because he took pride in what he did. And he actually had the money! This meant a great deal to him.

He looked over to Carter and smiled. He was surprised when the two men in the red polo shirts grabbed Carter by his arms.

"Hey!" Carter yelled. "Shit! Victor!"

"But—" Laamb said.

Harriman had removed a revolver from inside his shirt. He turned this on Laamb.

"Victor!" Carter shouted.

Harriman nodded to one of his people. Laamb wasn't sure which it was until Caroline stepped away from the others.

Harriman said, "Kill him, Caroline."

Carter was pinioned between the two men. Before Laamb could catch his breath, Caroline stepped toward Carter. She hit the bridge of Carter's nose with the side of her hand. Laamb heard something snap. Caroline hit Carter again, this time with the heel of her hand, driving Carter's nose bone into his brain. Carter slumped.

Laamb opened his mouth. He was in shock. He recognized the symptoms. His eyes were wide, his nostrils wide; he couldn't think or react. All he could do was stutter, "M—m—money. But the money. We have the money."

"I don't give a damn about the money, you idiot," Harriman said. "It's not mine."

He fired. Laamb was amazed even as the bullet broke through his skull. He died without hearing the sound of the shot.

/ 3 /

"As far as we know, the only lead the authorities have so far," John Chancellor was saying, "is the positive identification of one wanted man. It comes from a gas-station attendant in West Depford."

Once again the refinery fire was being shown on the television screen.

"Not much to go on," Marcia said.

"No," Pauling said.

Chancellor's voice continued, "NBC has learned that the FBI now believes this man, whose name and description have not been released, to have lived for several weeks in the West Depford area, and to have been a member of the Symbionese Liberation Army. The SLA, of course, was responsible for the kidnaping of Patricia Hearst. What baffles observers is that usually in cases of terrorist attack," the screen now showed a close-up of the refinery burning from the riverside, "the group responsible rushes to take credit for the act. So far the authorities believe they have not heard from the group responsible. Obviously nothing on this scale has ever happened before in the continental United States."

Chancellor let the public watch the burning refinery for a few seconds without adding a word. Then it was time for a commercial.

Marcia got up and moved the tape ahead. David Brinkley was saying, ". . . the only potential for a guerrilla war lies in a disaffected populace. The people of this country are, in the main, not disaffected. The overwhelming majority of Americans love America and have shown again and again that they will fight to prove it. If this is the first move of a stronger, more resourceful revolutionary cadre of the kind that had its infancy in the nineteen sixties, then the best and surest defense against it will be our own vigilant and courageous people. Time, of course, will tell, but if the attack in West Depford this morning is followed by further assaults against our property and our lives, then it will be ordinary Americans themselves, not their police, not their National Guard, not their federal bureaus and agencies, who will quash it. We will all be constantly on guard for men and women who are armed, or who are surveilling sensitive targets. Within days or weeks we will have stopped them."

"Good for him," Marcia said. She turned off the machine.

Pauling rubbed his head. "Well," he said.

"Well?" Marcia said.

After a moment he said, "They were good. They were really good." He meant the people who had blown up the refinery.

They were in the study where Pauling had watched the tape of Grace Argent the night before. Pauling had a drink by his elbow. He had made no move to touch it. The dog was asleep on the rug; Michael asleep upstairs.

"Do you think this man McGraw is right?" Marcia said after a few moments.

"Do you?" Pauling asked.

She shook her head. "I don't know. From all you've said, he made a good case. Grace believed him, didn't she? But she couldn't help it. A right-winger, a McCarthyite, blaming not another country or subversives or Communists but the CIA. Grace was already committed to a conspiracy theory. Unfortunately . . ."

"Yes?"

"It all fits, doesn't it?"

He nodded. "All right. I'll call John. You're in favor of that, aren't you?"

She nodded.

Pauling looked at his watch. He was stalling. He knew what time it was. He sighed and reached for the phone.

It rang on the other side of Washington. Finally a voice Pauling recognized came on and said, "We're out at the minute. If you'll leave your name and number we'll call back as soon as possible. At the signal please." Then the recording device signaled; Pauling hung up.

He bit his lower lip. He shook his head.

"You might as well," Marcia said.

"Yes." He lifted the receiver again and dialed.

He could imagine what was happening at the other end. The recording devices were automatically activated, the tracer was locking on. There would be immediate computer verification of his voice pattern. On the second ring, always on the second ring, the call was answered.

"Yes?"

"This is Pauling, Thomas Pauling."

"Sorry. You must have the wrong number."

"I am deactivated."

"Sorry, what number are you calling?"

Pauling sighed. "This is Hale Fellow," he said.

A moment later the voice on the other side said, "Very good. Go on, Hale Fellow."

"I want Gray Leader. I want him now. I'm at home."

"Reason?"

"Now," Pauling said. "No one else. He'll know where."

"You could have called him at home."

"Have I ever done this before?" Pauling asked.

For a moment there was silence at the other end.

"I'm just an operator, Hale Fellow."

"Sure you are," Pauling said. He hung up the receiver.

They waited. Five minutes later there was a single ring. Neither of the Paulings reached for the phone. The single ring was not followed by another one.

Pauling got up and put on his jacket. He went to the kitchen for his pill and half a glass of milk. Marcia walked with him to the front door.

Chapter Four

/ 1 /

There were no signs of life in the immense, empty truck lot adjoining the factory. After Pauling killed the lights of the Porsche, the only illumination came from a single sign at a door beside a row of loading platforms, and from a few dim bulbs over a sign at the side of the brick building, black letters on a white background: Werner Furniture.

Pauling got out and slammed the door of the car. He had parked near the door with the exit sign over it. He walked toward it. In the old days he had a key, but the chances were that Smith was already there and had left the door open. He pulled the door toward him, and it came.

It was darker inside than it had been out, but he knew the way. He found the light switch and used it, saw that the corridor to the exposed elevator shaft was empty, and turned off the light. His footsteps, as he made his way in the black, sounded exactly as they had on the several other occasions when he had called or had been called to a night meeting in that factory.

He kept his hand on the wall until he found the buttons for the elevator. He pressed the top one. Immediately the heavy machinery was set in motion. The freight platform above began to descend.

The light came first, a wide crack five feet above Pauling's head filled with bright yellow; it grew as the car descended. As his eyes became accustomed to it, Pauling was able to make out the grating, and behind it, feet first, John Smith seated in one of two straight-backed chairs set in the center of the platform. The elevator reached the level and stopped with a metallic slam.

"Hello, John."

"Good evening, Thomas. Good to see you. Come in, won't you?"

Pauling opened the grating, entered, closed it again behind him and pushed the controls. The car started back up. He stopped it between floors and went to take the other straight-backed chair.

"I assume this is still a safe place to talk," Pauling said. "It wouldn't be—"

John Smith held his hand up and nodded. "It's fine," he told Pauling.

Smith was a short man with a leprechaun's face and stark white hair. He had a leprechaun's smile too, and was wearing a neat summer-weight plaid suit. As usual he looked as though he had shaved and dressed only minutes before. He had deep wrinkles around his eyes and across his forehead. He was smoking a Players cigarette. Perhaps he had actually just shaved and dressed.

"How's the bride?" Smith asked.

"Fine. The family?"

"Can't complain. Arnold got into Yale Law School."

"Congratulations."

"For a long time I thought he was going to be an interior decorator or a hairdresser. I still have my fears."

Pauling snorted.

Smith added, "At least his sister is . . ."

". . . conventional?"

"Yes. Blatantly heterosexual. And yours, Thomas?"

"Michael is visiting. He's having trouble with his mother."

"As who would not. Well then, why are we suspended between floors on a bare freight elevator in the middle of a summer night instead of home in bed curled up with a good book and a good drink?"

Pauling smiled. He was extremely fond of John Smith; he had been for some time. In the mid-sixties, when it became clear to Pauling that he was not going to remain in the agency, that he would soon begin to work for himself, Smith was the man he had chosen to talk to about it, not because Smith was his senior officer, but because Smith understood him and trusted him. It was too bad that now Pauling had to take an adversary position, but he thought Smith would understand again.

"John, there's a very good chance that an important agency operation has gone bad."

Smith's expression did not change, but Pauling became conscious of his eyes; it was as if Smith had put the full force of his restraint into them.

"Thank you for not saying it's impossible, John."

Smith snorted, much as Pauling had a few moments before when Smith had made light of his concern for his son.

"We've known each other a long time," Pauling said.

"Twenty years. Twenty-one."

There was silence in the elevator. Except for the two straight-backed chairs the car was empty. The light came from a single bare bulb in a socket hung from a thick black wire. It was like a large interrogation chamber.

"All right, tell me about it, Thomas."

"I'm talking about the Texaco refinery," Pauling said. "I may be talking about a great deal more."

Smith's wrinkles seemed to Pauling to deepen. Pauling noticed lines on either side of the corner of Smith's mouth. He had not remembered them.

Pauling continued, "There was an agent aboard the tanker

who may have been hypnotized or programmed, or something even better. He doesn't sound like the hypnotized assets we've used or run into in the past. He seems to have been impervious to pain. He took a bullet and kept coming. Another one like him is operating elsewhere. There is suspicion in certain circles that there are more still. John, Texaco would be a beautiful first target in a nonadmitted war."

"Certain circles," John Smith said softly; he had a habit of picking up a word or phrase and handing it back.

"Sorry," Pauling said. He had no intention of telling Smith more about his sources.

Smith said, "I've not had anything to do with the Texaco thing. We've been on it, of course, but I haven't been asked to lend a hand."

Pauling knew the personalities to whom Smith was referring. He could guess who had been asked to study the Texaco fire.

"However," Smith went on, "if I were running a large-scale nonadmitted war, I would strike several targets simultaneously, not one at a time. You're jumping to conclusions, Thomas."

"Maybe, but I'm following good agency procedure in expecting the worst, and I have more."

"More," Smith said.

"I know there's a deep cover program to create assets different from any ever used before. I was there when the project was begun."

Smith didn't answer.

"Let's assume the project is ongoing," Pauling said. "Let's assume it's been subverted. Let's assume it's not yours but that you know a great deal about it because you're on the project review committee. You would understand immediately that there wouldn't be a better way of running a nonadmitted war against this country than to subvert that project. Agents who can't be traced because they can't be broken, until, finally, you find they came right from the agency."

Still Smith said nothing.

"The certain circles I mentioned have speculated there may even be a coup in the works, an agency coup."

Smith sneered. Pauling could not remember ever having seen him do that before.

"What would you want to do, Hale Fellow, blow the operation? Tell the world that the CIA has been manufacturing untraceable assassins? If you could prove you were right, it would rock the entire structure of American intelligence. It might even bring it down."

"No, I wouldn't want to blow the whole operation, even if it's been infiltrated. Here's what I'd want. I'd want the files. I'd want them all, and I'd want them now. I'd want my people in there making damn sure they had nothing to do with Texaco, to make damn sure they're clean."

"You want your company to vet the agency," Smith said. "Pardon my incredulity."

"I'll tell you what, let's call Warren Burger, let's call Leon Jaworski; let's have them check it out."

When Smith laughed, the promise that he was a leprechaun was almost fulfilled. He opened his mouth wide and slapped his thigh.

"Go ahead," Smith said when he finished laughing. "What else would you like? Perhaps the director could deliver the files to you personally. Perhaps—"

Pauling held his hand up. He pointed at Smith. "I want the file, John. I want entrée for my people. I won't accept an in-house cleanup, and neither will—"

"Certain circles?"

"That's right. It's too big, too immediate. What we're talking about may be a potential coup launched by a disaffected intelligence network. If that project is rotten, where does the rot stop? Where does it start?"

Smith stared at him.

"I want clearance from your office to go in there in my own way. I want a piece of paper to be somewhere in your office that says that on your authority, circumventing all superiors, all procedures, my people have been sent in to check this out. If I go down, you go down. I want a copy of that piece of paper."

Smith snorted again. His English cigarette had long since been extinguished under the leather soles of his lightweight Oxfords. He lighted another and replaced the colorful cardboard box in his jacket pocket.

"You're actually trying to blackmail me, to blackmail the agency," Smith said.

"That's right. Because my only alternative may do it worse harm. If I don't get what I want, I go right to the White House, to the press if I have to. Does the president know about the program? If he does, I'll bet he thinks it's to teach agents to beat polygraph machines."

Smith's eyes came up quickly. Suddenly his face held no hint that he was capable of humor. He had turned cold.

"What's it called, John? I want that now."

Smith said nothing.

Pauling didn't raise his voice; he simply made it harsher. The effect was much the same. "I'm talking about a war against this country. I'm talking about someone working from inside to bring us to our knees. Depression maybe, maybe worse. The Chinese, maybe, maybe something more subtle, the Japanese may be exponentially escalating their trade war against us. Maybe the Shah of Iran wants to knock down our stock prices below real value, and go on a shopping spree. Maybe it's the Russians, and maybe what our own men have planned for us next will cost a lot more than Texaco cost."

"Fuck you," John Smith said very softly. "Fuck you, Hale Fellow. What have you got?"

Pauling took a deep breath. "I've got the agent on the tanker. I've got a report of another one elsewhere, with a polygraph, a man who pain didn't affect, who acted as if he were in a trance."

"Where?" Smith said.

"Sorry. I've got the name of an agency expert in narco-synthesis, and a handle the agency may not have on how that expert can be made to dance, and I mean dance. And most of all I've got the news this morning out of New Jersey, and maybe I'll have the news tomorrow morning or next week. What do you call it, John? What's the name of the operation?"

"They're someone else's assets, not ours," Smith said softly.

"It's not someone else's expert in narcosynthesis! They're tied together!"

Again there was a long silence in the freight elevator. Finally John Smith sighed. The leprechaun lines crept back into his face.

"It's not a coup," he said. "It can't be."

"Good," Pauling said.

"At first we called it Alphadeath," Smith said. "The assets were recruited on the basis of their ability to produce alpha waves. You could have known that yourself, from your own time in."

Pauling nodded. "All right."

"It's in Cambridge," Smith added. "The Weldmore Institute."

Pauling let about a gallon of air out of his lungs.

Smith nodded. "All right, wise guy, you've maybe just cost me my career, maybe my life. Now you give. What's the name of the expert, and what don't we have on him?"

"Her," Pauling said. "On *her*. As you probably know, her name is Rita Facett. She bore a child. He was adopted at birth, but she kept in touch. The child is missing."

"Are you certain? Absolutely certain?"

"My source is."

"Damn you."

"Her original FBI government clearance was doctored."

"You're going to have to give me more than this!" Smith said. He did not say it nicely.

"Precisely. Don't do anything, John. Don't take any risks. You can't trust anyone inside. Don't even tell the director yet."

Smith laughed shortly.

"I'll take it. It ought to be fairly simple. All I really have to do is establish that they're it. Get me the files. When and if we can prove they're bad, you and I and . . . certain circles . . . can take it personally to the president if we want to. Heads will roll. Not ours. Twenty-four hours from now, we ought to have enough to go forward."

"Sure," Smith said. "It ought to be fairly simple."

This time Pauling laughed.

"You'll get us both killed," Smith said. "Will you go to Cambridge yourself?"

"No, I'll stay here—at least until I've studied the files. Can Facett be brought outside to report?"

Smith sighed and nodded. "Any of them can be called out if you have the Weldmore code. If I remember correctly, Facett is the liaison."

"That might simplify things. We'll go right to her. We'll take it right to her."

Smith was staring at his Oxfords. He said, "I'll take this on my own, on my own authority, for twenty-four hours. I'll get you the code tonight. You vet Facett. After that, if these suspicions aren't strengthened, I'll go upstairs through conventional channels. If they are, we'll do it your way."

"All right," Pauling said, "If I can have the files."

"I'll be in your office in the morning."

"John?"

"What?"

"You seem to think our suspicions won't be verified. You understand I don't. I think they'll be verified all right."

"I understand," Smith said.

"One more thing."

"Anything, anything," Smith said sarcastically and waved a small, white hand at Pauling.

"Has the agency been trying to kill a congressional investigator named Frank McGraw?"

Smith raised his eyebrows, which made his forehead crease in about a dozen lines. "Unlikely," he said. "Weldmore's control may have had Duane squelch a report. That would be all. So it's McGraw who brought you this. The Weldmore control may have wanted to talk to him because of the report. Killing him is a little romantic."

"Someone in the agency may want to," Pauling said. "May want to very much."

He got up and went to the controls. The machinery started. The elevator started down.

/ 2 /

In the wide dirt drive on the south side of number 400, a drive skirting the lawn and ending at a carriage house converted into a four-car garage, the five brown Ford vans baked in the morning sun. They were pulled off onto the grass at the far side. The Chevy van was also there, parked in the middle of the drive near the carriage house. Between the carriage house and the closest neighbor to the back—an angular three-story modern gray structure with long windows and steep roofs and board-and-batten siding—was the two-and-a-half-story hands' house where some of the kitchen staff and the laboratory technicians lived.

Mark Harriman was leaning against the side of the Chevy watching this building disinterestedly. Beside him was a woman of about twenty-five with short blond hair, an Irish face, and a turned-up nose. She was Jean Harcourt, the wife of the man with the bad complexion who had gone with Harriman and the others to Victor Laamb's.

Jean Harcourt's expression was not much different from the angelic one Frank McGraw had seen on the outsized man who called himself David, or the one Chief Stevens had seen on Lawrence Douglas. It was much the same as the expression on the faces of the two men who had carried Lawrence into 400 Brattle Street the previous day, and who had accompanied Harriman and Jean's husband to Laamb's farmhouse—the same expression usually worn by Ted, the man with the red moustache, and Caroline, the woman in the Orphan Annie hairdo. It was the usual expression of the trainees the Weldmore Institute had graduated in the previous eighteen months.

Rita Facett was standing at a second-story window of the main house staring down at Harriman and Harcourt, and she thought if she had to be near someone wearing an expression like that for five minutes more than was absolutely necessary, she would open the locked medical cabinet and swallow about two-dozen Nembutal capsules. About two dozen would do it. She had just found Harold Berger in his office in trance and had finally understood how Harriman had controlled Berger. He had drugged and hypnotized him; Berger had been Harriman's hypnotic subject for months. It had been stupid of her not to have understood that before.

Harriman must have sensed her watching, because he lifted his gaze easily to the second-story window and waved to her. Before he lowered his hand, he touched his nose and wiped his imaginary moustache. He had told Facett that if she tried to leave 400 Brattle, or tried to use an outside line, he would have her killed. But Harriman had told her that, he had claimed, only because she had not yet recovered from the shock of watching Laamb and Carter die, and because he had not yet had the opportunity to explain things to her. She did not wave back.

As Facett watched, Harriman turned his attention to Jean Harcourt. In the bright path of the early summer sun, which just then peeked over the rooftops, he looked like a high-powered young executive, full of confidence, expensively and tastefully dressed, lean and athletic. If he hadn't been pale, he could have passed for a tennis pro. Clean cut, successful, he might also have been the son of the owner of an enormous corporation, an heir to millions and to power. Watching him from the window of the institute, Facett hated him without apology. He was inhuman; his good looks, his success, his perfect pitch, his attitude about money, his languages, everything about him was insulting.

Raising his hand to shield his eyes, Harriman stared intensely at Jean Harcourt and smiled. "You and John are the only team we have," he said.

"I know, Mark."

"I like it. It provides a fail-safe system. At first I didn't like it. I'm not sure Harold did either. Harold decided it was necessary because you weren't effective without each other. But with you acting as his conscience, and with John prepared to do the bulk of the field work, it works well, doesn't it?"

"Yes, Mark."

"In the future we may use many teams."

"Did Harold say that?"

"Oh yes."

"I'm so glad, Mark," Jean said.

"Harold wants to know something, Jean."

"Yes, Mark."

"If it became necessary, if Harold asked you, would you end this round of John's existence, would you shoot him?"

"Yes, Mark."

"Oh good. Would he shoot you?"

"I think so, Mark."

"Good. Now I want you to come down a few notches because the drive is going to be a long one. You must remember—and keep reminding John—that long drives can send you into state four, even into total, and because you don't go in with a preset instruction, it can be a long time before you come down again. You could find yourself stopped at a tollbooth with a line of cars stretched behind you for miles and eighteen policemen asking you to please snap out of it."

Jean Harcourt chuckled.

"Well you could, Jean."

"I understand, Mark."

"Remember to keep your mental clock on during all drives. Every half hour I want you to say to yourself, come down a few notches, Jean. Then when you're down, you're to turn to John and speak sharply to him. Say, 'Come down a few notches, John!' I want you to take responsibility for that, Jean."

"If that's what Harold wants too, Mark."

"That's what Harold wants, Jean."

The back door to the main building opened and John Harcourt came out carrying a large, leather suitcase. He was a foot taller than Jean.

"Hello, Mark," he said when he was within a few feet of the Chevy van.

"Take the suitcase to the first Ford, please, John, and then come back."

"Certainly, Mark."

Harcourt walked to the first of the brown vans. He took the ignition key and went to the back doors to put in the leather suitcase. Leaving the doors ajar, he returned to Harriman. With great effort Harriman took another leather suitcase from the rear of the last Ford.

"It's extremely heavy," Harriman said. He straightened. Although he could put himself into a trance and perform remarkable feats of strength and endurance, Harriman did it very infrequently and never before one of his assets.

"Now, John, you are to drive very carefully, maintaining the speed limit at all times, never exceeding it."

"Yes, Mark."

"What is your call-in time, John?"

"Eight fifteen, Mark. Will Harold be saying good-bye?"

"No, John, but he wishes you well, and you know he's looking forward to speaking with you each day, twice a day. Have you memorized your route?"

"Yes, Mark."

"You seem very well this morning, John. Are you at level three?"

"Yes, Mark."

"You will drive at level two."

"I understand, Mark."

"Jean will remind you every half hour."

"All right."

"Those were Harold's specific instructions."

"All right, Mark."

"Driving is a little like sex, John. There is always the danger of exceeding your level without a preset instruction."

"I understand, Mark. I'll be careful."

"That's fine. Go directly to the rented apartment. Bring the suitcase with the charge to it until we go to foreign, when you are to place it in the chamber in the van. Eat and relax. Then drive the route. Park the van and leave it for an hour, come back, get it, return to the apartment, and wait to have sex until after you've called in, until after eight fifteen."

"Yes, Mark."

Harriman turned to Jean Harcourt.

"I understand, Mark," she said.

"The rental agreement is in the glove compartment. There's also a map of the route from the Automobile Association of America."

Jean Harcourt chuckled, and her husband's smile lengthened. Harriman had chosen the AAA at least in part because it was ironic, and this was not lost on either of the Harcourts.

"All right, have a good time," Harriman told them.

The Harcourts each met Mark's eye a last time and then went toward the first Ford. John carried the lead-lined suitcase easily, as though it weighed no more than the one containing their clothes.

As the Harcourts left, a large U-Haul truck slowed on Brattle Street in front of number 400. Harriman heard its brakes as it came to a stop on the far side of the mansion. Harriman then turned because Ted, the agent with the bushy red moustache, had exited the rear of the building and was walking toward him. He looked up to see if Dr. Facett was still watching, but she was gone.

"Hello, Mark. Hot."

"Yes. Go to the first van in the line, Ted. The key's in the ignition. Your suitcase goes in the rear."

"All right, Mark."

Ted walked to the van, as Harcourt had done, and went through the same motions. When he came back, Harriman lifted down another of Laamb's bombs, again with considerable effort. He gave Ted much the same instructions he had given the Harcourts.

"Will Harold be saying good-bye?" Ted asked.

"No, but he told me he looks forward to speaking with you twice a day," Harriman told him. "You have the longest drive, Ted. You won't be there for days. Make sure to get plenty of rest, and not while driving."

"Yes, Mark."

When Ted had driven away, another agent—this one named Martin, with a full black beard and protruding ears like F clefs—came out of the back of the mansion. The procedure and much of the conversation were repeated. By eight fifteen— Harriman checked his watch to see whether his estimate of the time it would take had proved accurate, and it had—each of the brown Ford vans was en route to its target, and each of the Weldmore assets to a rendezvous with an agent already in place.

John and Jean Harcourt were making for downtown Washington where a gaunt Mark II who resembled the angel of death had infiltrated the anti-Castro Cubans; Ted was heading for a farm outside Los Angeles; an agent named Stephen who had a face like a cherub and wavy auburn hair was driving to Brooklyn; Caroline, who had killed Carter, Laamb's assistant, was making for New Orleans and the team of relocated SLA people whom Lawrence had helped to destroy the Texaco refinery; Martin was on his way to Detroit.

In part, the operation in Detroit depended on the weather. In Detroit, according to the weather reports Harriman had heard that morning, it was even hotter than in Cambridge.

/ 3 /

The man at the wheel of the U-Haul truck had a nose that had been broken at least twice, a scar on the lid over his right eye that continued across most of his forehead, and a complexion like garnet paper. He had a cigarette stuck in the middle of his mouth as if he wanted to knock someone down with it.

His name was Finn, and after he got back into the truck in front of 400 Brattle Street, he turned the ignition and started up toward Harvard Square. He took Massachusetts Avenue out of the square and stopped finally near the corner of Ellery Street. He turned around partially in the seat and rapped on the back of the cab. Then he got out of the truck and looked up the street carefully. Believing he had not aroused the suspicion of anyone at the Weldmore Institute and had not been followed, he opened the back of the truck.

Another man jumped down and joined him in the street. Together they closed the back and went to get into the cab, where Finn put his cigarette out in the ashtray over the heater controls.

The man who had been in the body of the truck was only a little better looking than Finn. His mouth was much too small and his ears much too big. His name was Stein; he was younger than Finn and looked less athletic.

"I don't see anybody," Stein said.

"So he's late."

"We've been up half the night getting here and getting ready for this, and he's late."

"What we were up half the night getting ready for, we

already did," Finn said. "I didn't pull away exactly at five minutes."

"I didn't notice," Stein said.

"I figured it might look strange if they were in the habit of timing it. I got out of the cab, walked away and up the street, into the side street, and I came back after six minutes, not five."

"What the hell do you think it's all about?"

"I got no idea," Finn said. "What did you get?"

"I got some pictures and a conversation on the tape that was bouncing off something behind the building. Those vans kept pulling out. One as we got there, remember, one while I was using the camera so I got a shot of it, and one just as we were pulling out. Brown Fords."

"What's on the tape?"

"Weird stuff," Stein said. "Salespeople or something. They call each other by name all the time. Mark this and Mark that."

The men fell silent. Finn looked at his watch and then stared straight ahead. A black Corvette Sting Ray was driven past, and two children—they looked like brother and sister—hurried by holding hands.

After a minute Finn checked in the rearview mirror on his side of the truck, then leaned back to check the one on Stein's side. A car with a woman at the wheel, a late-model Buick, had pulled up behind them. It might have been a rental. Finn couldn't be sure because he didn't know how the plates ran in Massachusetts. He and Stein worked out of New York. He made a mental note of the license number, as he had of the two van plates he had seen, the one leaving 400 Brattle as they pulled up, and the one that left just as they were pulling away. He had marked both those numbers down on a pad, the first while he had been in the side street, supposedly leaving the truck unattended, the other while he was maneuvering through the traffic in Harvard Square.

"If that's him," he said, "it's a her."

Stein used the mirror on Finn's side of the truck and nodded. He saw a woman with bright blond hair and a shoulder bag get out of the car behind them, apparently forget something, and get back in. A moment later she pulled out into the street and proceeded down Massachusetts Avenue.

"That's her then," Finn said.

He turned on the engine and started after her.

"Ugly," Stein said.

"Oh yeah," Finn agreed. "Ugly."

The men were being funny. The woman in the car ahead of them was Marcia Pauling, and she looked especially pretty to them. She drove up Massachusetts Avenue until she found a place where she could pull over leaving room for Finn behind her. Finn parked. He and Stein hopped out, went to the back of the truck, and opened it. Stein jumped in. He came back carrying a manila envelope and a small tape recorder and went with Finn to get into the Buick.

Immediately Marcia pulled away.

"Which of you is Finn?" Marcia asked.

"Me. He's Stein."

Finn was next to her, Stein in the back. Marcia pulled into a tree-lined side street and parked in the shade. Stein handed forward the manila envelope with Polaroid pictures he had taken. He also switched on the recording machine.

While Marcia looked at color photographs of Weldmore from across Brattle Street and at a shot of a brown Ford van, they all listened to Mark Harriman and the agent named Ted, the voices distorted by a slight, immediate echo.

". . . plenty of rest, not while driving."

"Yes, Mark."

"I don't have to tell you about the dangers of driving, especially for long periods of time, do I, Ted?"

"You don't have to tell me, Mark. I'm looking forward to this."

"Good. Remember that Harold wishes you well and keeps you in his thoughts."

"Of course, Mark."

There was silence for a moment, broken by the sound of something scraped on the gravel, someone's foot perhaps.

"Have a good trip, Ted."

"Of course, Mark."

"You'll find everything you need, the rental agreement and the route in the glove compartment. When you get there, I want you to pay special attention to everything that Frank says. Frank has made very good progress with the people in Los Angeles. Harold wants you to take responsibility for trusting him. He's an extremely effective person."

"I know that, Mark. I admire Frank greatly."

"So does Harold, Ted. Good-bye."

"Good-bye, Mark."

Marcia was looking at the photograph of the van. It had been taken through a fisheye lens placed against a hole drilled in the side of the U-Haul truck. Like the photographs of the building and grounds, the shot of the van was greatly distorted. The plate number was clear, however.

Finn said, "Here are two more numbers."

He handed a piece of paper to Marcia, who put it into the envelope that had held the photographs.

"Both other vans looked just the same as that one, and there were two more in the driveway, not counting the one that left, and one Chevy van," Finn added.

The tape was still running; there was a sound of footsteps, and then voices again. The conversation they heard was much the same as the one between Mark and Ted, except this one was between Mark and someone called Martin. Martin was going to Detroit to meet a man named David and his call-in time was nine o'clock.

The voice that Marcia now recognized as Mark's said, "Harold has every confidence in David. Everyone is waiting for the Detroit thing with great enthusiasm, Martin."

"I know, Mark. I'll be sure to help him every way I can."

"What are these people?" Stein asked.

Finn shrugged.

Marcia said, "Are the two numbers you gave me in order?"

"The first is from the van that pulled out as we drove up, the other must be this Martin's," Finn told her. "A definite creep."

"Really," Stein said.

The tape ended with some background sounds that may or may not have come from inside the institute, but with no further conversation. A white truck with a red stripe around it rambled past them.

"You want us to set up and do it again?" Finn asked.

"Yes. Try it around noon from another spot."

"All right," Finn said.

"Meanwhile I'm going to check into a motel. Maybe we got lucky, getting those license numbers."

"Maybe. There's a motel on the far side of I-93," Finn told her.

"All right, you go there. Use your code names. I'll call you."

Finn smiled. "Careful, aren't you?"

Marcia patted his hand. "You've worked with my husband before."

"You're his . . . you're Mrs. Pauling?"

"Yes."

"All right!" Finn said. "He's a lucky bastard. I always said so."

Marcia beamed. Then she got tough again. "Get another truck and get it ready. Wait for my call at the motel. What's it called?"

Finn told her, and she started the car to take them back to the U-Haul.

A half hour later Marcia was talking on a pay phone in a booth in a Howard Johnson's. A waitress, with nicely turned calves and wearing a pink dress, was standing in the aisle between the tables talking to a customer who was almost twice her height.

"Did you like Finn?" Pauling asked.

"Yes. You're going to laugh, but he reminds me of my father." Marcia's father had worked with Donovan in the OSS. It was one of the reasons she had first been recruited. "He looks very tough."

"He is," Pauling said.

The customer walked away to pay his check, and the waitress went to clear off a table.

"Do you know Stein?" Marcia asked.

"I never met him. I've talked to him on the phone."

"I haven't told them a thing, of course, and they haven't asked."

"Of course."

"There were five brown Ford vans in the lot when they got there this morning. They're all gone now. Each seems to have gone to a separate destination; each asset sent out with excruciating care. We have three license numbers."

Marcia gave them to him.

"All right, maybe we got lucky; and so far we're on schedule."

The waitress passed close to the phone booth. She was strikingly pretty.

"Yes," Marcia said. "I have a tape to play you."

"Then I'll switch you to Ann. John's on his way up."

"All right."

"Be careful."

Marcia turned, putting her back to the front of the booth so she could get set to take the tape recorder from her shoulder bag without attracting attention.

"Yes," she said. "You be careful, too."

Chapter Five

The elevator doors opened onto the top floor of the office building on F Street, and John Smith stepped out looking like a boy on his first date, a boy with prematurely white hair. His face was smooth and shining, his blue suit hung on him as it might have on a tailor's dummy, his blue eyes were unusually wide. He walked down the well-lighted corridor toward the double glass doors marked: Pauling Consultants.

A blond girl with large, tinted lenses was sitting at a reception desk on the far side of the glass. She received clearance over the intercom from the hidden security guard, pressed a button, and the heavy glass doors parted. John Smith stepped between them. It was as if they had opened for him because it had been ordered in heaven.

There were lilacs on the girl's desk. She smiled.

"Hello, Mr. Smith. Mr. Pauling says to go right in."

"I'll go right in then."

He took a short walk along a wood-paneled corridor to the door to Pauling's outer office. Harriet, the Paulings' secretary—she was in her fifties and looked a little like Bette Davis—had lilacs too. She waved Smith onward. He went through the last door that separated Pauling from the world.

Pauling was seated. His shirt sleeves were rolled up, his heavy forearms on the desk in front of him as though he wanted to wrestle. Behind him, to either side of a window, were book-shelves filled with bound industrial reports. Smith sat in a leather chair. While Pauling watched, Smith took out his package of Players, extracted and lighted one.

"There was a meeting this morning," Smith blew smoke into the level air between them.

Pauling nodded.

"The subject of your connection with the Saudis was raised. It's common knowledge that you work for them occasionally."

"Of course," Pauling said.

"I was asked to come over and speak to you about it. We don't feel it would be a good idea for you to get deeply involved in the refinery thing. We'd like you to keep at arm's length."

"I understand," Pauling said.

"I told the committee I thought you would. Especially if I came personally."

"You don't want me messing around in there. You're on to something."

"That's right."

"As it happens, I had no intention of continuing my investigation. I'm glad you're getting somewhere." Pauling leaned forward and hit the switch that Smith knew shut down the tape machine in the cabinets under his bookshelves.

"Put it back on," Smith said.

Pauling frowned but did as he'd been asked.

Smith said, "Thomas, as an old friend who still maintains close ties to the agency, I want you to do something for me, something else."

"All right."

"I'll give you the details in a moment, but for the record,

I want you to surveille a covert operation in New England. I am, in fact, partially responsible for the security of that operation, and I want a fresh hand to have a look at it."

"To mix a metaphor," Pauling said.

It was Smith's turn to frown. "Yes."

He nodded, and this time when Pauling turned off the tape, he let him leave it off.

"Anything definite yet from Marcia?" Smith asked.

"No."

Pauling lighted a cigarette of his own, not a Players, and leaned back in his chair. He had bought a pack the night before, just after leaving Smith at the furniture factory; he had already smoked most of it.

"I think I get the picture," he said.

"I assume so," Smith said, "but just in case, understand that there will be no piece of paper of the kind you asked for last night. If Marcia does more than take a few pictures of Weldmore, and of course she will, you two are on your own. I don't see why I should hang my ass any farther out the window than it already is." He paused. "On the other hand, I've done some research."

Pauling put his forearms back on his desk.

"The news report last night about the SLA connection was accurate. It looks as though we're dealing with a conventional terrorist group. My guess, frankly, is a group of disaffected young people who have been living and loving in New Orleans. Unfortunately our principal means of keeping up with that group in the last twelve months has been—"

"Weldmore?" Pauling suggested.

"Yes," Smith repeated. "But just hold your water. You need to know a great deal more about what's going on. Weldmore was originally set up to produce the kind of assets you described last night, and they succeeded. Their first use was eighteen months ago when one of these Weldmore operatives infiltrated the international terrorist organization that press services used to say was run by a gentleman called Carlos. The real leader of the group is known by the code name Field Marshal.

"Damn," Pauling whispered.

"Of course you've heard of him."

"Of course."

"Our asset convinced Field Marshal he could organize American terrorists and, we think almost as a joke, thinking it impossible, Field Marshal got him entrée to five Stateside organizations. Black Panther holdouts in Detroit, SDS transplants near Los Angeles, Puerto Rican nationalists based in New York City, these New Orleans people I spoke of, and—this is really bizarre—anti-Castro Cubans here in Washington."

"That makes no sense."

"No sense. Of course. Their politics are wrong. The Cubans don't fit. Nevertheless each of these groups, thanks to the success of the Weldmore psychiatric and biofeedback team, has been penetrated. Each now contains a nontraceable and damn hard to destroy loyal American intelligence agent who was introduced to its inner core by the original Weldmore man, the one who got next to Field Marshal."

"Then I—"

"I said hold your water, Thomas. I think I played the fool last night . . . because of all the time we've known each other, because I trusted you to have better judgment. Now I see it this way: even if one of those groups, the New Orleans one for instance, turns out to be responsible for the refinery fire, who's to say the Weldmore Institute asset had any more to do with it than necessary? How are you going to prove that he did anything more than go along with it because he had to? How are you going to prove that he's an agent provocateur, subverted—"

"Is that what you think?" Pauling said.

Smith did not answer immediately.

"Obviously not," Pauling continued. "What kind of asset would allow fifteen million dollars worth of oil refinery to be destroyed to keep a secure position in a small-time group of defunct subversives? You're with me on this; you see it the way I do because it's the only way to see it. That's why you're here and talking. There's been no report from the asset, has there? Either before or after the event. The control at Langley must be nervous as a kitten. Who is it? Spencer? Does he assume his man is dead?"

Smith drew back deeply on his Player. "I don't know."

"I need more," Pauling said. "I need descriptions of all the Weldmore people. With descriptions alone we might be able to link Weldmore to the man who blew the tanker yesterday morning."

"Lawrence Douglas?"

"Yes."

"We got to Chief Stevens shortly after you did."

"You took your time."

Smith stared. "Maybe," he said.

Pauling sighed. "All right. The liaison, Facett, has got to be in on this. We'll have her back on our side by tonight or running to ground. Then we'll know. We'll be able to move."

Smith shook his head. "If you're right, they'll be way ahead of us."

"Not necessarily. Some goddamned head-in-the-clouds intellectual might be behind this with money from an Arab emirate, Kuwait, or—"

"Ibn Saud?" Smith put in.

"Lots of luck. Or these Weldmore people may have turned themselves on with some new drug. They may be hearing voices or may have gotten away from their programmers. It wouldn't be the first time some stupidly simple operation blew the top off a whole network or a—"

"You're wrong, Thomas," Smith said. "The organization at Weldmore is secure. The people involved are first rate. There's been no easy perversion of that operation. If it's been turned around, it's been done brilliantly, and we're in for a fight."

"Then I must have the files!"

"You have me," Smith said. "I'm here."

"All right," Pauling said again. "Let's take it from the top."

Smith put his cigarette out and shifted in his seat. "From the top then," he said. "Weldmore is set up as an institute for the study of biofeedback techniques, especially alpha-wave experimentation, but walk through the front door or around back, and you're on camera and covered by rapid-fire weapons. They have a Rand computer in the basement hooked into a telephone network and codes to the fielded operators. It's worked through voice verification systems as sophisticated as Langley's. Mark Harriman, a Weldmore shrink, might be the man they got to first or even the man behind any turn around, except . . ."

"What?" Pauling said.

". . . except that he's apolitical. He's a maverick genius whose interest is in what he can do, what innovations he can produce in the human mind, and he's too young to be disillusioned; he's thirty-seven. If we're talking about nonadmitted war, we're talking about allegiance and betrayal. If Harriman has gone over to someone else, he's an unusual kind of defector. His salary is excessive; he has position, success; he's doing what he always wanted to do, work on human guinea pigs."

"Go on," Pauling said.

"It makes sense that he's a satisfied man. His assets can do things never done before, like beat the polygraph machine consistently, like absorb pain without flinching or faltering. Harriman himself can put knitting needles through his upper arm."

"I see," Pauling said. "Who else have we got?"

"There are three executive-level personnel and five lower level: a computer operator, a head security officer, a general secretary, and two biofeedback technicians. I think we can eliminate the last five; they will simply follow orders. There's a security staff of four, a domestic staff of four, and of course the trainees, most of them graduated and fielded or ready for fielding. Everyone but the domestic staff—they commute—are housed in the main building or in the smaller building behind it."

"It will be one of the top three or some combination of them," Pauling said.

"Yes. The director is Harold Berger. His record is clean, absolutely unblemished. He's diligent, if unimaginative. Then there's Facett, who you think is being blackmailed. Facett is the liaison now because her work load was cut back when her technique was determined to be less effective than Harriman's."

"Explain that."

"Originally Facett's technique was thought superior. She uses drugs, and it was thought that drugs would work, but Harriman abhors drugs. He's shown that drugs don't produce reliable operatives—their effects are not lasting, or they last too long. His techniques do succeed. He turns the Weldmore trainees into what he calls 'Mark II's.' "

Smith made quotation marks with his fingers and held them there for Pauling to look at. " 'Mark II's' because the first round of attempts, Facett's, failed."

"All this is in the files?" Pauling asked.

"Yes."

"Then it's Berger and Harriman together. Who was the original liaison officer?"

"His name was Newell. He was Harriman's assistant when Harriman was at the Yale Psychiatric Institute. He died in a car crash over a year ago."

Pauling said nothing.

After a moment Smith went on, "We thought no one in the country knew more about hypnosis than Harriman. We believed that if anyone could use biofeedback techniques like training in the specific production of brain waves, hypnosis, and self-hypnosis to produce programmed operatives, Harriman could. And he did."

"There's something more, isn't there?"

"Yes. It's very far out."

"And the rest of this is routine?"

Smith didn't smile. "It has to do with Eastern mystical paths."

"What?"

"Harriman claims to have decoded ancient Eastern mystical psychological texts and made them fit Western psychological disciplines. He says he uses biofeedback hypnosis and self-hypnosis to take those trainees who can make it up the yogic ladder to complete self-control."

"I'll bet he tells that to all the girls."

Smith took out another Player, lighted it, and stared at Pauling balefully.

"And I'll bet he says it the other way around. I'll bet he says the Western techniques fit the Eastern paths."

"Who gives a shit?" Smith said.

"It's an idea whose time has come. Which Eastern tradition? Is it Buddhist, Hindu, or Taoist?"

"I don't know!" Smith said.

After a moment he added, "Harriman speaks Chinese, so maybe it's Zen. He studied in Hong Kong for a year before he went to medical school. He's also lived in France and in Germany and is fluent in French and German. He's an all-around bright boy. He could have been a professional musician. He could have been anything he wanted."

Pauling stared out his window at the summer sky. He felt what he had felt over and over again the day before: neither he nor Marcia was going to like this operation very much.

"Look, these 'Mark II's,'" Pauling made the quotation marks with his fingers Smith had made just before, "are dancing around the country, infiltrated deeply into subversive, five different subversive groups, maybe *controlling* five different subversive groups, up to God knows what and for God knows whom. We could be deep in a guerrilla war tomorrow morning, and you've come up empty."

"Empty?" Smith whispered. The sarcasm was heavy.

"The files, John! The descriptions of the agents! The full personnel files on the three executive-level people!"

"No!" Smith said.

Pauling reached into his desk. He threw Lawrence Douglas's personnel record at Smith, who caught it.

"Is that one of the 'Mark II's'?" Pauling made the little quotation marks with his hands again.

"I don't know," Smith said. "There's no picture."

"There were pictures with the Weldmore file?"

"Yes."

"John!"

"You've got enough! I gave you Facett's code last night. Now you've got the basics of the whole damn operation. I'm not giving you any fucking pictures."

Smith got up and brushed his suit off as though he had spilled ashes on it. He hadn't. He looked across at Pauling.

"You could be wrong," Smith said. "The whole operation could be clean. We're just going to have to slow this down a little. We'll wait and see what happens in Cambridge."

Smith's lighted cigarette was in an ashtray on Pauling's desk. He extinguished it and went out.

He passed the two women, both with lilacs on their desks. The one with the lenses put her finger on the button that parted the doors. From the back, Smith looked like a tired, old man.

/ 2 /

When McGraw's call came in, Pauling was in the office next to his own—Ann Gold's office—listening to the tape Finn and Stein had made in Cambridge. Gold was listening too. Like Pauling's, Gold's office was furnished in dark wood and overstuffed leather chairs.

Ann Gold was a short, dumpy woman in her fifties, with a faint line of hair above her upper lip and brown eyes almost as big as Marcia's. She had been an administrative assistant at Langley and ought to have been promoted to the rank of the man she worked for—which would have put her on a level with John Smith. She had never been promoted. Before she had been an administrative assistant, she had taken a few years off to raise a family to school age, and before that she had been a field agent in Eastern Europe. When Pauling had gone into business for himself, Gold had come with him happily.

When the phone rang, she turned off the tape from Cambridge.

"Put it on the speaker," Pauling said.

Gold pushed a button; there was a dull thud from a speaker on her desk near a photograph of her grandchildren. The phone rang again, amplified this time. She pushed another button and turned the speaker to face Pauling.

"Yes?" Pauling said.

"McGraw," McGraw said.

"This is Pauling. Go ahead."

"I'm back. I'm at the Hilton, using the name we agreed on. I'm calling from a pay phone. Any progress?"

Pauling looked at Gold, who had turned in her chair to stare at the wall. In profile she was handsome.

"Some," Pauling said. "Your man's first contact out there was probably with people once connected with the Black Panthers."

"You're talking about 1967," McGraw said. "You're more than a decade off."

"There would have to be enough of them to be a group . . . disaffected, hanging on to a revolutionary philosophy."

McGraw said, "Let's say I believe it."

"Don't do anything but locate them."

"Locate them?" McGraw was angry. "What happened there? How about an address, a name?"

"There's been no verification . . . we can't be sure yet which end is up."

For a moment McGraw was silent. Gold made a tent of her stubby fingers and peered inside it.

Pauling said, "Are you there?"

"I hear you."

"There's a firm in Detroit I've done business with. There's a man named—"

"Forget it," McGraw said. "I don't want private help. When do you expect verification, verification that will *satisfy* you? When will you give me something solid?"

Pauling disregarded his tone. "Soon. There's no way to tell. By tonight or early tomorrow."

"Let's hope that's not too late. The files ought to have—"

"They didn't," Pauling said.

"I see. Your source washed entirely."

"Panthers," Pauling told him again.

"Christ," McGraw said.

"It's firm."

Again McGraw took his time answering. "I'll have to live with that. I'll call in when I have something."

"Make it hourly, if you can," Pauling said. "Anything may happen. We have someone out, something may break inside the agency. Or . . ."

"Or there may be another news show like Texaco. Look, it's not just Detroit. How many others—"

"Four."

"And you have them? You know who they are?"

"Yes."

"Nifty," McGraw said.

"McGraw," Pauling said. "We've learned from Cambridge that these assets look with unusually high regard to a man named Harold. Harold Berger. Given what they are . . . what kind of—"

"I understand. Anything else?"

"No."

After a moment there was another thud on the speaker.

McGraw had hung up. Gold turned, hit a button, and looked at Pauling.

Gold's husband had been a field officer too. He had died in the early sixties in central Africa. When she looked at Pauling that way, he guessed she was thinking of him.

"Angry, isn't he? Do you want me to put on the Cambridge tape again?"

Pauling shook his head. He got up, went to a small television set on a wall shelf, turned it on, and quickly went through all the channels in the Washington area. He found kids' shows, talk shows, and a movie.

"You're looking for trouble," Gold said.

"Yes."

"It would come over the Associated Press first. And you're worrying about Marcia."

Pauling nodded. A buzzer sounded, and a light came on on Gold's telephone.

"Someone's calling the main number," she said.

A moment later Harriet's voice came over the interoffice intercom.

"It's Representative Argent, on five."

Pauling went to the intercom. "I'll take it in my office."

He turned to Gold. "The minute Marcia calls, Ann, interrupt me."

"Of course."

Pauling hadn't moved yet. "Ann, what do you know about Eastern mysticism?"

"Next to nothing."

"Then you wouldn't know how to pervert it."

She shook her head. "Shall I do some research? One of the boys spent a summer at an ashram a few years back."

Gold's sons were in their early twenties. It was her daughter, twenty-eight, who had produced the grandchildren.

Pauling shook his head. Finally he went next door. He put himself behind his desk and lifted the phone to deal with Argent.

"Grace?"

"Thomas, Henry Duane just called me, the committee counsel."

"Yes, I know who Duane is."

"He said he might be able to get in touch with Frank Mc-Graw."

Pauling began to drum his fingers on his desk. His eye fell on the cigarette pack that was now nearly empty. "Grace, where are you calling from?"

"From my office. I—"

"Grace, your telephone may be bugged. Just repeat the conversation you had, please, word for word if you can."

"Everthing might be bugged," she said. "Look, Duane just asked if I wanted to talk with Frank McGraw."

"And?"

"And I said maybe."

Pauling took one of the last three cigarettes out of the pack. "Grace, are you sure it was Duane? Do you know his voice?"

"Yes. It was Duane."

"Grace, listen carefully. I'm sending a man over, a body-guard. He'll be there in an hour."

"What?"

"Don't leave your office until he gets there. Don't see any-one you don't know. Stay put, *please*." He lighted the cigarette.

"Now, Thomas, surely you're—"

"Please, Grace. I'll be in touch."

Pauling hung up. He dialed his home number quickly. After it had rung several times, he began to drum his fingers again. Finally Michael lifted the receiver on his end and said, "Hello."

"Mikey, pack your things and go to a hotel. No, go home, go back to your mother. Don't wait to ask questions. I'll call you as soon as I can, I'll call you tonight and explain."

"But—"

"Don't give me an argument!" Pauling shouted. "This is not a joke, and it doesn't have anything to do with us, with you and me." He imagined Michael nodding on his end of the line. "Just do it, *right now!*"

"All right, Dad."

Michael replaced his receiver. As soon as he had a tone, Pauling dialed another number.

"Harding Associates."

"Jason Harding; Thomas Pauling calling. It's urgent."

"One moment, sir."

Pauling inhaled deeply on the cigarette and stared at the opposite wall.

"Hello, Thomas?"

"Jason, I want a bodyguard for Grace Argent, congress-woman, right now. She's at her offices. I want someone on my home, preferably someone I know, right now. There should be no one home. Someone damn good on Argent. Have you got Brideswell?"

"Yes."

"Use him, alternate with Balke if you can."

"Can do, Thomas."

Pauling hung up. He used the intercom. "Get me Henry Duane, counsel for the congressional committee investigating the intelligence community. Quickly, Harriet."

"Yes, sir."

He stood up and went to the window.

When Harriet buzzed back she said, "Mr. Duane's not in today, Mr. Pauling. I've got his home number and address. The number is ringing. It doesn't answer."

Pauling didn't respond.

"Sir?"

"I'm going out," he told her. "Tell Mrs. Gold we're on a security alert. When Mrs. Pauling calls, if you can't put the call through to me in the car, have Mrs. Gold tell her to sit tight. What's Duane's home address?"

Harriet told him.

"Get Jason Harding back. I just spoke to him. I want some-one to meet me there. Now."

"At Henry Duane's?"

"Yes."

Pauling went to get his jacket and his gun.

/ 3 /

Harding's man was there ahead of him, across the street and a half-dozen houses down from the address. It was Balke, medium height with a big shining bald head. Standing sturdily on the sidewalk between two parked cars, Balke looked like a human artillery shell. When Pauling found a spot for the Porsche, Balke got in next to him.

"What've we got? Harding said to get my ass over here fast. He said you'd fill me in."

Harding headed a Washington firm of private investigators. Balke, like many of Harding's people, had once been with the FBI.

"What we've got," Pauling said, "is the head counsel for a congressional committee. His name is Henry Duane. Number two thirty-five, apartment twenty-one." Pauling looked toward the row houses with high stoops. "He might be in trouble, at least I think he might have been in trouble about half an hour ago."

Balke nodded and pulled on his nose. "How do we handle it?"

"Are you armed?"

"Yes."

"I hate playing cops and robbers," Pauling said. "I didn't always, but I do now."

"Who are the bad guys?"

"Don't be surprised if they speak Spanish. They may be right-wing Cubans, slightly fanatic, and if one of them smiles like an angel, be ready for anything."

"I don't get it."

"Someone I know shot a man a couple of days ago, but the man kept coming."

"The guy who got shot?"

"Yes."

"Jesus, am I glad I was around when the boss called. Why don't we just call the police?"

Pauling shook his head.

As they had talked, he had checked the street. There was no one waiting in any of the cars parked in front of Duane's row house. No one suspicious was loitering. Because of the heat, there were lots of children around, most of them black. A few houses away, three men in shirt sleeves were sitting on a stoop, smoking and talking; they looked right at home. It crossed Pauling's mind that Duane could have afforded a more expensive neighborhood. Maybe he thought he was Ralph Nader.

"Anytime you say," Balke said.

"If we can help Duane, fine. But what I really want is to get hold of one of these people who doesn't mind bullets."

Getting out of the air-conditioned Porsche was like stepping into a sauna.

"Are you relieving on my house tonight?" Pauling asked. He was walking slowly toward Duane's house. Balke was right next to him. Pauling kept checking the neighborhood and the parked cars. It still looked all right.

"First I heard of it," Balke said.

"If Duane's in trouble, then Grace Argent might be. Harding has someone on her now. Probably Brideswell. They may be after me, too. My son Michael was at home—seventeen, tall, blond. I told him to clear out."

"Kids have a way of disobeying."

"That's why I mention it."

They went up the stoop calmly, watching the glass doorway above them, just two men paying a call on a friend. Balke was wearing a lightweight green suit. He had his right hand inside the jacket.

When he was forced to do something like this, Pauling always felt as if he were physically denser than usual. During the early 1960s, when the CIA had stationed him in what was now Ho Chi Minh City, he had been constantly aware of impending danger. That was the first time he had this feeling of increased density. More important, it had taught him that fear, like grace, has to do with what is inside a man, not what's outside. It was his final break with Catholicism; at times like this, it helped enormously.

"You weren't in Vietnam, were you, Balke?"

"Korea," Balke said.

"Did you know that most of the self-immolators were Zen Buddhists?"

"Self-what? Oh. Great way to talk at a time like this."

They had entered the narrow foyer and found the door to the corridor open. Numbers on either side began with one, so they took the stairs. There was no noise and no one in sight. On the second floor they found number twenty-one straight ahead at the rear.

They stood to either side of the door, Pauling facing it, Balke covering his back by facing the stairs. Pauling put his ear to the door, then pulled it back. He had heard nothing.

Balke took out his lock picks; Pauling shook his head, and he put them away again. If there were someone in there they would certainly hear the lock being picked. It was time to knock or to shoot the lock away and go barreling in, hoping there was no chain or police bar.

Balke leaned forward. He ran his eye down the crack between the door and the casing. "It's open," he whispered.

They got set. Balke turned the knob. The door swung open, and they went in, Balke first, then Pauling, both low, like hockey players breaking to either side of the goal, sliding to either side of possible fire. Then Pauling slammed the door closed behind them with his heel.

It was a living room, furnished with heavy Spanish-style chairs and a green velvet Victorian couch; there was no one in it. A window at the rear was open. An air-conditioner was silent in the window next to it. The breeze coming in the open window moved a chintz curtain toward them.

If he had felt like talking, Pauling would have commented on the open window, but he didn't feel like talking. He covered Balke, who went into the room on his right. He came out again shaking his head.

Pauling went to his left. It was a kitchen, unusually large for a city apartment, and there was no one there either. It was probably because of the letdown, the relief that there was no one to kill or be killed by that Pauling missed it the first time around.

"No one," Balke said. "No one in the bedroom and nothing disturbed. That window opens on nothing, no fire escape."

"Someone hated air-conditioning," Pauling guessed.

Pauling had seen it—them—just as Balke had spoken. He saw the heavy kitchen knife still on the little chopping block and the chopping block on the kitchen table. The table wasn't very far from the wall phone. One of them would have dialed for Duane, then handed it over to him. They might have used a drug to kill the pain, and each time he refused them, chopped off another one.

"Jesus Christ," Balke said finally.

There were three of them, next to the wooden block, still bleeding a little. Fingers. A pinkie and two large ones. Probably Duane's. Certainly Duane's.

"Let's go to Capitol Hill," Pauling said.

"You mind telling me now what it's all about?"

"In the car," Pauling said.

"What about those?" Balke asked. "Freeze them? Who knows, they might be able to sew them back on the poor bastard."

Pauling shook his head. "He'll be dead. He'll already be dead," he told Balke.

/ 4 /

Grace Argent looked as angry as McGraw had sounded. "Please explain all this to me," she said. She probably thought she was being charitable.

Pauling drew a deep breath. "Try this: there really is a nonadmitted war on. Whoever is behind it really does want to kill McGraw, probably to buy time. Whoever they are, they don't want our government to know yet that Texaco was only their first target. But they didn't know who McGraw was. Their man in Detroit had seen him, and they knew he was on to what they were doing with the polygraph. If just that part got around, the CIA would suspect the worst. That was probably their real worry. When clips of your committee hearing were shown on nationwide television, they must have guessed that the missing investigator you wanted so much to see was the man they wanted too."

Argent leaned back in her desk chair and stared balefully.

Pauling continued. "They guessed that Duane stifled McGraw's report because of CIA pressure aimed at preventing any mention of Weldmore—that's the name of the place that makes the agents we're interested in. They hoped that Duane knew where McGraw was. When he didn't—they tortured him until they were sure he didn't—they made him guess who might know. He guessed you. Who's a better choice for McGraw to try to persuade that a CIA operation went sour? They had Duane call to verify the suspicion, and you said the wrong thing."

Now she looked at him incredulously. They were alone in her inner office—a surprisingly small room. Given the meticulous way Argent kept her apartment, it was surprisingly cluttered, mostly with piles of papers and files. Balke had come in with his equipment; he and Pauling had checked the place for a bug. There hadn't been one. Then Balke had gone to keep

Brideswell company. Brideswell had arrived earlier, angering Argent, to act as her bodyguard. So far neither Argent, her secretary, nor her assistant had noticed anyone or anything threatening.

Pauling took another deep breath. Argent was still staring at him. "Grace, its time to take precautions. The conclusions I've reached are more than reasonable given our hypotheses."

"That there's a nonadmitted war, beginning with West Depford yesterday? That the CIA is involved?"

"Yes. Isn't that what we all have to be afraid of?"

Argent nodded reluctantly, unwilling, perhaps, to admit she was afraid of anything.

"What did I say that was wrong?"

"When Duane asked you if you wanted to see McGraw, you should have said you wanted to see him. Instead you said maybe."

Argent leaned across her desk at Pauling, placing her arms on her blotter. It was exactly the gesture Pauling used when John Smith thought he wanted to wrestle.

"So they know, or think I know, where he is?" Argent said. "Now look, I could have said that because I suspected Duane was up to some trick. I—"

Pauling was shaking his head. "They'll come after you to make sure. They took three fingers from Duane's hand. By now he's certainly dead. His corpse will never be found."

"Who are they? How did they move so fast? How do we—"

Pauling held up his hand. "In Washington there may be a strike force of anti-Castro Cubans infiltrated by Weldmore."

"Weldmore," Argent repeated harshly.

Pauling nodded. "Programmed Weldmore personnel called Mark II's, working, theoretically, to undermine an international terrorist conspiracy, have infiltrated five American-based operations."

"That's *illegal*," Argent said. She was getting angry again.

"Maybe."

"That's damn hard to believe," Argent said. She sat straight back.

"I'm having my home watched," Pauling told her. "I've alerted my people downtown, but unless I've missed something, they're not on to me yet."

"Just Duane and me?"

"Yes."

"How long do I have to have that man watching me?" She meant Brideswell.

For the first time Pauling noticed there was a picture of Lincoln on her office wall, taken when Pauling's style of beard had been more popular.

"I don't know. Marcia is in Cambridge. She's to make contact with the Weldmore liaison soon, if she hasn't already. That's all it may take. Once we're sure, we can bring it all out into the open. That'd take the heat off. Otherwise McGraw may learn something, or something may break inside the agency. It can't be long. If it's what we fear, it's too big an operation."

Argent slammed her palm on her desk. "No! There's no point waiting for proof. I'm going to tell someone now. Once they know they're exposed, they'll have no reason to kill Henry Duane. He might still be alive."

"Who will you tell?" Pauling asked. "There isn't enough evidence. We can't be sure yet. There might be something we don't know . . . too much we don't know. Besides, Duane is dead."

She changed expression again. This time she looked worried and quizzical.

"Grace, if you tell the wrong person, you may be killed. If you go right to the president on the little we have, you may not be taken seriously. Worse, there might be a leak and the wrong people may be warned prematurely. Maybe Weldmore has not been subverted. Then you'll have blown away an important agency project and ruined lives and careers for nothing. You may destroy the credibility of the intelligence community. That's one of the reasons McGraw brought me into this. He knew I wouldn't act hastily."

"What do you mean 'not subverted'?"

"So far there's too much conjecture. Maybe, despite the way it looks, Weldmore people are going along because it's the only thing they can do. It may only be a matter of hours."

"I insist that if there hadn't been a Weldmore, none of this would have happened."

"Maybe."

She leaned forward and lowered her head about a half inch. Pauling guessed it was, for her, a gesture of defeat. "What am I supposed to do now?"

"You're supposed to disappear for a few days, from any-place you might be expected to be. Like McGraw. I'll instruct your bodyguard to put you in a car and take you to a motel in Virginia."

"He's not that pretty."

"Don't go back to your apartment. Do everything he tells you. He may engage in evasive maneuvers after you leave here, in case you're being followed. They may not try to kill you, but to kidnap and question you. Keep down. This ought to be over in a little while, but in case . . ."

"What?"

"I'm going back to the office now. I'll dictate a letter containing all the information I have, specifying sources, and then I'll speculate a little. I'll have Jason Harding keep a copy of that letter for you."

"Who's he?"

"A man who runs a firm of private investigators. Balke is one of his people. Your bodyguard Brideswell is another."

"All right."

"If anything happens to me, check with Ann Gold at my office. Then go to the White House alone, shout your way in if you have to."

She smiled.

Pauling said, "Have you been listening to the news?"

"I heard a radio broadcast about a half hour ago."

"I haven't heard the news since before I left to go to Duane's."

"Nothing yet. Maybe we're all crazy after all. Maybe Texaco was an isolated incident. The president issued a statement through his press secretary, and that's what he's saying, in effect; that there's no indication it was anything else. The stock market opened late yesterday, but now it's business as usual. Trading in Texaco is still suspended. You know the Dow is down a heap. Fifty points."

Pauling nodded.

"Maybe the president's right," Argent said. "Maybe Wall Street is acting prematurely too."

"Three," Pauling said. "A pinkie and these two." He showed them to her. They were like John Smith's quotation marks.

/ 5 /

McGraw got out of a cab in front of the building that housed FBI headquarters and took the elevator to the tenth floor where a man he knew named Hendricks led him into a private office. It was the Special Agent's office, but the Special Agent was out. There were venetian blinds on the two windows and steel filing cabinets on the wall between them. Behind the desk were a half-dozen framed photographs of politicians and high-level bureau personnel, a portrait of J. Edgar among them, full face, glowering at the world.

"I'm glad you're around," McGraw said.

"Where would I be? You're getting famous, Stub. I read a newspaper article about your committee today. No one seems to know whether you've been fired or just missing in action."

"Neither," McGraw told him.

Hendricks was in his middle forties; like McGraw he was overweight. He put himself into the chair behind the desk as though it belonged to him. He and McGraw had worked together on several cases, Hendricks as McGraw's subordinate. That might help.

"Then you're still with the committee?" Hendricks asked.

McGraw nodded. "I need something."

"Name it."

"If the CIA is playing around in the bureau's territory, will you help me find out?"

Hendricks cocked his head to one side. "CIA operating internally? Here in Detroit? I'd *love* you to find out."

"Have you got a current file on the Black Panthers?"

"Current?" Hendricks seemed stupified. "Man, that stuff is dead."

"Could be," McGraw told him. "But there will be something on the people who used to give us trouble here."

"Sure," Hendricks said.

"I want an address. A name. Better: lots of names. Lots of addresses."

"You mean you want everything we have."

McGraw nodded.

Hendricks made a face at him. He popped his eyes and compressed his lips. "You serious?"

"Will you look into it?"

"This is asking more than you did before."

"Yes."

"What about the other thing? The informer I gave you. Was Harvey straight with you? Was that the man you were tipped to? The one Harvey told us was using a polygraph?"

"Harvey was straight," McGraw said. "Yeah, that was the man I was tipped to."

"What's it all about? Are you telling me the big guy is involved with the CIA?"

"Maybe."

"Come on, Stub, give."

"It works this way," McGraw said. "An agent volunteers to turn the machine on everyone inside a criminal or subversive organization—like this Mr. Johnson's—to see who's loyal, who's not, and who isn't sure. That gives the agent a toehold which he then exploits. Harvey says there's a big job about to come down. Johnson was using the big guy to make sure everyone who had a part in it had the right attitude."

"That machine's not infallible," Hendricks said. "What if they use it on the agent himself?"

"That's the point. He can beat it. He's trained to beat it."

Hendricks made his face again. Then he said, "All right, let's suppose that's possible. So what? How does the big guy fit in? He's white, right?"

"Oh yeah."

"How does Johnson find out about him? Why does Johnson think he's doing it? Does he get a fee or what? Is it a new syndicate service, the traveling truth box?"

McGraw smiled. "That's what Harvey thought. But let's say he actually uncovers a plant: police or one of the bureau's people."

"Lovely," Hendricks said.

"I thought you'd like it. But it makes sense that the big guy is involved with these former Panthers, that he got to Mr. Johnson through them."

Hendricks sat waiting for McGraw to continue, looking skeptical.

"He may be part of a plan to activate terrorist groups."

"What?" Hendricks said.

McGraw said, "Do you like what happened in West Depford yesterday?"

Hendricks had been leaning back in the Special Agent's chair. He brought himself forward heavily. "Okay, let's have it, Stub."

"It's awfully hot in this town. It feels to me like the kind of weather when Panthers or ex-Panthers might try to start something."

"Oh hell, man, this isn't sixty-seven or sixty-eight. Things are different. The mayor's black. Things are different."

"Sure," McGraw said, "unemployment is real low and the ghettos are filled with contented ladies and gentlemen, boys and girls playing happily in the water from fire hydrants. Look, West Depford may have been the first of several targets. Detroit may be next. All of it. The big man with the polygraph machine may be part of it. Harvey, the informer you say is straight told me that automatic weapons are involved."

"Yeah, he told me that too," Hendricks said.

"You did nothing about it?"

"I didn't believe it."

"West Depford," McGraw said.

Hendricks sat very still, thinking it over. When he was finished doing that, he said, "The boss is out of town; that leaves it up to me. I'm going to put a team on it. Since yesterday we've been looking at possible sabotage targets and possible saboteurs. I'm going to put two men on this Mr. Johnson angle."

"How about the Panthers?" McGraw said.

"I just can't believe there's anything to that. It's hot, yeah, but it's not the sixties, there's no Vietnam War, the mayor's black. But I'm not going to get caught with my pants down. If you want to know about ex-Panthers, go back to Harvey."

"He'd know?"

"Mr. Johnson's people aren't the only ones he keeps us up on. Yeah, he'd know."

McGraw got up.

"I think you're nuts," Hendricks said. "Let's say I hope you're nuts." There was disbelief in his tone but friendliness overrode it. He clapped McGraw on the back as they came out of the office.

Chapter Six

/ 1 /

The call came in to 400 Brattle about the same time Balke was asking Pauling whether to freeze the fingers. Because communications within the building were excellent, Harriman was alerted before the phone rang a second time. He was in the computer room in the basement with the machine operator, Levine. Levine was sandy-haired and baby-faced. He had a faraway look in his eyes and a benign smile, but he wasn't a Mark II. He was a Mark I, one of Dr. Facett's trainees, a failure as a field agent, and an addict. Harriman kept him at Weldmore because of his expertise with computers. He would do anything his supplier of drugs asked him to do, and Harriman was his supplier. He was twenty-five years old.

Lawrence Douglas was in the room too, wearing a sling. He and Harriman were standing near the printout when a metallic sound on the wall intercom made them look up.

The woman's voice that came over the box sounded crisp and professional.

"Call on thirty-four. Repeat. Call on thirty-four."

Harriman walked to the wall and hit a button below the speaker. "I'm in the computer room. Put it on the intercom and answer it."

Immediately there was a sound of a ringing phone; then the voice that had alerted Harriman said, "Good morning. Weldmore."

"This is Savage," a woman said. "Put me through to Dr. Facett."

"Right away, Savage."

There was a click, which meant that the caller was on hold. Harriman pushed the button again. "All right, put it through. Don't cut me off."

There was a buzzing, then Facett's voice. "Yes."

"Savage for you on thirty-four."

Facett took a moment to respond. "All right. I'll pick it up here."

There was another click on the speaker, then Facett's voice. "Hello."

"This is Savage. Is this Rita Facett?"

"Yes."

"You're being paged, Dr. Facett. One, two, one, five."

"But this isn't—"

"One, two, one, five," Savage repeated; she hung up.

"Get her, Lawrence," Harriman said.

"Yes, Mark."

Lawrence left through the glass doors. Harriman turned to Levine. "We'll run it through again later. Looks good so far."

"Thanks."

"You'll have a chance to sit in as the calls come in. We'll be fielding twice as many people. If the strain is too much on Berger, I'll want you to bring the machine in on line. I'll want it running dry and the machine responses recorded even if we don't need to bring it in. It'll be the first test of the full system."

"It'll go well, Dr. Harriman. If the agents stick to procedure."

Harriman nodded. He wasn't thinking about the computer, he was thinking about Facett. And he was wondering how long they had.

Levine put in a series of instructions, using the machine language panel at his desk. The tape decks started to wind and the printer to bang out a summary readout. Levine had been running an automatic response program cued by voice identification and testing an override emergency procedure. He didn't know what the emergency procedure meant, and he didn't care.

Lawrence appeared with Facett in the corridor outside the computer room, and Harriman went out to them.

"Go back into the computer room, Lawrence."

"Yes, Mark."

"I want to talk to you alone," Harriman said to Facett. "Do you mind if we take the elevator up?"

"I just came down."

"I thought my office would be better, or yours. Shall we go to your office?"

"All right."

She looked at him fearfully. He didn't want that. Fear was precisely what he had to dispel.

"Come on, Rita. I've been meaning to talk to you since last night, but first you were upset about Laamb, then I had the people to send out this morning, and the procedures to go over with Levine."

She said nothing. When the elevator door opened, she got in. He pressed himself against the side wall and stared at the ceiling. He didn't want her upset; he kept his distance.

"I'm supposed to leave here within fifteen minutes," she said.

"I know. It's all right."

"You'll let me go?"

"Yes. After we talk, I'll let you go."

"You mean to kill me, don't you? You don't need me now."

"Now is when I do need you. Before, I didn't."

They stepped out onto the first floor. Facett's office was down the hall from and on the same side as Harold Berger's. They went to it.

Harriman sat in front of the desk. Facett seemed tentative. She stood, not taking her seat.

"Please," Harriman said.

She sat.

With the desk between them, with Facett's chair slightly higher than his, with her in the seat of authority and he as her guest, he hoped she would understand what he wanted her to understand. He looked out her office window at the lawn and trees and the drive beyond them. Her office was much smaller than Berger's or his own, but it was more pleasant. It was painted light blue; Facett had hung several framed watercolor seascapes on the walls.

"I'm letting the boy go," Harriman said.

"I don't believe you."

"He'll be back with his adoptive parents in a matter of days, as soon as it can be arranged."

"It doesn't matter. You could kill him or have him killed any time you wanted."

"No. You could get him moved by the agency, secured somewhere else. You know you could. I want you to know I don't need him any longer. You're going to come around to see things my way. You're going to be on my side soon. That's what I told you yesterday, wasn't it? Now try to understand. I have the bombs. If things don't go well, I have a far greater threat—not just to you but to anyone and everyone—than the death of a small, black child."

Facett swallowed.

"Look, would you like to visit him? I'll arrange it. We can tell him you're a friend of the people he's been with. Then we'll let him go."

She sighed but did not answer.

"Listen to me, Rita. You have no idea how big the stakes are, what I expect to win."

She shook her head.

"You haven't even tried to guess," he said.

"I've tried."

Harriman got up and went to the window. He looked intense and especially handsome. His black hair had fallen over his forehead on both sides, which set off his face to advantage. Whenever he concentrated hard, he lost the overmothered look Facett hated.

"In a few minutes more you have to leave, so I'm going to be brusque," he said. "I'm going to threaten you. Then I'm going to give you something to think about. Then I'm going to promise you something. Then I'm going to tell you what I want you to give me of your own free will and in no other way. Then I'm going to promise you something else."

He had ticked the points off on his fingers. He held his outstretched hand in front of him as if it contained notes, as Laamb's yellow pad had contained the points he wanted to make the night before.

"I don't know who this Savage is," Harriman said. "Your usual contact is a man, isn't it?"

"Yes."

"All right. If this is special, if this is anything but a routine check or a meeting to acquaint you with new procedure or personnel, and if you say anything, or give any hint that leads to trouble for me and what I am trying to do here, I will blow up a major city. Clear?"

"Dear God," she said.

"Clear?"

"Yes."

"You know I'll do it?"

She didn't answer.

"Quickly now!"

"Yes. You would do it."

"Good. That's one, the threat. Two, what I want you to think about. Rita, imagine a country is at war with another country, let's say in the Middle Ages. The first country, the invader, crosses the borders with a huge army and destroys several key border forts. All right?"

She nodded.

"What happens in the invaded country, Rita?"

"Panic."

"Yes! Panic made worse because the country invaded has no army equal to the hordes of invaders. All right?"

"Yes."

"Suddenly the invading army disappears."

"What?"

"Suddenly the invaders are swallowed up in an earthquake. What happens then, Rita?"

"What are you saying?"

He took a step toward her, bit his lip, and stopped. "What happens then?" he repeated.

"Things return to normal. There's relief, jubilation."

"Right. That's point two. The thing I want you to think about. Three: the first promise. I won't use the bombs unless I'm forced. Absolutely forced. It's far more important that they exist than that they be used."

"What?"

"I'm telling you the truth. They are my invading armies. Do you understand?"

"No," she said.

"I do not want to use those bombs!" Harriman shouted. He slammed the frame of Facett's window with the side of his fist. When he had finished staring at her to drive the point further, he lifted the hand with which he had slammed the frame, wiped his imaginary moustache with it, then held it out again, again as if it contained notes like Laamb's.

"I am not going to tell you, on the moment of your departure for a meeting with an agency control, why I'm doing all this. I tell you I'm moving against minor targets. When you get back, if you like, I'll take you downstairs to the operations room and lay them out for you."

"Why now? Why are you letting my son go now? Taking me into your confidence now? It's because you need me to fool the control! What if I tell Savage this?"

"I told you. Listen carefully. That would force me to use a

bomb. Rita, of course I want you to fool the control. But it's not really necessary for my survival or the survival of the operation. Of course I want you to fool the control. But I want you, period. I want you on my side. That's point four. I want you to come back to me, Rita, of your own free will. A few minutes ago you were afraid I might kill you. The reverse is true. I want to keep you alive and close to me. Very close to me. That's my intention, not to let you go, ever, not if I can help it."

She laughed mirthlessly. "Then you have to tell me something else now, something else, not everything. That might be a start."

He looked down at his hand again. He still had the fifth point, the other thing he was going to promise her. He sighed and said, "No." He dropped his hand. "Not now. When you come back, I'll tell you more. I'll tell you as much as I can."

"My God, you're a bastard."

"Something like that, yes. I'm also the best psychiatrist you ever met, on a one-to-one basis and in analyzing and predicting mass psychodynamics. And I'm even more than that, aren't I, Rita?"

She shook her head. She was staring down at her desk blotter, at a number of addressed envelopes all containing letters but none containing a breath of what she wanted to scream to the world. She thought she would break. She hoped she would.

"Yes," she said, "you're more than that. I don't know what. Whatever it is, I don't like it."

"You will. You'll like it. Now listen. My last point."

He held his hand up higher, waiting for her to acknowledge his ability to organize his thoughts and hold them. "Five: the second thing I said I'd promise you. I'll never call you Reets again. Never."

"Oh, go fuck yourself," she said. She said it with little conviction.

He closed his eyes for a moment. "Please go meet Savage

now. You're almost late, and that won't do. Please remember: I give you your son now, I return him to you now as a gesture of good faith. I believe you'll see that any murders I may be responsible for, before all this is over, are for the good. So I give him to you now. Irrevocably. He's as good as back in his home. But I can destroy a city. I promise you that. That will work to my benefit. I'll have four more bombs. I've set it up so that anything now works to my benefit. So be careful. Please. Be careful."

He turned back to the window.

She was crying. "I think I'm going to fly apart. Just fly apart."

"You won't. You're made of very tough stuff. Like me. Tougher than you know. Believe me, I can judge people. It's my business, isn't it? You get to the point of suicide, you either give in to it, or you go past it. You're one of the few who'll go past it. You and I will be like this some day." He held up two fingers of his right hand pressed together. "Sweet Rita."

She wiped her eyes.

"You're late," he told her.

She left without looking at him, expecting every moment to be called back, expecting worse.

/ 2 /

The last Mark II to leave 400 Brattle Street was Stephen, who had a face like a cherub and wavy auburn hair. Stephen was also the first of the Mark II's to approach his target. His van emerged on the Brooklyn side of the Brooklyn Battery Tunnel early that afternoon and moved easily up onto the Belt Parkway making for the Prospect Expressway.

Stephen kept exactly to the speed limit. Although it was as hot in New York as in most of the country, he had the air-conditioner turned off and the windows wide open. Like the other Mark II's of the Weldmore Institute, he deplored air-conditioning; he liked things natural.

Soon Stephen was driving in the extreme left-hand lane of the southbound half of a six-lane highway which cut through the interior of Brooklyn from Prospect Park to Coney Island. Mark Harriman particularly despised the interior of Brooklyn, when he took the time to despise anything, because he had grown up in it. If any of the five bombs had to be set off, he hoped it would be the one Stephen was transporting. To each side of the six-lane highway, called Ocean Parkway, apartment building after apartment building presented a bland, brick facade from the cement pavement past the numerous heavily laden trees to the deep blue summer sky. Beyond the apartment buildings in all directions were house after house after house, each much like all the rest, exactly as Harriman had known it. It would have pleased him to see Stephen barreling along in the van, his round face drawn taut by a fine, full smile, his auburn hair whipped by the wind.

Near the corner of the parkway and Avenue S, a corner nearly indistinguishable from all the others he had passed, Stephen slowed to negotiate a left turn. He proceeded north past Coney Island Avenue, past Ocean Avenue, and finally turned into a side street lined with single and attached private homes, relatively late-model cars in front of each of them. He found the number he had been told to find and turned into the driveway. Then he got out of the van, opened the doors to the garage, got back in the van, and drove in.

The garage was not like other garages. It had been cut away at the rear and extended into a garage that backed against it and belonged to a house on the next street over. All this had been arranged by a stocky Mark II named Carl, who joined Stephen and helped him lift out his two suitcases. Stephen carried the one with the charge.

The men put their suitcases down to draw a curtain across the back of the van and to pile a lawnmower, some cartons, three old tires, and a folding bed in front of the curtain. It now looked from either side of the double garage as though there were no vehicle in it at all.

When they were done, Stephen and Carl shook hands, lifted the suitcases, and went into the house.

"You were right on time, Stephen," Carl said. The shortest of the Mark II's, he was as cheerful but not nearly as attractive as Stephen.

"I hope everything else is going on schedule, Carl," Stephen said as he put his suitcase down near a table in a small kitchen.

"Oh, it is, it is, Stephen. Of course, as Harold has said, when you're dealing with so many unknowns, especially the personalities of the guerrillas, it's difficult to be dead sure of anything. So we can't be absolutely certain it'll go off at exactly the moment we would all like. But as long as it doesn't go off early, I know Harold will be pleased."

"Oh, I know he will," Stephen said. "Harold actually stepped into my room last night and told me. The World Trade Center. It's lovely."

"Very few people will die," Carl said.

"Yes, I know."

"We rented the office space, we made arrangements to store what we told them was boxed furniture—Mark was especially helpful with the engineering problems—and well, it's just all set. All we have to do, literally, is pull the plug on the freezing unit, Stephen."

Stephen nodded. He had put himself into a chair near a Formica-top table.

"Would you like some iced tea, Stephen?" Carl asked.

Stephen nodded.

"We're quite alone, you know. My group knows I'm here, of course, and they know you were expected. They may want to test you on the polygraph, by the way."

Carl laughed. He had gone to the refrigerator and was removing a tray of ice from the freezer.

"But if there's anything at all you want to tell me about things, now's the time."

"Nothing really, Carl. Everyone is fine. Harold is looking very well."

"Oh, good."

"Mark is slightly wearisome of course, but that's his job."

"Yes. I'm glad Harold is feeling fine, Stephen."

Stephen said, "Two spoons of sugar, please."

"Of course."

A few moments later, both men were sitting calmly in the heat, sipping iced tea. The suitcase with the charge was at Stephen's left. After awhile he put his feet up on it so he could be more comfortable.

/ 3 /

Harvey had been sound asleep, but when McGraw forced his way in past the woman he woke up immediately; he stepped out of the bedroom wearing nothing but Jockey shorts. He was as thin as but more muscular than McGraw would have supposed.

The furnishings were threadbare, but the apartment was as neat as any McGraw had ever been in. Everything was in place. The woman behind him was compact, in her early twenties, and prettier than Harvey deserved.

"Who is he, Harv?" she asked.

"Go on, go for a walk."

"But—"

"It'll be all right. You do it."

The woman left without another word. When the door closed behind her, Harvey went into the bathroom to brush his teeth. McGraw followed.

"It's mid-afternoon, Harvey."

"I was up all night. You know, coming right here could get me killed."

"Doubtful," McGraw said.

Harvey had squeezed some Colgate on a brush and went to work with it. When he was done, he gargled, tore off some toilet tissue, folded it, and blew his nose. "What?" he asked. He flushed the toilet tissue in the bowl. "What do you want?"

"Who else besides Mr. Johnson is the big guy involved with?"

"Nobody. Nobody I know of."

Harvey looked at his face in the mirror and then at McGraw. He obviously felt more secure in his own apartment than he had in McGraw's car two nights before.

"I see you still got your cold," McGraw said.

"I don't know any more about that monster than I told you already."

"The price is the same. One hundred. Right now. I want an address. A name." McGraw stepped well aside from the door of the bathroom so Harvey could leave it without brushing against his considerable bulk. Harvey went back over to the bed and pulled on his pants.

"Sorry," Harvey said.

"All right, let's try something else. What about Black Panthers, Harvey."

"You kidding?"

"No."

"Uh huh. That's dead shit, isn't it?"

"Is it, Harvey?"

"You better believe it, Mr. McGraw."

"Give me a name. Name someone who'd be involved if it wasn't dead shit."

"Yeah, well, maybe. Isaac Carver. He has a woman around the corner from here. And a place of business near the river. A warehouse."

McGraw described the area where he had almost been killed.

"That's right. You know the place then?" Harvey was putting on a tight-fitting, white V-necked T-shirt.

"Yes," McGraw said. "Stupid of me not to have gone there first."

"It'd have saved you a hundred bucks," Harvey said.

McGraw sighed and handed over the money. This time it was five twenties. He was running low on cash.

"If you need me again, don't come here," Harvey said. "I have a telephone; you have my number. And if you see Charlotte on your way out, pretend you don't know her, all right?"

"Sure, Harvey," McGraw said. "Sure."

He could have kicked himself. He left the apartment and went down the stairs as fast as he could manage them.

/ 4 /

"Dr. Facett."

Facett turned to stare at the blond woman with the shoulder bag who had accosted her as soon as she pushed through the heavy door. The lobby of the hotel was as large as a ballroom, ornate, and carpeted.

"There's a message for you at the desk."

Facett nodded and walked on. She did not look back but guessed the woman who had spoken to her was the new Savage, that she had gone ahead to set up the meeting. The desk was on the far side of a number of couches and chairs from a bank of a half-dozen elevators.

"My name is Facett. Have you a message for me?"

"Oh yes. Here you are," the desk clerk said. "It was handed to me only a moment ago."

Facett took the envelope and opened it. The message was a room number. She understood that she was probably being watched to make sure she told no one where she was going. There were over a dozen people in the lobby, some of them on the couches nearby.

Ordinarily there were no written messages. Facett had simply been met in the lobby by her control. From the lobby they had walked across the street to the park. Only once before had she been asked to come up to a room, when Savage had the flu and hadn't wanted to meet her outdoors. On that occasion he had explained the arrangement over the open line at Weldmore.

Facett got off the elevator, found the room, and knocked. There was no answer. Finally the elevator behind her opened; the woman who had told her there was a message got out alone and came toward her.

"I'm Savage."

"No, you're not."

"I am now."

The woman's blond hair was exceptional, Facett thought; she had a pleasant face, easy to look at. She was turning a key in the lock. When she stepped in, Facett followed.

"Please sit down."

The woman turned on a light. Apparently she wasn't going to draw back the curtains or pull up the shade.

Facett put herself in a chair near a large television set. The room was small, cramped with the necessary furniture. The walls were green.

"Look," the woman said. "You know this is special."

Facett stared at her, afraid to say anything.

"We found out you have a son," the woman said softly. "Your control never knew that. That's one of the reasons your usual contact isn't here, why I'm here instead."

Facett never changed expression. She never even blinked.

"I need, I'm sorry but I need *right now,* proof that no one has used your son to turn you around. I want you to go back to Weldmore and bring me the Mark II agent files. Even Weldmore could, theoretically, be turned against us. Go back, put everything in an attaché case, and bring it here."

Facett smiled. "I'm not sure I can do that."

"I'm ordering you to do that."

Facett drew herself up. "'Look, I don't know what this is all about. It's insane, right? I know you people can be weird, *but I have not got a son!* You must have me mixed up with someone else."

She knew she sounded vulgar, that she had suddenly adopted the speech cadence of a street black. She knew it, but she didn't know what to do about it.

The woman looked at her steadily. "Now you're making me think the whole place might be rotten. Have you got a problem, Rita? What's got you so upset?"

"Look, I don't know you, *right?* I don't know what you want. I can't just dance out of Weldmore with the files because you know the code name of my control. Why don't *you* just dance in?"

"Until a moment ago, I was thinking of doing just that."

"I don't have a son," Facett said. She got up.

"All right," the woman told her. "It looks like we do have a problem. I was hoping we didn't. If you're holding out because you've held out for years, just because it's become a habit, stop it. If you don't, I have to assume you're holding out for other reasons. Maybe you want a little time to think about it. I wish I could give it to you, but I can't. If something's gone sour at Weldmore, you have to tell me. I'll help you with it. Trust me."

Facett walked toward the door. "Hey, you've got it wrong. If you order me to get the files, I will. But they're just copies of the ones I already sent to Washington. And I'll have to call Washington to make sure you're who you say you are, right?"

"Of course," the woman said. "I don't love pressing you on this. I understand it's a shock to find we know about the boy. But now you've got to cooperate, don't you?"

"There's nothing to it," Facett said. "Someone's put you onto something crazy. There's no boy." She put her hand on the doorknob. "You still want me to go back and get the files?"

The woman shook her head. "Don't go yet, Rita. If you go now, I may not be able to help you. I'll level with you. We know he's missing. We know they have him. He must be alive, or they must have convinced you he is. Help us now, and we'll break our necks to get him back for you . . . for his adoptive parents."

Facett made her eyes wide and let her anger build. "Honey, you're nuts," she said. She turned the knob.

The woman took a revolver out of her shoulder bag and pointed it at her.

Facett froze. She had seen what a gun could do. She had seen what one did to Laamb's head.

"Finn!" the woman called.

A connecting door opened and two men came in. "We're going to have to keep you here, Rita," she said. "Please go inside with these gentlemen and make yourself comfortable. They'll have to watch you until we decide what to do next. While they're watching you, please reconsider. Don't hold out on us."

Facett felt faint and slumped against the man who had approached her. He held her, and she almost cried.

It wasn't fear that had her, it was relief. She didn't have to go back there. They wouldn't let her. Dear God, it was out of her hands.

/ 5 /

The phone booths were near the newspaper stand at the glass doors, and the man behind the candy and Kleenex was missing some of his front teeth. Maybe he had been with the Bruins, Marcia thought. He was waiting on a tall man with his arm in a sling.

"Where are you?" Pauling asked.

"At a pay phone in the lobby. She won't talk, but she's badly frightened. She's crying, has been for some time. We still don't have proof. She won't confess, she won't say anything. They've been turned all right. I'm sure of it," Marcia said.

"All right. That's good enough for me. I'll call John. Mc-Graw was right. By the way, the boy's adoption record can't be traced to her. We've checked."

"Will Smith move now?"

"I think so. I think he'll go on his authority alone. You bring in Facett."

"Right. As soon as I'm sure we're clear. Just in case Facett was followed. I'll assume there's a problem and have Finn set up a safe departure procedure."

"Good. Wait until we talk again. What's the room number?"

The man with the sling put a paper under his immobilized arm, and walked away. Marcia had not seen his face.

"It's room eight-twelve. Did you get the files?"

"No, not yet, but John came through with the names of five subverted groups," Pauling said.

"Five groups, five vans."

"Maybe. At any rate there's one here in Washington—Cubans. I've asked Harding to set up a surveillance, if he can find them. He had files on them. I'm studying them now. I wonder who the hell is going to get the bill for all this."

"Anything else?"

"Yes. We think Henry Duane, the subcommittee counsel, was murdered. I've had a bodyguard placed on Grace and one on our house. Michael got off all right; I was worried about him for a while."

"To his mother?"

"Yes."

"Damn it, be careful."

"You be careful," he said. "Set it up for after dark if that suits Finn. Get back up to that room."

She hung up, bought a copy of the *Boston Globe* from the man with the missing teeth, and went back toward the elevators.

The phone in Marcia's hotel room rang two hours later. She lifted the receiver.

"Yes?"

It was Pauling. "It's all right. John has acted. It took awhile, but he's put it under maximum secure surveillance. There's a great deal of activity inside the building, lots of people talking, lots of lights.

"Are you sure it's secure?"

"No one who leaves will get far, anyone who wants to can go in. I'd say in a matter of a few more hours, he'll take the next step."

"Then it's all right. Our part in this may be over."

"Let's hope so. Bring in that package. Have you set up a way to go?"

"Yes."

"Bring it in carefully. It's a little after nine now. I'll expect you in four hours."

"I hear you. I'll see you soon."

She went to tell Finn and Stein.

/ 6 /

Like the four other suitcases with fissionable charges, John Harcourt's was very heavy. Harcourt managed it with one hand, however, carrying it up the stairs and into the second-floor furnished apartment the Cubans had rented for them. The feat was especially impressive because Harcourt was so thin. He carried the suitcase through to the bedroom and put it down on the floor near the one Jean had carried up.

Jean came into the bedroom and went to the open window. From it she was able to see the brown van where John had parked it near a streetlight. The neighborhood—rows of four-story walk-ups with high stoops—was much like the one where Henry Duane, the committee counsel, had lived.

"It's almost time for our call, John," Jean said.

Harcourt looked at his watch, nodded, and took a seat on the bed near the telephone on the night table. They had been in that apartment less than a minute. Already they looked as though they had lived there all their lives. They were smiling and for a moment, Harcourt, who was not a handsome man— his features, his complexion were off-putting—actually showed a small amount of physical charm.

"It's always exciting calling Harold," Jean said. "You know, sometimes we get to talk to him longer when we're on the road like this than we do when we're in Cambridge."

"I know," John said. "But this is different. We were being tested before. This time what we're doing is really important to him."

Jean came and sat next to John on the bed. When it was time, John lifted the receiver, held it so Jean could hear too, and dialed. It took only a moment for the phone in Cambridge to ring. It rang once, then again, then it was answered.

"Hello."

"Hello, sir, this is John."

"Wonderful, John! How are you, John! It's good to hear your voice."

"Jean's listening."

"Oh good. Good!"

"It's good to hear your voice too, sir. Everything is going as it should, sir. You can tell Mark that there were no problems. Jean reminded me every half hour about my state."

"Good," Berger's voice replied cheerfully. "Good. Good. Have you made your first circuit?"

"Yes, sir. I let Jean come up to the apartment, then I did it, sir. There was very little traffic. I'm parked just down the block."

"Good. Good. John, listen carefully. It's time now to switch to foreign."

John smiled and leaned back a little. Jean looked at him curiously. He had moved the phone so that it was more difficult for her to hear. "All right, sir. I understand. We won't have any trouble finding you, will we, sir?"

"John!" Jean whispered loudly. "Come down. Come down now!"

On the other end of the phone there was a shrill sound, as if something had gone wrong with the connection, then Berger's voice said, "Good. Good."

"Sir?" John said.

"Yes, it's all right, John. I understand your concern. There will be no problem. John, listen carefully. It's time now to switch to foreign."

"Yes, sir."

"Good-bye, John."

"Good-bye, sir."

Harcourt replaced the receiver and sighed.

Jean stood up. "You weren't supposed to ask that. You aren't supposed to ask any questions like that. You have to stay within the parameters. You know he can no more allow himself to be concerned with your fears and psychological problems on the phone than he can in person. John, that was stupid, really stupid."

John smiled and nodded.

"There was a strange sound on his end," he said. "Did you hear it?"

"Of course there was," Jean answered quickly. Although her reply made no sense to either of them, Harcourt nodded, accepting it.

"We've switched to foreign," Harcourt told her.

"Well what's the difference? There's no difference, is there, John? It just means we are to arm the van and call a different number. There's no difference."

"No, Jean," John said. "There's no difference. We've moved. There's no difference."

"It just means he'll be somewhere else. It won't be more difficult to think about him, John. John!"

"I wonder how the others are taking it," John said.

"How should they take it? What's there to take, John? I sense that you think you have a problem, John. I want you to tell me about it. I want you to go into state three, John."

John sat still, staring straight ahead.

"Go on, I want you to go into three, John. Shall I take you up?"

John placed his hands on his knees and closed his eyes. A moment later he opened them again. "No need, Jean. I'm in three."

"All right. Now, John, where's the problem?"

"He's at another number," John said. "Harold's moved."

"Why is that a problem, John? What does it remind you of? Use your physical feelings. Your key word is moved. Moved."

After a moment or two John said, "I'm six."

"What's going on, John? Tell me what's going on."

"We're moving. We're all in the . . . in the car, and we're going to a new house. I hate to leave our house, that house. Nice old house, and mommy is . . . ."

John went on for some time. When he was done reliving the incident from his childhood, Jean made him lie down and helped him put himself into total, a deep state of anesthetic self-hypnosis, so sleep was deep and restful. Soon, although it was not particularly late, she lay down too. She fell asleep, self-programmed to awaken in exactly two hours, when, cheerful and alert, she would wake John and instruct him to arm the van.

/ 7 /

The calls had started coming in to 400 Brattle Street at eight fifteen, but it was not until nine, after six calls had been fielded by Berger himself, while the machine duplicated his efforts, that Harriman decided he could move. That meant it would be best to keep the computer room secure until nine the next morning. That way the least strain would be put on his agents, and each of them would have been instructed personally, either by Berger or Berger's voice. Possible trauma would be avoided. Preparations were made, and the room was vacated.

Empty, fully lighted, the computer room was eerie, an empty horror house, partly because of the artificial fluorescent lighting. The tapes sat motionless, waiting. The small lights on Levine's instruction panel flashed on and off beside three white phones.

Abruptly, there was an electronic thud on the speaker on Levine's panel, followed a moment later by the sound of a ringing phone. The phone sounded not just much louder, but much more real, much closer, than the sound of the phone that had come over the intercom for Rita Facett hours before. The computer tapes began to turn. The call was automatically answered.

Harold Berger's amplified voice echoed through the empty room. "Yes?"

"This is Martin, sir."

"Wonderful, Martin! How are you, Martin! It's good to hear your voice."

"I'm fine, sir."

"Oh good. Good!"

"Everything is fine, sir. I'm right on schedule. I was held up a little in rush-hour traffic on the New York State Thruway, sir, but we expected that and everything is fine."

"Good. Good. Martin, listen carefully . . ."

There was a slight pause during which the tapes moved back and forth, coming to dead stops before they moved again at great speed, a little like birds feeding—fast, alert, and awkward.

". . . it's time now to switch to foreign."

"All right, sir. I'll switch to foreign. Is there any problem, sir?"

The tapes began to do it again, measuring Martin's words,

searching for the right response. They came up with one very quickly.

"Problem? No, Martin, absolutely not. Everything's wonderful."

"I'll say good-bye then, sir."

"Good-bye, Martin. I look forward to talking with you again in the morning."

"And I with you, sir."

The computer cut Martin off, and the room became silent and eerie again until a few minutes later, when there was another electronic thud on the speaker. Once again, a phone began to ring.

Chapter Seven

/ 1 /

The war in Detroit began at exactly ten thirty-eight. The temperature was ninety-four degrees at City Hall and about three thousand degrees in the center of the first of the nearly simultaneous nonatomic explosions that knocked out most of the power in Michigan, Wisconsin, Indiana, Ohio, and Ontario. The lights in Grosse Pointe and Melvindale went out first. They were on, and then they weren't, as if they had been an illusion all the time. Everything went almost precisely as David, the former Panthers, and Mr. Johnson had planned it.

At the atomic generating plant ninety miles south of the city, near Blissfield, the four-foot-thick power exit cables, fifty yards from the reactor, were cut by carefully placed charges. As the saboteurs watched, pieces of concrete were hurled hundreds of feet into the air; warning sirens sounded. This meant the plant was automatically shutting down, the radioactive rods lifting up out of the water they warmed and sliding into their lead sheathings.

Simultaneously other saboteurs, using the kind of charges employed at West Depford, destroyed five transformer units that reduced the voltage coming in from the south. Near Pleasant Ridge a passing motorist saw a steam generating plant go up like a star in a nova; a refrigerated tank truck, disguised as an ordinary fuel oil carrier but filled with liquified natural gas was parked there until it exploded, only one minute behind schedule. At that moment the sudden power demands on systems in neighboring states and Canada burned out two generators before they could be shut down, and seriously damaged three others.

To prevent assistance from electric generating systems even farther away, each of the five separate overland power lines feeding the Detroit area were brought down in inaccessible locations; in all, ten steel towers were destroyed, leaving high power lines on the ground. For several minutes high-voltage arcs blazed white lightning and bent and melted the steel of the capsized towers. The explosive devices were claymore mines.

Thirty-four people were killed and several wounded by the various blasts, all but a few as a result of the Pleasant Ridge detonation, but the casualty list was going to mount.

The moment the blackout was total throughout Detroit, squads of armed criminals moved against the banks. Meanwhile the saboteurs themselves, members of a black-nationalist group who called themselves the Night Liberators, hurried back to the city to begin a triple action.

One group organized attacks on police stations. Others began a systematic distribution of automatic weapons to potential looters and members of teen-age gangs. A third group set fire to business districts near Renaissance Center with incendiary bombs. Intending to keep fire fighters away, the third group then took up positions on nearby roofs.

By eleven thirty, less than an hour after the blackout began, there was more blood on the streets of Detroit than had ever been spilled in an American city. Squad cars had been attacked by mobs, police had emptied their riot weapons into crowds in self-defense and had been murdered for their trouble. Over one hundred corpses lay bleeding in Highland Park where rival youth gangs had shot at each other and at innocent bystanders. At a precinct near the Ford plant, the streets were literally washed with the blood of men who had been cut down from the roof when they tried to rush the front door, the blood crimson and glaring in the light of the power lanterns set up by the police.

Near the old ferry slip for Belle Isle, a merchant who had tried to prevent looting had been shot and then hung from a light post. Everywhere in the dark streets, merchandise was being transported by hand, cart, wheelbarrow, automobile, truck, and bicycle from the stores of Detroit to homes and apartments. That night every automobile from every auto-mobile showroom in the city was driven off through streets which were without light or police.

The swiftest and surest part of the operation occurred at the banks. Mr. Johnson's men used explosives to break through the front doors and stationed guards, swept into the banks, blew the vaults, and emptied them long before police or the National Guard could retaliate.

The noise from explosions, incendiary bombs, and auto-matic fire in that first hour in Detroit was constant. Although the looting and several of the fire fights lasted throughout the night, most of the damage was done in those first sixty minutes.

Slowly, the people in the streets began to understand what had happened. The murder and death settled over them, and they realized that—like the power companies and merchants and businessmen and bankers of Detroit—they were victims. The looting and fighting continued. Someone would profit from a night of terrible loss.

Stub McGraw—four fingers of his right hand slipped into the pocket of his sport coat—watched that first hour's activity from the roof of the warehouse behind which he had almost been killed. It was a beautiful summer night. Above, the stars and moon were glorious. Below, the darkened city, its streets cut by head lights, ablaze at its center, was dying.

Three hours later Grace Argent was awakened in her motel

room in Alexandria by a ringing phone. She turned on the light, fumbling for a few seconds while she searched for the switch, then lifted the receiver.

"Yes."

"It's Thomas, Grace. You probably haven't heard. There's been a blackout in Detroit, there's massive rioting and looting. Automatic weapons are everywhere. There are fires, and the banks, most of them, have been emptied. It's what we've been waiting for. They blew up all the power plants, even an atomic one. So far the army has detected no radiation."

"Thomas."

"There's more. It's Marcia. She was bringing in Rita Facett, the liaison from Cambridge. She was coming with two men named Finn and Stein. Finn and Stein were killed, their bodies were found a half hour ago by Boston police in the car they were using to get to Logan."

"Thomas!"

"They've taken her captive or killed her."

"Thomas!" Argent pulled herself up and rubbed her eyes. "Oh, Thomas."

"I've called John Smith. It's time. I told him you were coming too. Wake up your bodyguard and have him drive you to the White House. We're to use the rear gate."

Pauling hung up, leaving Grace Argent staring at the rug on the motel room floor.

/ 2 /

From a distance the White House looked artificial, like an ornament for a wedding cake. Inside the illuminated Cabinet Room there was no question of unreality. The atmosphere was grim and foreboding.

John Smith looked wilted for the first time since Pauling had met him. There were bags under his eyes. A few strands of his ivory white hair hung over his forehead. Smith was seated between the director of the Central Intelligence Agency and Robert Spencer—Savage—the Weldmore control.

Spencer could not expect to enjoy this meeting; Pauling knew him well enough to know that his cheeks hadn't always been that red. He was about Pauling's age and chinless as a frog. The director, Nelson, was an athletic, handsome man, square jawed, his eyes constantly, unblinkingly, on the president.

Grace Argent was seated on Pauling's right, directly across from Smith, near the head of the long, elliptical table. The attorney general was on Pauling's left. The head of the FBI, the chairman of the Joint Chiefs of Staff, the secretary of the army, the president's chief administrative assistant, the vice-president, and the secretary of state were ranged down the far end of the ellipse—judges, jury, and execution squad. There had been absolute silence since everyone had come in and been told where to sit by the president himself.

The president sat with his hands flat on the table, his light blue, merciless eyes moving from face to face until they had made the complete circuit of the people present. When he started speaking, his eyes began the circuit again.

"Central Detroit is burning," he said. "Provocateurs from the CIA itself may be responsible. They may also be responsible for the Texaco incident. They may have been turned against us by a foreign power."

His gaze had come to rest at the far end of the table. He was letting his people down there know, in case they didn't already, why the hell they were up in the middle of the night, and whom, as judges, jury, and execution squad, they could thank. He did that by turning to Nelson and then to Spencer.

"I want this in perspective, and I want it fast," the president said. His voice was low and very dry.

"Three years ago," the director said, "a program was begun by the CIA to create hynotized and programmed agents who could be used as instruments of future policy, even as assassins—assets who could fool polygraph machines, withstand truth drugs and torture. Originally coded Alphadeath, the operation was based in Cambridge, at the Weldmore Institute. The cover was experimentation with the production of alpha and other types of brain waves, and with biofeedback equipment of all kinds. At first there was little success. The assets produced were no better or worse than hypnotized agents of the past. Then we had a breakthrough. A man named Harriman, a psychiatrist with an interest in Eastern yogic technique, began to produce people who could do everything we had hoped. One of these people was fielded. He was sent abroad to infiltrate an international terrorist cartel, and he carried with him the polygraph machine that he eventually used to dispel an Interpol agent from that group and place himself in it instead. The operation was so successful that five internal groups, groups like the Weathermen and the old SDS . . . and the old Black Panthers . . . were infiltrated in the same manner by Weldmore assets. They're called Mark II's. This was done through, *through,* Mr. President, the original, European-based operation."

The director looked across the table at Pauling and then at Grace Argent. He frowned. Obviously he didn't like it that they were there, but he had been forced by Smith to tell the president that they had vital information, that they had precipitated activity within the agency that might be of enormous consequence. He lifted his eyes back to the president. When he was not told to stop, he went on.

"Two hours ago, Robert Spencer, the Weldmore control, came to me to tell me that John Smith," he looked at Smith, "had been going through the Weldmore files—he has the rank and the right to do that—and it became obvious to Spencer that Smith thought Weldmore had been subverted, that we had lost control of it, that Spencer himself might be . . ." the director paused, ". . . rotten. Spencer guessed that Smith had decided to make sure himself that Weldmore hadn't been behind Texaco."

"Is one of these five internal operations Weldmore infiltrated located in Detroit?" the president asked. His voice
was still low, but the question fell like an ax.

"Yes," the director said.

"Smith," the president said.

John Smith pushed the strands of white hair that had fallen
across his forehead back in place. He looked at the president,
then at Pauling. "If you don't mind, Mr. President . . ." He
turned his palm over in Pauling's direction as if he had a
bomb in it, and he preferred, after having thought it over, to
roll it over there.

"Grace Argent called me two days ago," Pauling said. "I
went to her apartment to find myself staring at a revolver held
by a man named Frank McGraw, an investigator of long
standing for various congressional committees, once with the
FBI. McGraw had circumstantial evidence that a man involved
in a possible crime in Detroit was a hypnotized or programmed
CIA asset. In part because the man tried to kill him, in part
because the CIA stifled his report to the subcommittee, he
suspected an agency operation or that the agency itself had
gone bad. McGraw learned that a CIA GS seven named
Rita Facett was being blackmailed. He knew that Facett was
an expert in narcosynthesis. He thought we might, together,
be able to find out if an agency operation had been subverted.
As it happened, I was investigating the Texaco incident and I
was beginning to suspect that programmed assets were being
used to wage a nonadmitted war against us. McGraw and I
couldn't go to the CIA through channels because someone
there might be involved. So I sent an agent to Cambridge. I
convinced John Smith that there was reason to suspect Weldmore. There was still a great deal of doubt that our suspicions were correct, and we wanted to be cautious. If we were
wrong, we didn't want to blow Weldmore's cover or its operation. But now we have Detroit. After making contact with
Facett and partially substantiating our fears about Weldmore,

my agent and Facett have disappeared. Their bodyguards are dead."

Grace Argent looked at Pauling with enormous eyes.

"Two of Mr. Pauling's people were found dead by the Boston police," the director said. "The agent he's talking about is his wife."

"This afternoon," Pauling continued, "because of a phone call Representative Argent received from Henry Duane, her committee counsel, I went to his home. I found three fingers, three human fingers, near a butcher block on his kitchen table. I believe whoever is behind the subversion of Weldmore, which I no longer doubt, tortured Duane to find out where McGraw was, and failing that, to try to find out who might know and be tortured in turn. That's why he called Miss Argent. We put a bodyguard on her very quickly. Those people were then, and still may be, trying to keep the subversion of Weldmore quiet. Probably they are operating on a timetable. They weren't ready for us to learn that Weldmore is their base."

"But now they know we know; they know *you* know," the president said. "Your operation will have alerted them."

"No, sir, not necessarily. The operation was set up to look like a vetting by a company control. The agent was to tell Facett she had found out about the blackmail, that her former control," he looked at Spencer, "had not found that out and had therefore been relieved. My agent will be able to stick to that story for some time . . . if she's still alive," Pauling said.

John Smith said, "Mr. President, Weldmore has been surrounded and secured for three hours," he looked at his watch, "going on four. No one has tried to leave it. Unfortunately," he looked at Pauling, "no one has tried to get in. Of course the army intelligence agents there are instructed to be invisible, to let anyone in who wants to, but to arrest anyone who comes out as soon as they're clear of the building. Pauling is right; there's still a chance they don't know we're on to them."

"And?" the president asked.

"I've got a helicopter coming to the White House lawn," the director said. "John Smith will fly to Cambridge immediately and take over the army operation. If that's all right, Mr. President. I know your immediate concern is with Detroit."

The president had turned back to Pauling. "Mr. Pauling, who exactly are you? You run an intelligence what?"

"I'm for hire, Mr. President. I was with the CIA once. I'm on my own now. I do intelligence work of all kinds."

"For hire," the president repeated. He looked at the director. "What is being done about these five groups?"

Nelson said, "Army intelligence and the FBI, cooperating with local law-enforcement agencies, have moved against them all, sir, including one here in Washington, Cubans, anti-Castro Cubans. But they've all gone to earth. We have not been able to find one member of the inner corps of any of them. We now believe the Weldmore intelligence, our principal source for intelligence on their activities, must have been doctored for some time."

"Spencer?" the president asked. If anything his voice was even lower than it had been before.

"I was fooled," Spencer said. "I was duped. We all were. I resign, sir. Here and now."

"Duped had better be all you were."

"Pauling," he said after a moment, "where's McGraw?"

"Detroit, Mr. President."

"I take it he reports to you."

"We've been working together since yesterday. He calls in, yes."

The president spent several more moments staring at Pauling. Then he spoke directly to him. "I assume you want to go with Smith. I want you to go with him. I want you two to go now. To Cambridge. The rest of us will stay here and continue this discussion." He looked about the elliptical table. "Does that suit you people?"

When he received no negative responses, he said, "You're for hire, Mr. Pauling. You're hired. Since you've been working for us anyway, and doing it well—as Nelson has made clear—we'll make it official."

"If that's the way you want it, Mr. President."

"That's the way I want it," the president said.

/ 3 /

After the first hour of blackout in Detroit, there was a lull in the action. There were no more explosions. Entire blocks of buildings near Renaissance Plaza were in flames, but the fire fighters had taken losses and had given up trying to move in their equipment. The shooting there had stopped. The state police and National Guard troops, stationed on the edges of the looting and rioting, had been ordered, for the moment, to hold their fire. There was still plenty of shooting, sporadic gunfire from the besieged precinct houses, and more than an occasional high-pitched screaming siren as ambulances tried to move casualties to the hospitals.

For some time, McGraw watched the fires in the center of the city from the roof of the warehouse. Flames leaped from roofs like birds trying to take off; headlights sliced up the otherwise black streets. He guessed that the president had asked the governor not to use the National Guard as a fighting unit, but only to cordon off the besieged areas, that the army itself, probably a Special Forces team, would shortly move against the men with automatic weapons positioned near the downtown fires. He also guessed that there would soon be loudspeaker trucks moving through the city, possibly armored loudspeaker trucks.

He would like to have spent the night right where he was. When the helicopters came, they would have lights so bright anyone below would be blinded. McGraw really wanted to see that; he wanted to see the sons of bitches wiped out. But there was something else he had to do.

He was running on luck and on instinct. He had never felt both so strongly in him before or felt that it had ever been more important to trust them. He now believed the warehouse he was standing on had been the storehouse of the automatic weapons that the militants had distributed. McGraw had found a small room built against the wall of the lower level of the building outfitted with a cot and a desk. He believed it to be David's. He felt if he could be patient, if he could wait him out, David would return. Sometime tonight David would get his ass out of trouble in the streets, abandon the militants he had persuaded to destroy their own city, and come home to his lair.

Although the warehouse was as high as a four-story building, it had only two levels. A steel staircase climbed a long wall from the ground level to a small landing and went from there to the second floor where another staircase went up to a cat-walk below the roof. From the landing between floors, McGraw had seen that it might be possible to jump to the ceiling of the small room. He left his bird's eye view of the city and went down to the catwalk, closing the skylight behind him quietly.

As soon as the skylight was back in place, everything about him seemed to shift. It was as if the whole world had moved a fraction of an inch while he had been looking the other way. It wasn't just the increased dark—there was moonlight and starlight out there on the roof—it wasn't that the sounds from the streets were suddenly muffled, it wasn't the closed, dusty odor. Something else was happening. McGraw could sense a peculiar tension in the warehouse, or a foreboding of death more real than the death in the city outside. Perhaps it was all inside him, perhaps it was what he wanted, what he intended. He was ready, after all, to commit murder. He left the catwalk for the stairway down, descending slowly to the landing above the small room.

He had not used his flash during his descent. Now he took it out and played the light over the roof of the room. If he could land on the joists, he would be all right; but if he hit the Sheetrock ceiling, he would go through. He decided to avoid both and land on the top of the side wall, on the header, and fall forward, catching the joists. He would have the flash in his hand and would have to release it in time to catch hold. He was standing about five feet above and two feet away from the place he would have to land.

McGraw climbed over the railing, aimed his light, and leaped. He landed on the header as he had hoped, but when he dropped the light in front of him it went out. Instead of bending forward as he had planned and grabbing for the joist, he tried to balance on the header. He almost went over backward.

Finally he steadied himself. He wasn't as agile as he had once been; he had never been an acrobat. He was too damn bulky. Then he knelt, lowering his center of gravity, and felt the Sheetrock at the tips of his shoes give way just as he found the joist he had wanted in the first place. He got both forearms against it, caught his breath, and then, balanced awkwardly on the header and the joist, he found the flash, shook it, and it went back on.

The holes his toes had made in the Sheetrock might be obvious to anyone lucky or paranoic enough to look for them. That was a chance McGraw decided to take. Using the light carefully, he crawled laboriously from joist to joist to the center of the ceiling. An electric cable, an old-style BX line, went to the light fixture there. He moved over to avoid it. If his memory of the room below was good, he was just above the desk. He settled down.

He was stretched lengthwise across three joists, none of his weight on the Sheetrock nailed to them from below. He had maneuvered so there was one joist under his thighs, another under his stomach, a third near his shoulders. Occasionally he could push up on the last for relief or let his feet down easily until he found the joist behind him, and ease his leg muscles. For the most part he could just wait there, uncomfortably, and occasionally clear his throat. Soon he would not be able to do even that.

At times he heard gunfire from the streets. Once or twice he heard a car go by. But after about an hour, which seemed much longer, the warehouse door was opened, a flash played across the floor, and footsteps crossed toward him. The door to the room below opened and closed.

McGraw heard someone dialing a phone and the voice of the man who had almost killed him, sounding again as if its owner was in love.

"Hello, sir. This is David . . . Yes, sir, it's good to hear your voice too, sir. . . . No, isn't it wonderful the lines are still open? I was afraid we wouldn't be able to talk tonight . . . Yes, sir. Just as it was planned. I'm totally in the dark . . . Thank you, sir . . . All right, sir . . . No, I wouldn't mind . . . And you too, sir.

"Hello, Mark . . . Yes, just as planned . . . No, I understand he wants you to talk to me, that the operation is important to you too . . . Yes, Mark . . . No, I had no feeling about going to foreign, why should I? . . . All right . . . Yes. I understand the van is very important, and I have confidence in Martin . . . Of course I'll be waiting for him here, but I doubt he'll get . . . Oh, I see. All right. I'll be here. Please tell Harold I'm pleased to have talked to him again today. It's special to hear his voice three times . . . Yes . . . Of course . . . Thank you, Mark. Congratulations to you too . . . Goodbye."

The phone was replaced, and for a long time there was silence below. Then McGraw heard a series of loud sighs and guessed that the man was doing self-hypnosis or going into trance. But it sounded like David was having sex; it made McGraw feel he was at a dirty movie.

When he had taken up the position on the roof, he had thought to lure David out onto the warehouse floor by throwing something down. If he had done that, he would have turned his

flash on David and then shot him. He thought to blow David's
head off. The man might not feel pain, he might be able to
smile after a kick in the groin, but he would bleed all right,
his skull would burst all right, if a bullet went through it.
But now there was another of them coming and a van. McGraw
had to think. If he waited, there was a chance he would learn
something else. Also a chance he would be found and killed.
The militants David had conned and armed might arrive.
McGraw doubted that. They'd all be out there fighting their
war.

McGraw stretched one limb at a time, very carefully, and
tried to figure things out. He wondered whether he could stay
up there much longer without going crazier than the Marquis
de Sade.

/ 4 /

The dark highway was virtually without traffic, and the
big car moved down it at high speed. In the front seat, twisted
so he could see Pauling and Smith, was an army major, pale,
gaunt, and worried. The major had already told them that his
orders were to obey Smith, that he understood Smith out-
ranked him.

"We're in two houses," the major continued. "One directly
opposite them on Brattle Street, another behind them. The
residents are not allowed to use the phones."

Smith nodded.

"Thirty yards down the street is an operations truck with
a communications and surveillance unit and a squad of com-
mandos. There are plenty of people in there, in number four
hundred, and they're making plenty of noise. No one's come
out or gone in since we set up."

"Very good," Smith said.

"We went into the two buildings we occupy from the

enemy's blind side. With any luck at all they don't know we're there. Our communications and commando unit looks like an ordinary moving van."

"All right," Smith said.

"Sir, could I know what's going on?" the major asked.

"How much time have we got, Major?"

The major looked out the windshield to get his bearings. The driver was keeping to an even seventy miles an hour.

"Five minutes."

Pauling stared out the side. They were approaching greater Boston and would soon turn off into Cambridge.

"The place you've got surrounded," Smith told the major, "was set up to produce controlled agents. Five terrorist groups were infiltrated by them, two of those five groups may be responsible for West Depford and Detroit."

"Set up by the CIA, sir?"

Smith didn't answer.

"Internal groups?"

"Yes, Major."

"Good luck when this comes out, sir."

"You're jumping to conclusions, Major."

"Yes, sir. Can we expect trouble from the three groups we haven't yet heard from?"

"I don't know," Smith told him. "Army Intelligence, the FBI, and local police have been alerted. Suspects are being rounded up, but the ones we want most are in hiding."

The major said, "That means all five groups are coordinated and we can expect anything, doesn't it, sir?"

"Yes," Smith said.

"What do we do now at Brattle Street? Do we go in shooting or ask them to surrender?"

"First we get them on the phone, then we'll see."

"Who's in there, sir? Is this their headquarters?"

"I don't know the answers to those questions either, Major."

"It's going to look like hell in the morning," the major said.

"When the country wakes up to find what happened to Detroit. They say entire blocks are in flames."

"Jesus," the driver put in.

Pauling was still staring out the window. The black car turned off the highway, headed toward Boylston Street.

"Who's behind it, sir? Who's in control of the operation?" the major asked.

Smith said nothing, and after a moment the major turned back to look out the windshield. It was two fifteen, and the streets were deserted.

"May I know more about what's going on in Detroit?" the driver asked.

"I don't know," the major said.

"Special Forces units were ordered against pockets of armed men who have been keeping fire fighters from the central city," Smith said. "Otherwise nothing's being done. The president ordered a containment action. The National Guard has cordoned off the area."

"If Brattle Street's an agency operation, this'll be the end of the CIA," the major said. He was still staring out the windshield. "Sorry, sir, but my guess is you'd be out of a job in a month."

After a moment the driver said, "Jesus," again.

They turned a corner at speed, and they were on Brattle Street.

"Slow it down, Lieutenant."

"Yes, Major."

"Slower!" Pauling said. It was the first time he had spoken since he'd entered the car.

The major picked a hand mike off the CB unit in front of him and spoke into it.

"This is Reed. Are you there, Colonel?"

"Yes, Reed."

"Hand it back here," Smith said. He leaned forward and took the microphone. "What's happening, Colonel?"

"Nothing, sir. Absolutely nothing. We know there are people in the house because the phone's been used and there's noise."

"Are you taping the calls?"

"Yes, sir. We have you in view now. Please come to a stop behind the van. That's us."

"That's the building, the big one," the major said. "It looks like a damn, what, historical monument or something."

"Don't let it fool you." Smith handed back the mike. "There are heavily armed guards. Your men could take them, of course, but you'd have casualties. I'll get them on the phone and give them a chance to surrender."

"No," Pauling said.

"Thomas, don't be a damn fool."

"Get them on the phone, John," Pauling said. "Get Berger if you can. Someone or something may tell us where Marcia is, where they've gone to ground."

"Damn!" Smith said.

The car had come to a halt behind the truck as the colonel had asked. Pauling got out and started diagonally across the street in a straight line for number 400. He went up the two cement steps from the sidewalk and marched down the path that sliced the lawn from the steps to the porch. He went up the porch and into the shadows of the entranceway. He put his finger on the bell and left it there.

/ 5 /

McGraw didn't even move to look at his watch. He remained stretched across the two-by-sixes, his short-barrel .38 in one hand, the flash in the other. He concentrated on the man in the room below just as a poker player concentrates on the deck when it's in the hands of a new player. It might have been two o'clock in the morning, it might have been three. McGraw didn't know, he didn't care.

Most people in Detroit were looting, mourning, or asleep, but not David. David was content to sit in complete darkness, awake and alert, waiting for something. McGraw felt it. He felt he was inside David's head. The dark didn't frighten David. Nothing, McGraw guessed, frightened David. He was hypnotized or self-hypnotized and would stay as still as a cat until it was time for him to move.

The time finally came. McGraw was numb; where he wasn't numb, he was sore. But his concentration hadn't broken. When there was the sound of the door opening at the far end of the warehouse floor, he wasn't taken by surprise.

The door was closed.

"Yo, David!"

In the dark below, footsteps crossed to the front of the room. The door opened. Then there was silence. No one breathed, no one moved.

"David? It's me, man, Jim. You got a light, use it. Yeah."

A flash went on almost before the man stopped speaking. The beam cut across the twenty yards of floor to the door and settled on the drawn face of a black man.

"Come on, man, say something."

"Put down your weapon, Jim."

Jim had been carrying a machine pistol. He set it carefully on the floor near him. Only then did the beam from the flashlight settle at his feet.

"All right if I come over there?" Jim called.

"Yes."

Jim hurried over. "Listen, you know what's happening out there?"

"No."

"Man, they wiped us out. We didn't have to worry about no damn National Guard or no damn SWAT. The army came, man. Those sons of bitches came down in damn helicopters with lights on them so bright we couldn't look up at them. They blew us away, man. You hear me, they blew us *away*."

"You're not the only one of the men left, Jim."

"The *hell* I'm not. I was two flights down or I'd be dead now, too. You hear me, the damn plan stank. What 'fade back' into the population like guerrillas, like Vietnamese guerrillas, David? How the fuck do a dead man fade back into the population, man? You want to answer me that?"

"You angry with me, Jim?"

"Damn right, man. Weren't for you—oh shit!"

"Look, Jim, I only helped you people to plan and execute what you wanted to do anyway. I put you in touch with a man who got you weapons. I got you a way to have Mr. Johnson finance the whole thing. I didn't make the plan. I didn't say you'd all live through it."

"Fuck you!"

"I fixed it so no one in your team or in Johnson's was liable to talk before tonight, didn't I? I helped you with the blackout. Now you turn on me, Jim."

"Damn right! Damn right I turn on you, motherfuck."

"That's too bad, Jim."

"Yeah, right. Too bad."

The shot came from over by the door, but David must have sensed it, must have known that Jim hadn't come in alone, because he had knelt down and in the same motion, clear to McGraw who peered carefully over the edge of the office roof, had withdrawn a revolver from his back pocket. David shot Jim high in the chest. Jim lurched and fell. Another shot rang out. David's light went out at once and there was a sound below McGraw: David was rolling over and over on the floor.

No one moved in the warehouse. The only sound was of Jim moaning, breathing heavily. Then nothing.

Suddenly David's light came back on, revealing a man at the warehouse door, his hand almost on the knob. David's weapon was fired again. The man fell.

David's instincts were very good, but now it was McGraw's turn. He turned on his light and held the beam on him.

"Don't even turn toward me!" McGraw said harshly. "I know you can handle a few slugs, David, but I'll blow your head off, *man*," he added sarcastically. "I'm not one of your bimbo terrorists."

"It's you, isn't it?" David asked softly.

"What?"

"I say it's you, isn't it?"

"If you mean the guy who kicked you in the balls, right, *man*."

"I thought we'd taken care of you."

"You did? What gave you that idea?"

"I was told it was being taken care of."

"Oh sure, you want me to collapse, so I just collapse. I just fade away to some convenient cemetery. Right! Now you drop that revolver, Mr. Castrato, and straighten easy."

David didn't move. He didn't drop the revolver. He didn't straighten. He had fired from a crouching position at the dead man near the warehouse door, and he stayed that way.

McGraw bit his lip. He wasn't afraid. He was ready to kill, confident he could accomplish it, but he wanted more than David's death. He wanted the man coming to Detroit who David had spoken about. He wanted the van that was important. He wanted a hell of a lot.

"Straighten up, David! Drop the piece and straighten up!"

David again declined. He remained crouching, as if he hadn't heard. He was deciding whether to shoot, or risk being shot. He was wondering whether he was accurate enough and fast enough to survive.

"I can put four bullets in you before you get off one. There's a light on you, David. Is it in my hand? If so, which one, *man?*"

David still didn't answer.

"Harold would want you to stand up straight. He'd want you to drop your weapon," McGraw said.

"What?"

"Harold would want you to do as I say."

David spun and fired. McGraw had already cursed and squeezed off a shot. It went through David's neck and ought to have sent his aim so far off the only danger would be from the bullet knocking something off the warehouse ceiling onto McGraw's head, or maybe hitting a chunk of star and sending that down out of the night.

Instead the bullet whistled by McGraw's ear. McGraw fired again. This shot hit David in the forehead. His brains splattered out into the wash of light still cast by the flash in McGraw's hand. At last McGraw could climb down off those damn two-by-sixes and stretch.

Taking care not to get blood on himself, he lugged all three bodies up to the second level of the warehouse where he piled them behind crates. The water was still working, so he cleaned up David's brains and blood and Jim's and Jim's friend's. Then he made himself comfortable in the small room, setting the clock he found beside David's cot for eight A.M. It was only two thirty-five, which would give him almost six hours rest.

/ 6 /

The man who answered the door at 400 Brattle wore a uniform like a museum guard's and a smile that threatened to rip his face. Incongruously, he was carrying a machine pistol loosely at his waist. Sounds of laughter and light conversation came from somewhere inside the institute.

"Yes, sir!" the man said, snapping to attention and saluting with his left hand. The right one now held the pistol. Obviously the man was not a Mark II but one of the Weldmore security personnel.

Pauling stared at him. "You've been drugged."

"Sir!"

"Berger! Where's Berger? Harold Berger?"

"I don't know, sir! In his room, sir! Maybe!" The man giggled.

Pauling stood absolutely still. He knew exactly how many

rounds the pistol the guard was carrying could fire in one second.

"You're a government employee," Pauling told him. "The officer in charge of this project is Savage. He's waiting outside. Go out to that black Lincoln with your hands over your head and wait for orders."

"Sorry, sir. I can't do that, sir! Savage or no Savage, sir!"

"Oh, you'll do it all right," Pauling said.

"Sorry, sir! I have hit the switch and must wait the full ten minutes, sir!"

"What switch?"

The man giggled again.

"I said what switch?"

The guard raised his eyes to meet Pauling's. They were gray. "The one in the security room, sir! In ten minutes we'll all come out with our hands up, sir!"

"Why did you hit the switch? I said *why?*"

"Orders, sir! If anyone came before seven thirty A.M., we were to hit—"

Pauling took the pistol with his left hand and hit the man at the navel with three fingers of his right. The guard doubled over. Pauling went past him and inside fast.

The sounds of laughter and conversation were coming from one of the rooms off the wide corridor. He took the first door to his right.

A battery of five television sets, all of them turned on, one of them showing the guard doubled up on the floor of the entranceway, was arranged on a wall over a desk. Another guard was asleep in a chair. This one held a machine pistol, too. Pauling took it, disarmed it, and threw it down. Then he went back out into the corridor.

All the rest of the doors opened on offices. In one of them Pauling found the laughter and conversation he had been listening to, and which the army surveillance team had been picking up. It was on a tape recording. Pauling shut it off and continued his search.

He checked his watch. He was as certain as he wanted to be that the ten-minute switch was a detonation timer. Something somewhere in that building was being done that took time, ten minutes. When it was done, there was going to be an explosion. Something. He had nine minutes to go. Or eight, or seven, depending on when the guard had hit the switch. Figure seven.

Pauling ran up the stairs and found a light switch. A floor of cubicles was illuminated, containing instrumentation desks, and in some cases examination tables. Nothing was moving, nothing was happening. He went up to the third floor and found a half-dozen empty bedrooms and an empty dormitory. He went back to the stairs and came down them two at a time. Smith, the major, a colonel, and three soldiers were waiting for him.

"No one," Pauling said. "But something's happening. Colonel, clear the area."

"Do it," Smith said. He turned to Pauling, "Have you checked the basement?"

Pauling shook his head and went back to the stairs. At the bottom he found the corridor to what Harriman had called his control room. He ran forward and threw the door open. On the front wall was a giant portrait photograph of Harold Berger. He turned and ran back to the glass doors to the computer rooms. Smith had just arrived there.

"Wait!" Smith said.

The computers were running. Tapes on a series of tall reading units were moving sporadically.

"It's erasing them," Smith guessed. "The telephone answering system must—"

"I understand," Pauling said.

"Then it'll be set to go off if we go near it."

"It's already set. Get clear!"

Smith stared at him.

"Get clear!" Pauling repeated.

Smith turned and went back toward the stairs, and Pauling

dropped to his knees to stare at the space between the door and the floor. He saw no trip wires. He pressed himself carefully against the glass, peered to one side, then to the other. He stared at the console table, at the phones, printer, and keyboard.

Smith was still on the stairs.

"Get out! Just leave a clear path," Pauling yelled.

"No."

"Get out!"

There was a transparent plastic cover over the tapes inside. He would have to get those out of the way, rip off the tapes, and get back to the door. If the door, the tapes, or the floor were wired, he would be killed; but if they had relied on the switch the guard had thrown, he might make it. If there had been seven minutes when he started, he still had forty seconds.

He pushed open the doors and went in, walking carefully, watching where he stepped. When he got to the console table, he saw a button marked H. He hit it. The tapes stopped.

Pauling went for them. He ripped back the transparent screens on the first set, yanked off both reels, repeated the same thing on the second set, then on the third. He ran.

He had just turned the corner into the hall when it went off. He was thrown ahead toward the stairs, gripping the reels of tape to his stomach.

/ 7 /

Stephen and Carl sat on a couch in the living room of the rented house in Brooklyn sipping their morning coffee. There were several pieces of pink overstuffed furniture in the room and framed paintings of big-eyed children on the walls. The Mark II's were watching Detroit burn on a black-and-white portable television set on the coffee table in front of them. The news films had been taken from a helicopter; they gave an overall view of the blacked-out city from the river to Highland Park.

Broad streets were cut by headlights of automobiles. Bright flames broke into the black sky from the burning blocks near Renaissance Center.

Carl said, "Is that all you usually have for breakfast, Stephen, coffee?"

"Yes. Sometimes I have a piece of toast, Carl."

"Don't you tire out in the middle of the day, Stephen?"

"No, Carl."

They stopped to listen to the voice of the television newsman.

"This was Detroit at midnight last night. Less than forty-eight hours after the refinery fire across from Philadelphia, a major American city has been attacked. So far the Justice Department, which is coordinating the investigations of both incidents, maintains that there is no evidence of a connection between them. But the similarities are striking. No one is sure yet who attacked the refinery Tuesday morning. Neither is anyone sure who caused the blackout, handed out the automatic weapons, or attacked the banks and businesses of Detroit. The president has called a press conference for one o'clock this afternoon. It will be covered by all major networks, including NBC. The stock market, which suffered severe losses since the West Depford fire, is as of now still scheduled to open. There is already evidence from London, however, where their market has been open for several hours, that Detroit-based stocks will take a bad beating. Trading in many issues may be suspended. The lack of power alone will severely curtail automobile production."

The announcer paused, then said, "We have an update on the casualty figures. It is now estimated that over a thousand people lost their lives in Detroit last night. Over a thousand people! There is no estimate of the number who may have been injured."

While the announcer spoke, the helicopter moved back and

forth across the city, the cameras continuing to focus on the fires near Renaissance Center.

"I'm going to get another cup, Stephen. Want one?"

"Sure, Carl."

"What you're watching, if you've just tuned in," the announcer said, "is Detroit last night, just after midnight. The blackout at ten thirty was caused by a carefully planned and boldly executed campaign of sabotage. All power plants in a hundred-mile radius were crippled and all cross-country power lines were cut. Within Detroit itself youth gangs were armed with automatic weapons, police stations were attacked, and criminals or terrorists invaded the banks. Looting went on most of the night. Over one thousand people have been killed by gunfire, in explosions or fires, and there is no report yet from the Justice Department as to who is responsible."

"I could make you some toast, Stephen."

"No, no. I'm fine, thank you, Carl."

"If you're sure, Stephen."

"I am. I am, Carl."

The television announcer's voice had become more urgent. He said, "At this point our helicopter was told to leave the area, and it did. National Guard troops had arrived to cordon off the city and a Special Forces unit was on the way from a base in Ohio."

The pictures on the television screen changed. The shot was now from ground level outside Renaissance Center. Fire trucks and police cars were grouped near a corner, at least fifty policemen, many armed with rifles, stood near them.

The announcer said, "The fires you just saw were burning out of control at least partially because fire fighters were unable to approach them. Groups of armed men, terrorists, were stationed at windows and on roofs, keeping the fire fighters away. What you are about to see now is something I never expected to witness in the United States."

To judge from the news film, the cameraman must have started to run very fast. When the camera was held steady again, it was aimed at a building down a dark, deserted stretch of avenue. The picture had a sound track.

"Don't stick your head out there!" someone shouted.

"Hey, that's where the motherfuckers are shooting from!" The last remark made Stephen laugh.

The sound of a helicopter grew loud. A light came out of the sky so intense that the film became white for a moment before a filter was fitted over the lens.

"Look at that," Carl said calmly. "Look at that, Stephen."

Fire came out of the sky and washed into the top floor of the building at which the camera was pointed. It may have been from a flame thrower or napalm. No one said. Whatever it was, it worked. After a deep silence, police and fire trucks moved into the avenue.

The face of a commentator appeared on the screen.

"Again, there is no confirmation that the people responsible for the blackout and distribution of weapons in Detroit were the same as those who destroyed the Texaco plant in West Depford, but the president has called a special news conference for this afternoon, which will be carried live by this network." He paused, then said, "We have more film ready."

Another shot of Detroit appeared on the screen, this one also from the air. The fires were still smoldering, but the sky was light now. There were no vehicles on the streets. Several stop zoom shots, one after another, revealed pile after pile of bodies. Another showed a man hanging from a streetlamp. It was one of those candid shots that become etched on the memory of all who see it. It was left on the screen for a long time. Finally the picture was taken off the screen and replaced by another film from a helicopter.

"This," the announcer said, "is Detroit about an hour after dawn this morning. The fires burned themselves out, were blown out, or were extinguished. Martial law has been declared. No vehicles except ambulances, police, fire, National Guard, and Red Cross trucks are permitted to move. Police announced by loudspeaker truck that a search would begin for weapons, and that anyone found to possess them would be jailed. We have a report that anyone turning in weapons voluntarily is being allowed to go free. There's a growing pile of them in front of some police stations."

The announcer paused. "There has been a carnage here unlike anything in recent American history. Somehow a city, my city, was made to turn against itself, people made to turn against themselves. There was madness in Detroit last night. Today, after the damage has been assessed and the dead have been taken off the streets, the entire nation will have to live with what happened."

"Are you sure, just for a change, you wouldn't like some scrambled eggs, Stephen?"

"I'm sure, Carl."

"David did remarkably well."

"Yes."

"I don't know if our action will compare, really, to what David's accomplished. Well, we'll do our best, of course."

"Of course. It's not time to call in yet, is it?"

"No," Carl said. "You remember we are to go to foreign now, Stephen."

"Yes."

"I wonder what that means."

"We've moved, that's all. Harold's moved. And of course we're to arm the van."

"I really like to know where he is. I don't like not knowing."

"He'll tell us, Carl."

"I don't like being out here alone."

"Believe me, we're not alone. Harold is with us. He'd never desert us. How could he?"

Carl nodded and smiled.

"Believe me," Stephen said, "you'll have television time too, Carl, really."

"I guess so," Carl said. "Although my people are getting

a little nervous. They're afraid the refrigerating devices will fail. A blackout in New York and . . . " He held up his hands, palms toward the ceiling.

"It will go off prematurely?"

"Yes. We won't have coverage of the actual blast, Stephen."

"Stop worrying. It'll be fine. There won't be any blackout here, Carl."

"I want him to be pleased, that's all. I want him to know we do our best too."

He went to get Stephen another cup of coffee.

/ 8 /

It was a private medical clinic, without a neighbor for a half mile on a rural stretch of road in Wellesley. It was a two-story brick building with wide glass doors up a single cement step from a wide, green lawn. Several cars, including a blue Chevy van, were parked at the rear where there was another, broader expanse of lawn, ending at a wood. The lawn was long enough for a light plane to take off or to land on it; there was a low wooden outbuilding near the wood wide enough to house one.

The phone rang in the basement of the clinic. It rang once, it rang again, and then it was answered by the same type of computerized instruments that had answered the phones at 400 Brattle Street.

Levine and Harold Berger sat at the control panel; Rita Facett and Mark Harriman stood nearby. Neither Facett nor Berger looked well. They heard Berger's computer voice answer the phone and Caroline's real voice respond. They heard Berger's computer voice tell her that it was good to hear from her, too, compliment her on calling "foreign" after receiving no answer at Cambridge, and instruct her to continue toward New Orleans as scheduled.

Caroline's call was the last Harriman had been worried about. When Caroline hung up, he breathed a sigh of relief. Now all of the Mark II's, even those who had not been told to call "foreign" had done so anyway. Switching phone numbers, as Harriman had known for some time they would have to do, had presented his agents with an unexpected problem, a problem compounded by the premature evacuation of the Brattle Street headquarters. It seemed the Mark II's needed to visualize Berger at his end, in surroundings they knew. Now that hurdle had been overcome. Smiling, Harriman went out of the small computer installation to find his personal bodyguard.

A minute later they were on the ground floor of the clinic and crossing the lobby, making for a set of double doors to a corridor with many rooms along it. At the last room the bodyguard dropped behind Harriman. He turned in without knocking, and nodded to the doctor and nurse who had operated on Lawrence Douglas. They were standing on the far side of a bed containing the sleeping form of Marcia Pauling.

"How is she responding?" Harriman asked.

"All right," the doctor said. "She's absorbed a great deal of the drug. She will be weak, virtually unable to resist your suggestions."

"Don't tell me my own business," Harriman said. "When will she be conscious?"

The doctor looked away.

"Soon."

"Good. We'll see if the equipment I had you install is functional. As soon as she's ready, wire her to the instruments. If you have questions, ask Dr. Facett."

The nurse looked frightened.

"Just do it," Harriman said.

He stood for a moment looking down at Marcia Pauling; then he turned and went back the way he had come.

He wanted to be back in the computer installation before the next scheduled call—Carl from Brooklyn. He wanted to be absolutely sure that Berger was dispensable. Berger was on strong drugs and at a deep level of trance; he wouldn't last forever.

But it wouldn't take forever. The Dow had fallen fifty points the day of the refinery fire and thirty the next. Key stocks in which Harriman was interested had already lost a large percentage of their value and would continue down. His contact on the outside had been reporting to him regularly. He had gone short on key securities. Although trading in some of them might be suspended for a time, they were sure to take a severe beating when it resumed. The dollar market abroad had also responded according to plan and would drop lower, much lower.

If everything worked well, in another week there would be total panic in America, reflected in all markets. Only Harriman would know at what point that panic would be relieved.

No matter what happened now, Harriman had won; he had brought it off. From now on it was all gravy. Even if one or two of the remaining operations failed, just the fact that they had been attempted would help to panic the country.

Harriman's bodyguard picked him up outside Marcia Pauling's room and escorted him, keeping three paces behind like Muhammadans' wives, back to the computer.

Chapter Eight

/ 1 /

Ann Gold didn't take any time to explain why she had come back into the field after twenty years behind a desk. As soon as Pauling opened his eyes, she gave him the facts as she knew he would want them. The hospital room was much like the one in which he had interviewed Chief Stevens.

"The room is secure, we can talk. It's in McLean's in Belmont outside Boston. You're going to be all right."

Pauling nodded. It hurt.

"Marcia hasn't been found, or any trace of her," Gold went on. "Or of the people who may have captured or killed her. Your son Mike called to say he wanted to come back to Washington, so I'm letting him stay at my apartment. He's there now. John Smith asked to have McGraw's calls transferred to Langley, and I said okay. I don't know if he's called in or not. It's now eleven fifteen in the morning."

"Detroit?" Pauling said. His voice sounded harsh.

"The saboteurs used some very sophisticated materials. Liquified natural gas, for one. Smith thinks the more difficult assignments were accomplished by Mark II's, but that's hypothetical. The city won't get full power for weeks. Block after block in the center of the city is gutted. Smaller fires were widespread. The Red Cross and the army have established aid stations. Generators are supplying hospitals with power. Millions have been allocated from federal disaster funds. The total damage hasn't been assessed. It'll be in the billions. There were so many bank robberies, there is discussion of an extraordinary measure to make paper money valueless. People may have to turn in their currency for vouchers and may have to account for what they have."

Pauling tried to laugh. It sounded like a grunt.

Gold smiled sympathetically. The smile didn't take. "There's an immediate problem about the automatic weapons. No one knows where they came from, so no one knows how many there were or what percentage has been captured and turned in. A house-to-house search was threatened; it hasn't come off. The press has suggested that the terrorists may have been inspired by the Mafia or what they refer to as the black Mafia. Cart before the horse, except in this case cart before the cart and the horse is invisible." She made a tent with her fingers and touched the top of it to her chin. It meant she was thinking about something.

"When can I get out of here?" Pauling asked.

"You were concussed, and you have a fractured wrist. It's bandaged, but your hand should work. Your doctor—not agency—wants to keep you here for observation. I pressed her on it; she's just being cautious. She's worried about the concussion. Do you feel nauseated or dizzy?"

"I'm going back to Washington."

"I thought so. I brought clean clothes for you, and I have a bottle of aspirin in my pocket."

"Anything besides Detroit?"

"No. Nothing else, not yet."

"New Orleans, California, New York?"

"I'm not told everything. Apparently there's been some progress in California, but the other groups have covered their tracks. No one can guess when they'll strike or where. It's assumed they'll each do something soon."

"It was almost two days between Philadelphia and Detroit. I think they're on a timetable."

"They may be."

"No word from the terrorists? No statements taking the credit? Threats? Demands?"

"Nothing Smith believes authentic."

Pauling pushed against the bed. He got into sitting position. His head throbbed and his stomach tightened. "Thank you, Ann. Thanks for taking in Mike."

He looked at his left wrist. As Gold said, it was bandaged. The bandage went all the way up to his elbow. There was a splint that felt as though it was made of plastic. He found he could make a fist.

"Much pain?"

"No."

"Do you want the rest of it?"

"Yes. And I want to talk to Smith."

"He's back in Washington."

"What about the tapes I got off the computer?"

"I don't know."

"Are Harding's people still trying to find the Cubans?"

"Yes. I told them to double their efforts, to put every man they had on it. They keep running into government people. Smith set up a special team operating through the Justice Department to coordinate all agencies. Tom, our firm, you, have been placed at the top of the pyramid with Smith and the various directors. The president wanted it that way."

Pauling nodded. It hurt again, so he stopped.

Gold said, "I'm glad you're still with us. It's good to see you with your eyes open. Are you sure you want to come home?"

"Yes."

"You know, I've had little to do since I got to Boston. I've been in touch with our office, of course, but since there's been little real news for hours, I've spent the time going over the total situation, trying to guess who we're up against and why."

"And?" Pauling said.

"The terrorists Weldmore was supposed to subvert apparently subverted Weldmore. That's the first possibility, and I don't like it. The second is that a foreign power subverted Weldmore *and* the terrorists through Weldmore. That makes more sense and that's the theory to which you, Marcia, and Smith subscribed. It's almost too frightening to deal with."

Pauling tried to laugh again, not because he disagreed.

"We may never learn who's fighting us," Gold said. "Japanese or Russian or Chinese or Saudi wealth may be used to tear us apart, and we can only strike at their foot soldiers, these subverted groups. We can't aim a missile at their capital city. Which capital would you aim at?"

"There's been no statement yet," Pauling said.

"What?"

"No list of demands."

"Then you're going back to theory one? Terrorists after all."

"No," Pauling said. "I'm concerned with Weldmore, with the man behind the subversion, the guy who has Marcia if she's still alive."

"Harriman?"

"I'd guess so," Pauling said.

He turned the sheets down and got out. He had been put into a hospital gown. He took it off while Gold stared out the window. When he had his pants on he sat down on the bed and bent over to put on his shoes.

A woman in a white coat came in the door and glared at him.

"I'm your doctor," she said, "and you can take those shoes off. You'll be staying here for observation, Mr. Pauling."

"I'll be all right once I get some food."

The doctor became even colder and more authoritarian. "You've suffered a severe blow to the head—"

"Quiet!" Pauling told her.

He took the shirt Gold was holding out for him. A few minutes later they were in the back of a cab heading for Logan Airport.

/ 2 /

"You'd be Martin," McGraw said. He was lying on the bunk looking up at a short, wide, smiling young man with a full beard and extraordinary ears. McGraw was in his shirt sleeves, his shoulder holster conspicuous. Light came into the small warehouse room from a barred window right up against the ceiling over which he'd spent part of the night. The room was dusty, the desk took up most of it.

"That's right," the man said. "Where's David?"

"Out of town."

"Why?"

"He had business. I'm supposed to bring you to him. He had to meet with some people. You're supposed to know what that means."

McGraw got off the bunk and stretched as if he had been asleep. In fact he had been wide awake in the chair behind the big desk when the warehouse door opened. He had been there for hours. Except for a quick walk to find a meal at an army mess truck, he had kept to the warehouse.

"I'd have been here earlier," Martin said. He sat on the edge of the desk. "But there are roadblocks. I left my van and hitched in with some Red Cross people. I told them I had family here I thought I could help."

He snickered. "I don't know you. Who are you?"

"I'm with a man named Johnson. Ring any bells?"

"Maybe," Martin said. "But you're white."

McGraw looked at the palms of his hands. "Damn," he said. "You're right."

Martin laughed. "You look more like a cop of some kind."

"Yeah, well I am a cop of some kind. You want to go with me to find David now, or do you want to sit here and wait for him by yourself? It's your choice. I couldn't care less. The thing's over, pal. I don't know why you're even here."

"What did David tell you?"

"Just to bring you. It's over. Now we all sit back and enjoy what we got. All I have left to do is pick up mine."

"Your share?"

"That's right."

Martin nodded. "I'm still surprised David isn't here. Mr. Johnson is holding him prisoner, is that it?" He was still smiling.

"Well, whatever Mr. Johnson wants, Mr. Johnson . . . you probably know the song. And he wants no loose ends." McGraw cleared his throat. "He wants David and his friends with him during the split and maybe for a few hours while everyone moves away from the city. There's a lot of money being divided, pal, but you'd know that, if you're David's friend."

"That's not the part of the operation I was interested in."

"Oh."

"Is it true the army killed the men who were keeping the fire fighters from downtown?"

"I wouldn't know," McGraw said.

Martin's smile grew. It gave McGraw the eerie feeling he was talking to David.

"Where's this van of yours? You might want your own wheels. I haven't signed on as a full-time chauffeur."

"It's south of town."

"It'll be on the way then. You coming?" McGraw put on his sport coat.

"There are roadblocks. Maybe they won't let you through."

"I already told you," McGraw said. "I'm a cop. Mr. Johnson has to have someone on the side of law and order, doesn't he?"

"I suppose it makes sense," Martin said.

"Are you coming or not? Either way suits me."

"You're awfully easy with all this. You don't know me. You can't even be sure I'm who I say I am."

"Look pal, it's all over for me. My share is bigger than anything I ever hoped for. I'm on my way to South America. Doesn't it look it? What's the matter, you can't tell a tourist when you see one?"

"I don't think I like you," Martin said.

"Fine. Stay here. I did what I said I would."

"I asked you how you could tell I was David's friend."

"You freaks ever look in a mirror?" McGraw sounded angry. "You ever see the way you smile? You and David could be twins from the nose down and the chin up. I don't know where it is you come from, so I don't know what you want to hide, but those damn smiles of yours are a giveaway."

"Oh."

"Coming?"

Martin hesitated, then nodded.

"My car's in the street," McGraw said. "Just you walk in front of me, all right? You make me as nervous as David does. Come on, come on. If I wanted to do something terrible to you, I could have done it already, right?"

Martin laughed.

"Jesus, that too. The both of you think you're invulnerable, don't you?"

"Maybe we are," Martin said. "Not the way you'd think."

"Yeah. Well, come on, the sooner I get you to David the sooner I never see either of you again and the better I like it."

Martin looked at McGraw and finally pushed up off the desk. They went out of the office, Martin first. McGraw was breathing about as tightly as he ever had. They passed the place where he had killed David. They went into the alley where David had almost killed him.

"Straight ahead," McGraw said. "Don't get nervous when I flash my identification. You're with the good guys now. Try to look the part."

Martin looked back over his shoulder at McGraw and

laughed. When it came to it, McGraw thought, he was going to have no more qualms about this one than he'd had with the other.

/ 3 /

When the bell rang, Pauling asked Balke to turn off the video tape of the president's press conference. Balke did it and went to get the door. Pauling still didn't feel well enough to move if he didn't have to.

"Come in," Balke said, and Ann Gold appeared. She had delivered Pauling home, then returned to her apartment to see about Michael.

"Michael's all right," she said. "He understands there's a slim chance you may be in danger here. He's agreed to stay at my place."

She took a seat on the couch.

Balke said, "There are men across the street in the Fieldings' house. The Fieldings have vacated for the duration. There are men in the Whitestones', across there, in the Whitestone study. The Whitestones haven't vacated, but they're cooperating. Even so, someone might get in here."

"I'm just hoping, Ann. I'm just hoping they come," Pauling said.

Gold nodded.

"We're watching the press conference," Pauling told her. "The president has requested a joint session of Congress. I want to hear what he said."

"I know. I heard. I'm not sure it's a good idea."

"Neither am I. But before we watch it, I want you to know what I'm thinking about. I'm thinking about Cubans."

"It would be nice to get a step up on them," Gold said. "Do you think they'll try something on the scale of Detroit?"

"It'll be something big, something to generate massive publicity."

"I agree."

Balke said, "Maybe the Cubans are being kept incommunicado so they don't get the idea they're in this with Maoists?"

"Maybe," Pauling said.

"All black nationalists in Detroit may have been killed," Gold said. "All of them. I got that from one of Smith's people."

Pauling lighted a cigarette. They sat for several moments, not saying anything.

"So what've we got?" Pauling finally said. "A suicide mission, maybe, somewhere in Washington, maybe, attempted by anti-Castro Cubans. Maybe some of the same people Nixon used during Watergate."

Balke nodded. "Or close to the Watergate people," he said.

Pauling motioned to Balke, who went to the television. The president stood at a lectern in front of the press corps.

". . . there isn't any hard evidence to discount the possibility that these are isolated incidents. It wouldn't be smart to leap to conclusions. We're dealing with something we've never had to deal with before. On the other hand, these two incidents may not be connected. More sophisticated matériel was used in Detroit. As a whole, the operation was more ruthless. Yes, Mr. O'Hara."

"Mr. President, there's been considerable speculation that all American terrorists have banded together, even talk of the possibility that a Communist power may be behind it. Is there anything to this?"

The president said, "I repeat, so far we have no hard evidence that the two incidents are related. They may be. We're even assuming that they are, but it remains an assumption. Mr. Rosen."

"Mr. President, there has been a congressional investigation in the last few weeks, as you know, into possible CIA-Mafia links. We understand that the Mafia may have been involved in the Detroit riots. The banks were looted by trained criminals. Congresswoman Argent was speculating only last Friday that the CIA was unwarrantedly operating inside the domestic United States. Sir, my question is: has the CIA been operating on domestic soil because they feared what happened last night and last Tuesday morning?"

Mr. Rosen sat down, the president smiled, then became somber. "No, the CIA has not involved itself with domestic matters. No, we cannot look to the CIA to help us. Unless, and this is very speculative, unless the CIA can turn up something outside the country, the source, perhaps, of the money with which these terrorists were financed, or the source of the terrorists themselves."

There was the usual raucous sound of reporters shouting, "Mr. President," in something more or less like unison. A question was asked and answered about the relief efforts in Detroit.

A reporter asked, "Mr. President, what can we expect next?"

"One of the reasons I called this press conference was to make an announcement," the president said. "I want the country to know that everything that can be done is being done. For that reason I have asked that a joint session of Congress be convened tomorrow morning. I'm going to ask for a symbolic declaration of war against the kind of terrorism we've witnessed at West Depford and in Detroit."

There was a great deal of commotion and some applause from the press corps.

"I am not going to allow this country to become prey to terrorism, not even on the scale we're accustomed to in most of Europe. I'm going to request emergency legislation—which I will outline in my speech—to grant increased police powers to the FBI and additional personnel, specifically for combating terrorism. Now, not six months from now." There was more shuffling among the reporters, but the president hadn't finished speaking. He proceeded calmly and deliberately. "As to what else we're doing: every police officer, every member of the armed forces stationed here, every officer of the Federal Bureau of Investigation is working around the clock to uncover the people who were behind the refinery fires in Philadelphia and the people who are responsible for the Detroit riots. And all of us are alert and on guard against more of the same."

"Sir!" a reporter shouted. He was recognized immediately. "Sir, have demands been made on you or on the Congress that we haven't heard of, demands to give up our support of Israel or to remove our troops from Western Europe? Is there anything, sir, which you know about which may point to an organized drive to influence our policy?"

"No," the president said. He added, "There have been several calls. Most have gone to newspapers and television stations. But there are none we take to be authentic. No, we have no one to point at," the president said. "Not yet. I might say this: we can't be blackmailed. We won't be threatened. It's that simple."

"Mr. President!" a hundred people shouted at once.

A woman in the third row was recognized. The camera held her while she asked, "Mr. President, are there any plans to close the stock markets or to act to stop the fall of the dollar abroad?"

"No. On the contrary, if the dollar falls far enough, we may buy. It's a good investment. Any depression of the price of the dollar based on what's happened in the last week may help us in the long run. It's not as if the dollar was down because of a deficit in the balance of payments. We've had that problem, and it's a serious one. This is different. The true value is not reflected by the present price."

A voice shouted, "Thank you, Mr. President," and the president walked off the rostrum to more applause.

Balke got up and switched off the television.

"Have you seen the coverage of Detroit, Thomas?" Gold asked.

Pauling nodded. His stomach was growling, but he said nothing and made no move to go to the kitchen.

He said, "What are the Cubans going to do, Ann?"

"I don't know."

"Balke?"

"I don't know," Balke said.

Miss Margo was standing at the door wagging her tail without enthusiasm. Pauling stubbed out a cigarette and got up to let her out. It was time for his pill anyway.

When he got back, he said, "You'd think she'd stay out a little while. She did this before. She goes to the yard and then comes right back."

No one responded.

"All right, let me know if you think of anything, Ann, or if anything comes in over the office lines. Smith knows I'm here. I'm sure he'll let me know if there are developments. Go on, get clear of here, just in case."

/ 4 /

McGraw drove south out of Detroit with Martin, both hands on the steering wheel of his rented Ford, his eyes straight ahead. He wondered whether Mark II's could read minds. If they could, he didn't have very long to live. He cleared his throat and concentrated on what he was doing.

Smoke was still rising from the central city behind them. There were damn few cars on the highways. They passed an army convoy and three Red Cross trucks going north toward Detroit. Then the far side of the highway, too, was empty of traffic.

"You'll hit the roadblock in about three miles," Martin said. "They'll be looking under the seats, in the trunk, under the hood and chassis. It's guns they're after, I guess. And cash."

"I guess," McGraw said.

Martin laughed. It made McGraw's lower spine and the backs of his thighs tingle. He thought of something else. Martin probably had no intention of driving that van to a place he knew nothing about. If he had gone to the trouble of hitching a ride to avoid a roadblock, whatever was in that van was too important.

"Did you have a long drive in?" McGraw asked.

"Yes."

"Well, whatever you do, don't tell me about it. Don't tell me who you are, who David is, where you come from, or what you have in common besides the way you both smile. I don't want to know about it."

Martin chuckled. "Suits me."

"Fine."

"There's the roadblock. Slow down."

"I thought I'd fly right over it."

Two khaki canvas-covered trucks were parked in the highway, the space between them just wide enough for a car. There were four jeeps in the breakdown lane and over a dozen soldiers standing around the first of six cars lined up to pass through. McGraw's car became the seventh.

"In case I don't get a chance to tell you this later," McGraw said, "you make me goddamn nervous."

Martin didn't respond.

By the time it was their turn, ten cars and a pickup truck were parked behind them. McGraw looked at them as he got out from behind the wheel to hand a young second lieutenant his government ID. Martin got out on the far side and stood clear. He was watching McGraw and the soldier. Of course he was smiling.

The lieutenant nodded. "We have to search the car anyway."

"Sure," McGraw said.

"We have to look in the trunk and under the seats."

"Fine."

McGraw took his wallet back and reached into the car for the ignition keys. He tossed these to a private who had been standing near the second lieutenant. Then he stared into the lieutenant's face.

The lieutenant said, "You wouldn't happen to know what happened back there?"

McGraw laughed. "When I figure it out, I'll write you a letter."

The lieutenant lifted a clipboard and wrote something on it. He walked over to the front of the car and took the license number. The private, with help from a friend, had gone through the trunk and the back of the car. They went to peer under the front seat. When the private and his buddy got up, McGraw and Martin got back in.

"Have a nice day," the lieutenant said ironically.

"Yeah." McGraw slammed the door and started the motor. He would have liked to tell the lieutenant, "Pray for me, pal."

It was an ordinary summer day, but it had a strange feel to it. It was almost as if the sky and the clouds held a subliminal message about what had happened in Detroit. McGraw found it queer. The highway ahead of them was empty again.

Martin said, "Tell me where David is now, please."

McGraw thought: so this is it. He'll kill me, take the car, contact his headquarters, and wait. He's not in any rush to see David. But if he can get information out of me, it works to his advantage.

"Sorry," McGraw said.

"So am I," Martin said.

Out of the corner of his eye, McGraw saw Martin reach into his jacket.

"David said to take you to him, not to tell you how to get there. He said to bring you and to bring the van."

He looked to the left, away from Martin, and kept his foot even on the accelerator. He could have hit the brake. He could have pulled his own gun. He did neither.

"He said to bring the van?"

"That's right. How do I know for certain you're who you say you are? Maybe I'm letting your smile fool me. Maybe there isn't any van."

Martin remained silent for some time. Finally he said,

"We're coming to a turnoff; take it. There's a motor inn up there. We'll go to it."

"Is the van there?"

"Just do it, all right?"

McGraw realized he'd been holding his breath. He let it out. When he came to it, he took the turnoff. The motor inn was on the opposite side of the road a half mile from the highway exit. McGraw saw a chocolate brown van in the lot. Martin still had his hand in his jacket.

"You're making me nervous again," McGraw said. "I'll look at your license plates. They're supposed to be from Massachusetts. If they are, I'll tell you where David is."

"Good," Martin said. "Good. Good."

McGraw had brought the car to a full stop to make the turn. He was staring hard at Martin. He thought he would never forget the blankness in his eyes. David's eyes had been that way too.

McGraw put his foot down softly on the accelerator to move across the road into the lot of the motor inn. When the car was going ten miles an hour, he hit the brakes as if there were a rattlesnake on the pedal. The tires squealed, and the car came to a stop. McGraw held the wheel hard to keep from being flung forward. He went for his .38.

Martin recovered and fired first. The shot broke the window behind McGraw's head. McGraw had his right hand on his gun and his left hand on the door handle. He threw the door open. He leaned back as he brought out the revolver.

There wasn't enough time to roll all the way out, but he was on the way down and Martin's second shot went over him. McGraw was half out of the car and half in. The car was moving again. He kicked at Martin's gun. The car kept running. The blankness in Martin's eyes hadn't changed at all; he was still smiling.

McGraw fired twice. He hit Martin in the chest both times. Martin got off a shot that hit McGraw's cheek. He would have gotten off still another if McGraw hadn't done what he had done to David. He shot Martin square between the eyes and took off the back of his head.

/ 5 /

Although he had been expected since early evening, John Smith did not arrive until three in the morning. Pauling and Balke were sitting in the darkened living room when the doorbell rang. Pauling went to answer it, while Balke covered him from the hall. Both had a view past Smith of his people in a car across the street. Pauling asked Smith to wave them in, and he did. They waited with Balke, while Smith and Pauling went to Pauling's study. Smith had never seen it before.

"Nice," he said. "Very fancy. Maybe I ought to go into business for myself too."

"Come in with us. There's room."

"Maybe. How're you feeling?"

"I'm all right."

Smith took a seat on the couch and took out his imported cigarettes. He tamped one down on the box as Pauling continued.

"It wasn't a severe concussion. It just put me to sleep for a couple of hours."

"Not just a couple. You ought not to fool around with something like that."

"What was on the tapes, John?"

"A coded program. We broke it. It's a phone response system. The caller can't get too fancy. It'll exchange set pleasantries, record a report, encourage, give further instructions, all in the voice, Berger's I would guess, that these agents respond to with such total dedication. Unfortunately the voice tapes were destroyed in the explosion. Dedication may not be the right word. I think the voice itself must trigger certain responses."

"Deepen or reestablish their programming."

"Yes."

"The tapes gave no clue—"

"Where headquarters is? No. Anywhere with a phone, and Berger or a computer. Anywhere," he repeated. "We might take all the phones out of service. Every one. All calls might have to go through an operator who'd listen in. Drastic, but it'd cut their lines of communication. We're ready for something drastic."

"What if they're programmed to go berserk if that happens?"

"That's what bothers the director. We may try it anyway. The stakes have risen exponentially."

"What?"

"Lean back, Thomas. Make yourself very comfortable."

Pauling had put himself into the chair behind his desk. He stared at Smith. Something in his stomach turned over, just as something in it had turned over when Marcia failed to call the night before.

Smith said, "Those vans your people saw pulling out of Four Hundred Brattle a few days ago, the ones you surmised were heading to each of the five subverted groups?"

"Yes."

"McGraw came through for us in Detroit. He killed two Weldmore assets, Mark II's. He got one of those vans. A bullet grazed his cheek, took some of it off, but he got one of the vans."

"What is it, John? What the hell is it?"

Smith had waited to light his cigarette. As he did it, his hand trembled. He looked up at Pauling and exhaled smoke toward him.

"Excuse the histrionics, Thomas. I'm practicing. In a few minutes you and I are going to the president. The director will meet us there. We're going to have to break it to him in person."

"Come on," Pauling said. "What was in the van?"

"An A-bomb. Our guess is there are four more."

"Holy Mother!

"We think a physicist named Laamb made them."

"Yes," Pauling said, "Laamb was seen in the company of Rita Facett and Mark Harriman. McGraw—"

"Yes. McGraw told me."

"It would work? The bomb would work?"

"We think so. We're dismantling it now. Trying not to lose one of our people by going too quickly. Or all of them."

"Where is it?"

"Nevada. We picked it up with an industrial helicopter, one of the big ones, and flew it to a cargo plane at an air force base in Michigan. It's in Nevada now. Our men who are trained just for this are getting a chance to show their stuff. If they do it wrong, if they start the trigger charge moving toward the pile and don't get in in time to pull it out—"

"It was rigged to go off?"

"McGraw guessed what it was. Without him we might have fooled with it right at the motel outside Detroit. Instead we put a Geiger counter on it. We don't know if it's rigged to go off, if there are safety devices or timing devices. But it's a bomb, all right. It may destroy a square block, a square mile, a whole city. We don't know yet."

"Holy Mother," Pauling said again.

"This is what I think, Thomas," Smith drew in deeply on his cigarette and spoke through the exhaled fumes. "I think you're wasting your time if you think the Cubans will come after you here. Even if they do, the Mark II agent, if you could catch him, would not be able to help you to locate Marcia. Not even if you could figure out a way to deprogram him. I think they went after that committee counsel, Duane, and were after McGraw, only to buy themselves enough time to get the vans moving toward their targets. Now that they've gone to ground and the vans are out, they won't waste their time or take unnecessary risks. You agree?"

Pauling nodded. "Yes."

"All right. How do you suggest we now proceed?"

"We try to figure out what the Cubans are up to, and the other groups. We search for those vans. The Cambridge tapes indicate the drivers are to make contact with the Mark II's already in place. We have three license numbers. I don't know what we can do to find their new headquarters."

"Three license numbers," Smith echoed. He leaned back and sighed. "You think Marcia is alive, don't you, that they're holding her?"

"Yes."

Smith looked at the blank TV screen across the room. He changed the subject. "There are thousands of vans like the one McGraw got for us. Chocolate brown Fords. Thousands. The four we want may be garaged or repainted or may have had their working parts removed when they reached their targets." He put out his cigarette. His hand was no longer shaking.

"There'll be an ultimatum," Pauling said. "We've been waiting for an ultimatum. We'll get it soon."

"When, in your estimation?"

"After the Cubans have struck, and the people in Los Angeles, and the people in New Orleans or New York. The three groups not yet heard from. When the threat is very, very real, we'll hear about those bombs. We'll hear what they want, or what they'll want us to think they want."

"We may have their people in California. May. We don't know. Why do you think there'll be an ultimatum? Why should the terrorists be more than pawns?"

"I don't think they're more than pawns," Pauling said.

"A foreign power has gone to war with us," Smith said. "An ultimatum would give them away. We'd wipe them off the earth."

"You misunderstand me. The ultimatum would come from the terrorists, or seem to." Suddenly Pauling felt very tired. "There are two triangles touching at their apexes. One triangle is the people who financed and planned this war, the other is the Mark II operatives and the five groups. I'm staring at the point where the triangles touch. It's their strength. There's probably only one person there, so we may never find out who we're fighting, and never be able to retaliate. But it's also their weakness. Because of the person he is—it's probably not Facett, it's probably Berger or Harriman, probably Harriman—this thing isn't going to go the way they want it. It'll go the way *he* wants. And he'll put out an ultimatum."

"Not Facett. Probably not Berger."

"Harriman. Gold has gone over it all and agrees. Harriman. The man who created these assets."

"Yes."

"He's the key."

"You're trying to guess what he wants, what he'll do?"

"Except to try to outthink the Cubans, I've thought about little else," Pauling said. "I'm sure his interest in mysticism is important. And I'm sure he wants to panic the country. Panic can do more harm than five atom bombs. That's why I think there'll be an ultimatum."

"Maybe," Smith said after he had thought about it for a moment. "You've been studying the files on the Cubans we delivered to your office?"

"Yes."

Smith looked at his watch. "The call is going to go in to wake up the president in five minutes. It's time to go."

Pauling nodded. His head hurt again, as it had in the hospital. "Right," he said. "Let's go."

/ 6 /

The president was seated behind his desk in the Oval Office. He was so still, it was possible to believe he wasn't breathing. Nelson, Pauling, and Smith were standing. There were lights throughout the White House offices. Aides were getting in touch with high-ranking officials.

Nelson had just said, "The bomb is functional. Our best guess, without actually setting it off, is that it's functional."

"Set it off," the president said.

"They want us to panic," Pauling said. "If the media learns of an unscheduled atomic blast it'll help them get what they want. We have to assume that even if one is a dud, the others aren't. I don't believe they intend to use them, not yet. Of course we have to assume the worst, but it gets complicated."

The president stared at Pauling without letting go an ounce of the several hundred pounds of tension behind his eyes.

Pauling went on. "I believe the strategy of the enemy is to panic us, not to use the bombs immediately if at all, to use the terrorists to establish their credibility, to prove to the country that they can do what they like, and then to hold the atomic weapons over our heads until we cower. The astronomical difference between the kinds of actions points to that. The refinery fire and the destruction of millions of dollars worth of property and hundreds of lives in Detroit versus the billion-dollar potential damage and millions of lives that nuclear blasts could cause. If they mean to wipe us out with their bombs, Texaco and Detroit are wasted effort. There's another argument to support my position. It has to do with the strategy of a nonadmitted war."

"Which is?" the president said.

Nelson said, "Mr. President, we are not being softened for a conventional blow, an air strike or missile attack, from a major power. We'd still have our total nuclear retaliatory force. So if it's a major power we're fighting, they must want to weaken us economically. For different reasons, the same holds true of a rich, small power. A financially crippled America would make a fine buyers' market, especially if the weakness were superficial. If we're fighting a small power like Japan, which competes with us for world markets, they may be trying to put us temporarily out of business. But our total destruction would hurt them, too. I agree with Pauling. So far we have more to fear from their terrorist groups than from nuclear attack."

"Until the ultimatum," Pauling said. "Until they've threatened to use the bombs to get maximum psychological effect."

The president was eyeballing Pauling again, as if he were responsible for everything that had happened. It made Pauling feel less than welcome. It did something else. Something in Pauling's head fell into place; two things in his head fell into place.

"There's something I want. There's something I want very much," the president said. He shifted his eyes to Nelson, his voice was not gentle. His face, which had turned red, got redder. "I want to know who it is! Do you hear me? I want to know who's doing this to us."

Nelson nodded. "Yes, sir."

"You do hear me?" the president said to Nelson.

"Yes, sir, I hear you. Every agent we have is on it."

Pauling said, "It's no good. There'll be false trails. There'll be several. We may find out eventually, but not now, not in time."

"You like being a lightning rod, do you, Pauling?" the president whispered.

"Sir," Smith said. "With four atomic devices being driven around the country, you mustn't go through with the joint session in the morning. Even if all this conjecture is right. Sir, I have to repeat, we believe one of those devices is here in Washington."

The president hadn't replied the first time Smith had said that. He didn't reply now.

Pauling said, "About the Cubans. It's not out of the question that they've been preparing for some time to attack either the White House or the Congress."

"Good!" Smith said. "The Congress. Anti-Castro Cubans and the Congress!"

Nelson said, "Sir, you might consider moving to the shelter headquarters."

"That wouldn't panic anyone, would it?" the president replied. "Neither would calling off the joint session. How big are those bombs, Nelson?"

"We estimate they'd take out a square half mile, sir."

"Then starting here at the White House and on Capitol Hill, starting at dawn, have the security people search every square inch of street and garage in a radius of a mile. Use Geiger counters."

"Yes, sir," Nelson said.

"I'll have the vice-president and the Cabinet take to the shelter, *quietly,* until after the sweep."

The president turned to Pauling again. "If you're right about the Cubans, this will give you a chance to get them."

"Yes, sir," Pauling said.

"Any more ideas, Pauling? Any idea how to find out who's doing this to us?"

"No, sir. That's the idea of nonadmitted war. It's rigged so you can't do it in time."

"There will be a Cabinet meeting at six," the president said to the director. "In the shelter. Six A.M. Please be back here for it."

The three men went out through the lighted offices. As they left, others were on their way in, among them the vice-president and the head of the Joint Chiefs.

Chapter Nine

/ 1 /

By dawn nothing had changed, and two hours later the search of the areas around Capitol Hill and the White House had turned up no Ford vans with special compartments under the rear seats. The sky over Washington was cloudless; the sun burned the eastern facades of the monuments and government buildings.

By nine in the morning, dozens of the top officials of government had been alerted to the president's strategy: a shadow government, the vice-president and the Cabinet, had been flown to the secret war shelter. To rally the nation and launch a counteroffensive against the terrorists, the joint session was on.

Pauling and Smith had spent the night going over the security arrangements with the Capitol Police, the Secret Service, and army liaison. Any and all vans and trucks passing within a mile of the Capitol or the White House would be rerouted. If drivers needed to go through, they would be searched and scanned with a Geiger counter. The bomb squad would do a thorough search of the gallery and the chamber for conventional devices. No one would be permitted into the building with a package of any kind. Even congressional and senatorial aides would be stopped and their briefcases and attaché cases searched. There would be double the usual number of security people. A First Air Cavalry troop would remain on ready alert a half mile away. Two Huey Cobra heligunships, jet-propelled and armed with rockets, would be in the air over the Capitol dome.

Pauling's personal responsibility was for an operation dubbed Mousetrap. If the Cubans were coming, the likely route was from the Senate Office Building by subway. This meant they would have real or forged security clearance, but they'd had months to get it. Pauling gave security personnel on the far side of the subway orders to let anyone and anything through that would pass ordinary, cursory inspection.

Twenty minutes before the joint session was to start, Pauling was in the corridor outside the doors to the gallery overlooking the chamber. He nodded to the guards and went in.

Most of the congressmen and senators were already in their seats. Pauling saw Grace Argent enter late and walk steadfastly down the aisle of the House. In a few minutes the president would be walking the same route.

One of the men who had accompanied Smith to Pauling's house the night before came over. He was as bald as Balke but paler and less friendly.

"Everything's copacetic," he said. Like Pauling, he was wearing a bright green laminated security tag on his pocket. If terrorists got this far or if any of the people already there caused a problem, he was there to handle it.

"Good," Pauling said. He recognized several wives of senators and the son of a high-ranking State Department officer who had gone to school with Michael.

"How many of them down there know, do you think?" the man said softly.

"I couldn't say."

"Razwell looks spiffy, doesn't he?"

The chairman of Grace Argent's committee was in an aisle seat, looking like a movie star. Since his committee investigation had begun, despite his cooperation with the CIA, he was not the favorite congressman of agency personnel.

"Keep on your toes," Pauling said.

He went out to the hall to a window overlooking the Capitol steps. John Smith was there, looking as though he had slept the night before. He was staring across the parking area filled with black limousines.

"Well?" Smith said.

"It's all set. Except for the basement, the security isn't hard to penetrate, it's impossible. I don't ᴊare what kind of weapons or credentials they've got or how many of them there are. There's only one way for them to come in now, the one way we've left them. That means they'll have to take the elevators."

"Then let's hope you're right," Smith said. "That they're coming. That they're all prettied up and have terrific ID's— but I'll give you better than automatic weapons, I'll give you grenades, and I still say they won't try it."

"Before Texaco I might have agreed with you."

Smith was still staring through the window. He not only looked as though he had slept well, he looked ten years younger than he had in Pauling's office on Wednesday morning. He was no longer caught between Pauling and the agency.

"I haven't said this yet, Thomas."

"It's not necessary," Pauling said.

"You know how I feel about Marcia."

"Of course."

"Will you watch from the gallery?"

"No. I'm going down to the basement. I want to be there if they're coming."

"The Secret Service can handle it. Stay up here and listen to the speech. Be there when we let them out of the elevator, sleeping soundly from the gas you've got ready for them."

Pauling shook his head. He went to a bank of three elevators. There were four uniformed police at the elevator doors and a Secret Service man, but if one of those doors opened and men jumped out already firing, Pauling would put his money on the attackers. They would kill the guards before they could draw their weapons. But, they wouldn't get that far. He nodded to the Secret Service agent as he stepped into the middle elevator.

Four more uniformed policemen, one a sergeant, were stationed between the elevators and the subway to the Senate Office Building. Pauling nodded to them and walked over to peer down the tracks. A sixth policeman and two Secret Service men stood at a flight of stairs beyond the elevator bank.

The walkie-talkie in the sergeant's hand crackled. A voice said, "There's a Mayflower moving van on Constitution Avenue about a quarter of a mile away from us. It seems to have stalled crossing the avenue. We've got army people checking it out. We had a negative Geiger reading on it a few minutes ago."

"Get it out of there!" another voice said.

One of the Secret Service men motioned to Pauling. He went over to them.

"The president's arrived," the man said. "He's about to enter the chamber. I don't like this moving van. They opened it, ran a Geiger over the roof. I still don't like it. I'm damn glad there are gunships in the air."

The other one said, "We're in control down here, Mr. Pauling. You don't have to worry. No one gets up the stairs or more than halfway up the elevator."

The man's walkie-talkie sputtered. A voice shouted, "Man, the whole damn side is coming off the van. There are cannon in the furniture! Christ! Those are 106-mm recoilless rifles! Two of them! Where are—"

There was a terrific explosion followed by the sound of something massive ripping and falling. There was another explosion, then a third. From the basement it would not be possible to hear it, but Pauling understood that the army people near that Mayflower van were now targets for automatic fire, probably from cars on Constitution Avenue.

There was a shattering somewhere above. The voice on the Secret Service man's squawk box shouted again. "Goddamn, here comes that Cobra! Right down the avenue!" There was a second shattering explosion. The voice shouted, "Good-bye, van!"

"I wish to hell I was out there," one of the men said. "I've never seen one of those gunships take out anything, let alone a moving van."

The other laughed nervously.

"Look out, now," Pauling said. "That was the diversion. Here we go."

The cartlike subway arrived, and two men got out. They were wearing business suits, but they might as well have been in fatigues with their faces blacked. Everyone knew who they were.

Another car was coming with a TV news team: three men, one with a camera, two carrying tubular black microphones.

"Take it easy," Pauling said. He went toward the guard at the elevator.

He was sure those microphones were converted grenade launchers, but he wasn't watching the news team. He was staring at one of the men who had gotten off the subway. As gaunt as the angel of death, the man was smiling steadily. The angel and his friend arrived at the elevator bank at the same time Pauling did.

"What's going on? What was that explosion?" the angel asked the sergeant.

"A gunship blew away a van with recoilless rifles in it," the sergeant told him. "But not before we took a shell or two."

"We?"

"This building."

"Damn!" the angel said. "Let us up there!"

The three men carrying the equipment arrived.

"Identification?" the sergeant said.

The angel pulled a wallet out of his jacket pocket and opened it. A card said he was from CBS. Another said he had security clearance for Congress.

"Let them up," Pauling said. He hit the button for the elevator. He stared at the man with the smile. The Secret Service agents were heading for the subway.

The sergeant's squawk box sputtered again. "It's over! We took seven casualties. Get us the medical unit. You can back off, Huey, you're just making it windy!"

"Roger."

"Jesus, let us up there!" the angel said to the sergeant again.

"Here's the elevator now," Pauling said. "Get on your walkie-talkie, tell them on the ground floor there's a news team coming."

The Secret Service agents had just sent a car of secretaries back to the Senate Office Building. They turned to look at Pauling, the police, and the five men about to board the elevator. They watched calmly as the men stepped in. The elevator doors closed.

Pauling counted aloud to three before he shouted, "All right, you bastard, you son of a bitch, you're stuck!"

He pointed to the sergeant who had already opened a panel on the wall between the first two elevators. "Pull it!"

The sergeant yanked on a U-shaped switch, and Pauling whooped. The Secret Service men came up and one of them clapped him on the back.

"Release the gas," Pauling said.

The sergeant took a remote-control device out of his pocket that looked like the kind used to open garage doors. He pressed the button. Gas would now be pouring from the light fixture in the elevator. There was a banging up there—then nothing.

"They'll sleep like babies," the Secret Service man said.

For the first time since Marcia had failed to call in, Pauling felt he could breathe. His head had stopped aching.

/ 2 /

John Smith was scowling.

"The Mark II is catatonic," he told Pauling. He turned his attention back to the phone.

Pauling and Smith were in Grace Argent's office, lent to them after the attack on the Congress. The president had been greeted in the chamber by sustained applause just after the shelling—three shells penetrated the dome of the Capitol, but no one in the chamber had been hurt. Another missed and exploded a half mile away on the far side of the Potomac in a parking lot. Then the Cobra, swooping from the sky, put a rocket into the asphalt under the van, and it was all over.

But there hadn't been seven casualties on Constitution Avenue, there were forty-six, including six terrorists. Seven army people were killed or wounded by two men with automatic rifles who opened fire from the street. The sides of the moving van had been ejected like the slide off a semiautomatic pistol. Smith, who had seen it all from the window, had described it to him.

Smith muttered good-bye and hung up the phone. He leaned back in Grace Argent's desk chair. He looked at home. He had been talking to someone on the specially secured CIA floor at Bethesda Naval Hospital, where the gassed terrorists had been taken after they had been removed from the elevator.

"The doctor says he's in a trance. He says he's never seen anything like it. I wonder where they got those recoilless rifles."

"Try to break him," Pauling said.

"Of course." Smith took out his English cigarettes and toyed with one.

When the phone rang, he answered it. He replaced the receiver to say, "Nelson offers his congratulations to you and assumes the president's will follow. 'A tidy trap,' he said. His words."

"Break him," Pauling said. "Berger's voice must exist on tape somewhere. Find it. Duplicate it."

Pauling stared out Argent's window at the statue of Ulysses S. Grant on the Capitol steps and thought about the angel with the gaunt face. When he brought his gaze back inside the office, he noticed the picture of Lincoln he had noticed the last time he'd been there.

"We'll do everything we can," Smith said. "You know that. But even if we can get anything out of him, with drugs or tricks, he may not know where she is."

Neither man spoke for some time. Smith had still not lighted his cigarette. In the chamber the president would be finishing his speech, and he would certainly get the legislation he wanted.

Pauling thought about the second thing which had occurred to him under the president's gaze late the night before. He decided to tell Smith.

"I'm going abroad."

"What? You said yourself we'd never turn up an enemy in time, that there'd be too many false trails too cleverly planted. I agreed with you."

"I'm going anyway. I think I can find out something—just me, no one else."

"You're serious, aren't you?"

"I don't know when I'll be back."

"We're going to beat these bastards here, Thomas. We've stopped the operation here cold. We're close in California."

"I'm thinking of Marcia," Pauling said.

"Of course you are. All right. But tell me where you're going. Who do you think is responsible for this? Who're we fighting?"

"You tell me," Pauling said.

"Nelson likes China," Smith said. "I prefer Japan. Remember the Japs've been fighting an economic war against us. They have few resources of their own. If they can weaken us, they can become the most important industrial nation in the free world. Then they'll have whatever they want. They'll just buy it."

Pauling nodded. "Maybe," he said.

"I want to know what you think, Thomas."

Pauling just shook his head. He got to his feet. "Wish me luck, John."

Smith stared after him. He finally lighted his cigarette. Smoking steadily, he stared at the wall over Lincoln's picture until he was fairly certain he knew where Pauling was going.

/ 3 /

Marcia opened her eyes to find herself strapped to an examination table. A nurse with a Mediterranean complexion was staring down at her. She had never felt weaker. It was as if her blood had been drained.

Rita Facett stood behind the nurse, far darker and far more beautiful. As if aware of the poor showing she made with Facett there, the nurse left Marcia's side.

"You're awake," Facett said.

Marcia said nothing.

"Look, we've got you wired to the equipment we use to test our people's responses. An electroencephalograph, among other things. He's going to come in a few minutes to question you. You won't be able to fool him. You've been given a heavy dose of drugs. They're going to influence you to tell him the truth. The machines will make it obvious to him if you lie and when he's asked something that makes you nervous. I'm sorry. I don't know what he wants you to tell him, but please cooperate."

Marcia closed her eyes. She had seen the wires taped to the palms of her hands and to her forearms. She felt the ones on her head.

"I don't know why he didn't kill you," Facett said. She

sounded genuinely confused. "I don't know why he hasn't killed me. Sometimes I think this is all just a game for him. He says that sometimes, and I almost believe him."

Facett bit her lower lip. She came closer to the examination table to touch Marcia's arm.

"Savage, cooperate with him. Please. Make it go all right for me. Do it for me, if you won't do it for yourself."

Marcia understood. Facett would do what she had to do to save her son.

A man in a white coat approached and put his hand on the nurse's shoulder. He smiled down at Marcia.

"I am Dr. Pahvleen. We don't want to see you hurt Miss . . . ?"

"Savage," Marcia said. Even her voice was weak.

"Miss Savage. Please cooperate. We'll do everything we can to help you."

A pale, handsome man appeared in the doorway. He came in on cue.

"Hiya," he said. "I'm Mark. Mark Harriman. You good at tests?"

He laughed. "You're terrific, honey. War's hell, you know. But damn . . . I think I like you with wires coming off your skull."

He turned to a machine near the examination table. The wires attached to Marcia's forearm went to various contact points on its face.

In an entirely different voice, he said, "Let's begin, shall we?"

He hit a switch on the side of the machine and watched as a number of gauge needles sprang into position. On a paper roll near the top of the machine, Marcia's heartbeat recorded a steady, jagged terrain.

Chapter Ten

/ 1 /

Mohammed Ibn Saud Imani was almost as short as John Smith. There the similarity ended. Imani was stocky, bearded, and sensual. His eyes were as big as olives, his skin dark, his lips full. He was one of the richest men in Europe, he spoke English flawlessly. He was an OPEC representative to the free world; he would have been at ease in a harem.

"It was good of you to meet me at the airport," Pauling said.

Imani waved a pudgy dark hand. "What's wrong? After what happened in Washington today, I expected you to be serious, but not this."

Pauling looked grim. The exhilaration of capturing the Cubans and their Mark II was gone. It had dissipated on the plane as he contemplated the difficulty of breaking the Weldmore asset.

"Marcia has been killed or taken captive," he told Imani.

"Your wife?"

"Yes."

"Your new wife!"

"Yes."

"By the terrorists?"

"Yes."

Imani grew extremely sober. He stared out the window. They were being driven past row after row of attached red-brick buildings. It was very early in the morning in England, and most of the people in those houses would be sleeping.

"Thomas, I'm not taking you home."

Home was Mayfair, a Victorian mansion that could have housed fifty Imanis.

"The house may be watched," Imani said. "I don't want to advertise our meeting."

"All right."

"We'll just drive until we finish talking. Then I'll take you back to the airport."

"They can survive without me in the States for a few days," Pauling said.

"It's not that. I think you'll want to take a flight to the Continent."

Pauling looked at the back of the chauffeur's head through the interior window of Imani's Rolls, waiting for the Saudi to explain what he meant.

"You don't believe your wife is dead, do you?"

"No, I don't."

"To find her you'll have to find the people who are running these people. They have struck now, what, three times?"

"Yes."

Imani moved his round head up and down and closed his eyes. When he opened them again he said, "How were things when you left?"

"We stopped them in Washington, as you know. What you don't know is we've taken prisoners. In my last conversation with our people, we seemed ready to stop them in at least one other location. That leaves one terrorist group unheard from; one which survived its mission—the refinery; and an unknown number of agents, perhaps ten, perhaps fifteen, who can independently do a great deal of damage. Four are especially dangerous."

"Yes?"

"Wiping out the terrorist groups may not be enough. The stakes are very high, Mohammed."

Imani clasped his heavy hands over his stomach and leaned a few inches forward. He looked as though he might be about to pray, but he just stared at the Rolls's built-in bar.

"You trust me, Thomas. I'm glad we're friends."

"Mohammed," Pauling said. "If it's your people, and you're having a case of conscience, you did the right thing to warn me."

"My people!" Imani seemed genuinely shocked. His eyelids went up as far as they could go; his mouth opened. "My people!"

"Of course!"

"Listen to me, Thomas. I'm a very rich man."

"Yes."

"Very rich men can have what they want. Well, there was nothing I wanted that I did not have. So I added something to the usual list. I decided to give myself an unusual bonus."

"Go on."

"I warned you, Thomas, not because I was having a fit of conscience, but because I decided to indulge my hatred. Hatred is sometimes worth indulging."

Pauling stared into Imani's eyes.

"I hate terrorists, Thomas. I especially hate terrorists I am forced to finance."

"The Palestinians?"

"Of course."

"If you're telling me the PLO has the finances, the intelligence, the vision, to wage a nonadmitted war against—"

"No! Listen! The Palestinians are only the weak link in the chain. You should be glad they are. Otherwise I'd know nothing at all."

The Rolls had stopped; the chauffeur was about to turn. Apparently Imani had instructed him to make a wide circuit of Heathrow. A police car passed them on the left. Beyond there was still another row of attached houses.

Imani leaned back in his leather seat. He arranged his stocky frame so that he was comfortable as he stared directly at Pauling.

"There is a man called Field Marshal. You've heard of him, of course. Over a year ago an American agent, CIA, came to Europe to infiltrate his operation."

Pauling said nothing. He let out some air, he took some in.

Imani said, "That is what I was told. An agent from America came here to infiltrate an international organization of terrorists affiliated with the Red Army of Japan, the IRA, the PLO, and the Baader-Meinhof gang."

"All right," Pauling said.

"His name, one of his names, was Lawrence Douglas. Field Marshal's plan was to send him back to contact your own, homegrown terrorist groups, to organize them, synchronize them."

Pauling remained silent.

"I believe you must know most of this already," Imani said. "Or some of it."

"Go on."

"All right. This man, Lawrence Douglas, was very special. He had a way of subverting subversives, of obtaining entrée to their inner core. He proved this to Field Marshal by infiltrating his. Then he told Field Marshal that he was a CIA agent, that there were others like him, that he and these others were ready to turn against the CIA and truly organize American terrorists—for a price. Lawrence Douglas offered Field Marshal a way to make American terrorists effective. In turn, Field Marshal would financially support the operation, plus. Field Marshal agreed. He sent his people out to raise the cash."

"Plus," Pauling said.

"Yes."

"The Palestinian came to you?"

"He didn't know me very well. Otherwise he would have gone to someone else. He talked too much. But not until a few days ago did he tell me enough."

"You gave him money?"

"Some, yes, not as much as he wanted. I knew my government would give it to him if I didn't. It's still our policy. They ask, they get. No questions. But since he did not go to the government, but to me, I insisted on hearing details of the plan."

"I'm grateful for your foresight," Pauling said. An edge had crept into his voice. He lighted a cigarette and put the match in an ashtray on the bar.

"You will be more grateful still if it helps you to find your wife, if it helps you to stop these people."

The chauffeur had turned again, this time onto a wide highway about ten miles north of the airport. He picked up speed.

Pauling sat absolutely still. There was a question he wanted very much to ask, but it was important that he get an honest answer.

"How much money was involved, Mohammed?"

"I gave him fifty thousand pounds."

"That's not enough!" Pauling frowned. "What does Field Marshal get? Does he issue a statement asking for money? For the release of prisoners? What prisoners? For changes in American policy? He's a gangster, a thrill seeker, a game player . . ." Pauling stopped.

Imani said, "I don't know about Field Marshal. I know about the Palestinian. When America is weak, she will give up Israel. When America is weak, we, the Saudis, he thinks, can step in and lend America money. Then, then she will give up Israel."

"Is that what would happen?" Pauling responded quickly. "Saudi Arabia would bail us out. We'd be so grateful we'd change our basic policy?"

The pace of the conversation had been accelerated, and Imani answered very quickly. "It happened after World War II. America lent millions to Europe. It helped 'to stave off Communism.' Isn't that the cliché? Of course it's possible that if she were in grave trouble, grave financial trouble, someone might come along and lend America a hand. You would have a love-hate relationship with these people, but you'd be their ally, very much their ally. If it were the Saudis, you might, eventually, give up Israel. But that is not the point."

Pauling stared at the back of the chauffeur's head again.

Imani said, "The point is that I hate these people. I hate these people who blow up airplanes and bomb schools. Two years ago an English couple was killed by a terrorist bomb in a theater in Tel Aviv. They were friends of mine. More than friends. The woman and I were lovers. Don't believe it, Thomas. Don't believe it, but I love her still. Don't believe it. Don't trust my motives. Just go to Amsterdam."

"Amsterdam?"

"The Palestinian I spoke of lives there," Imani said. "Will you remember a name and address if I give it to you?"

Pauling nodded.

Imani told it to him, sighed, and leaned toward the bar again. "We are only"—he peered out the window—"a few miles from the airport." He turned to look behind them. There was very little traffic. "Would you like to go there now? There's a flight for Schiphol in an hour. I'd lend you my aircraft, but I think the less contact we have just now—"

"Mohammed, Field Marshal may be involved in this, as you say, but there is also a country involved. There has to be. I think you'd better be sure your people don't know more than you make out, that if they do, they don't know we've talked."

Imani answered without hesitation. "Of course it crossed my mind, Thomas, that my king might want very much to be in a position to come to the aid of the United States. It crossed my mind *before* I gave you the note that, in effect, invited you here today."

"And?"

"I checked it out, of course. When we give money to the Palestinians, we ask no questions. We're not using them as our pawns. We have no understanding with Lawrence Douglas or with whoever he works for. It's not Saudi policy to take any pleasure or profit from America's trouble. If it were otherwise, however strong my feelings, I would not have told you any of this."

After a moment Pauling nodded. "I'm glad to hear it, Mohammed."

"Thomas, I suggest that when the time comes to look for a government that is secretly the enemy of your country, you don't concentrate on the obvious possibilities alone. There are even European nations that might consider it an advantage to see the United States weakened."

When Pauling said nothing, Imani sighed deeply and added, "I hope you find her, Thomas. Truly, I hope you find her."

/ 2 /

Pauling placed the first call from Schiphol Airport, from a courtesy phone in the VIP lounge in the departures terminal. Ann Gold answered on the first ring.

"Yes?"

"It's Thomas, Ann. I'm in Amsterdam on the way to the embassy. Our private codes won't do for this."

"I understand."

"How's Michael?"

"Fine. Sleeping."

"Any startling news that can't wait twenty minutes?"

"No."

"All right then. If we both leave now you ought to be there when I am."

Pauling replaced the receiver and went out through the building to the ranks of taxi stands. Two KLM stewardesses in blue uniforms were laughing as they jaywalked ahead of a bus pulling away from the curb. Pauling got into a cab. He told the driver where he wanted to go.

He had less trouble at the embassy than he expected. The agency attaché on duty placed the call to John Smith's office over the CIA line without argument. Eight minutes after entering the building, Pauling was alone and speaking to Gold again, this time over a scrambler. Smith was probably listening in on the other end.

"You'd better tape this," Pauling said.

"You're on," Gold said. The connection was so good she might have been in the next room.

Pauling repeated the name and address Imani had given him, then said, "It's a Palestinian friend of Field Marshal's. I was going to look into it myself. Up until a half hour ago, there was nothing else to do."

"I don't understand."

"I walked out through customs. I got as far as the cabs. I was bothered about what a long shot it was—that if I could find him, if he cooperated—after awhile—he still probably wouldn't have what I needed. I want to turn him over to the usual channels."

"All right," Gold said. She knew Pauling meant he wanted Smith's people to deal with the Palestinian, pick him up and question him—if they could. If they couldn't, it wouldn't be because the Dutch authorities had refused them or interfered.

"Ann, you know what I've been trying to come up with?"

"Yes."

"I think I've got it. I got to the cabs, turned around, bought a ticket to Zurich, and placed my first call to you."

"Zurich?"

"Yes. I leave in less than an hour."

"I still don't understand," Gold said.

"We've had our sights set on the man in the middle all along, while the agency worried about who was behind him and their own involvement, while the army and the Justice

Department concentrated on stopping them. Now we'll see if our strategy pays off."

"How?"

"What does he get out of this? He's a game player. No ideology will move him. Not by itself. Not if his method for programming his people derives from his own experience, and it must."

"I agree."

"We thought it'd be the payoff from both sides. From Field Marshal and from the country behind him. I thought that, didn't you?"

"Yes."

"Do you know how much the man whose name and address I gave you got from England? Fifty. Ann, that's not enough. No terrorists can afford both a large-scale operation and an enormous payoff. They must have spent a fortune getting those recoilless rifles."

"I'd say so."

"That leaves his original backers. But how much can any country give him without leaving a trail? The agency will be backtracking every sizable laundry job in the world. His backers expected that; so did he."

"I agree again."

"There were two days between the refinery and Detroit, another day between Detroit and Washington. Unless we force his hand, I think he means to keep us busy for quite a while. Five small—comparatively—forays, their pawns expendable, then—"

"I understand!" Gold said. "I've got it!"

"Ann, do you remember Claude Sternfeld?"

"Yes!"

"I want you to call him and ask him to have the information I'll need ready for me. Tell him I'm on my way."

"All right."

"How's the market doing?"

"Not very well. Trading in Detroit-based stocks opened

and they took a bad beating. The Dow closed down another forty points, despite the army's quick action this morning. That's one hundred fifty points since the refinery. The idea that the Congress could be attacked at all was not encouraging to investors."

"No, still, forty points is better than I thought."

"Market analysts feel one more Detroit and it'll break."

"All right. Is there anything new? Any success at Bethesda?"

"No. He's still catatonic."

"I've got to leave now; I've got a cab waiting."

"I'll see to it you're met at the airport in Zurich. I hope you're right. If you are, of course we'll find out who he's using. We'll check here while you're with Sternfeld."

"Yes."

"That much—however much it is—would mean a great deal to him. Nothing, really, to a major power. So he intends to double-cross his backers, he's intended it all along. But not so they'll really mind very much, depending on who they are."

"Yes. Keep your fingers crossed."

"Yes."

Pauling replaced the phone, thanked the attaché, and left the embassy. He walked down the cement walk to the open gates to get into the waiting taxi.

/ 3 /

The California night hid the platoon of men in the trees on the side of the hill. The thick growth over their heads kept away the moon and starlight. Even so, they had orders to keep low and well back. Only Balke and the major were standing. They were hidden by tall bushes a few feet in front of them and trees to either side. They were staring across a quarter mile of fields to a Spanish-style ranch house.

A private with a walkie-talkie hunkered near the major, the

same major with whom Pauling had moved against 400 Brattle.

"The fields are in tomatoes," he had said when Balke arrived. "It failed as a dude ranch, so the owners rented the house to our friends and the fields to a farmer who lives across the valley. Our friends are the dregs of the radical left, Mr. Balke, every one of them crazy, and one of Weldmore's Mark II's."

Balke shifted uneasily.

"They have rage, Mr. Balke, and without the Mark II, they'd have spent it on each other. With him, they've got the army out. I'd say Weldmore did a fine piece of work."

It sounded as though the major thought Balke was responsible.

"How many are there, Major?"

"Eight, four men, three women, one Mark II. He's named Millstein. They're waiting for a friend of Millstein's."

"The second Mark II?"

"We hope so."

"In a van?"

"Again, we hope so, Mr. Balke. We hope so."

"And if it is?"

"We think we'll be able to get in there fast enough to prevent a detonation. If we see the van, we'll wait until the driver goes into the house. We'll get as close as we can first, then hit them with automatic fire."

Balke's mouth went dry.

The major went on. "After the Mark II arrives, our informer is going to take a walk up that road."

The major handed Balke night glasses. A single-lane road, probably dirt, ran past the house to a long, low stable and went on into the hills. Balke brought the glasses back to stare at the house again. There were no lights and no movement.

"How did he fool the polygraph?" Balke asked.

"What?"

"The polygraph. How did the informer fool the polygraph?"

The major grimaced. "Ask the other civilian."

Balke went to his left, threading his way between the trees and around the soldiers hiding behind them, until he'd found a man in civilian clothes. He showed him the credentials he had received from the CIA through Ann Gold. The civilian nodded and walked a few yards into deeper woods, stepping over roots and stones. Balke could still see the moonlight on the dark tomato fields and the tile roof of the ranch house.

"My name's Balke."

"Justice," the man said. He had dimples and a deep tan.

"CIA?"

Justice nodded.

"Who's in there? On our side I mean."

"I never met him."

"But the polygraph?"

Justice shook his head. "He didn't turn on them until after he'd been tested. He just wasn't crazy enough to go along with the plan their Mark II helped them devise. He walked into the FBI office in Los Angeles when he was supposed to be in town seeing his dentist."

Balke laughed uneasily. From his new position on the hill, he had a better view of the moon. It was full. It, and the warmth, reminded him of the time he had spent in Hawaii, but he hadn't been this nervous then.

"If we can believe him, in the morning he and the others are to get into four cars, drive into Los Angeles, toss incendiary bombs into banks and offices, and kill as many civilians with their grease guns as they can manage. They're to drive through the streets until they're out of ammunition."

"Christ."

"He said they wanted to kill a couple of thousand people who were part of the problem because they weren't part of the solution. They have twelve specific target areas, three for each car. There are eight other vehicles parked around Los Angeles for them to trade off into, to keep ahead of the police. Each team has grenades and a launcher to keep in reserve in case they get pinned down."

Balke said nothing. He didn't really believe it. Then he thought about Detroit, Washington, and West Depford.

He was back up standing next to the major when a captain came over from their right.

"Everything's set, sir. The men in the woods on the other side of the road can take the cars out anytime you say."

The major nodded. "No one's to move."

"Yes, sir."

"Nothing is to happen until our man goes out the back and keeps going."

"I understand, sir."

The captain went back the way he had come.

"We've got a recoilless trained on the cars and the house," the major told Balke.

Balke's mouth went dry again; he felt light-headed and frightened.

A radio squawked; the private repeated the message. "Vehicle coming up the road, sir."

Thirty seconds later they saw the headlights. The major already had his night glasses up, but they weren't necessary. Balke could see it easily. It was a van, a dark van, probably brown.

"Pray it's brown," Balke muttered.

"That leaves three," the major said.

The van slowed and came to a stop outside the ranch house. A man got out, stretched, raising his arms well up over his head and bending his back. When he went to the door of the house, it opened for him.

"They've put the lights on. That's good," the major said.

A hollow, yellow glow appeared in one of the front windows after the van driver disappeared inside.

"Stay here if you like, Mr. Balke," the major said.

"I'll come along if you don't mind."

A door opened at the rear of the house and a pale light cut a swath across the ground toward the stable. A man came out onto the path. He closed the door behind him, removing the

swath of light from the ground. The soldiers around Balke got
to their feet. The man started walking toward the stable.

The major waved. The men moved forward.

At the edge of the woods, the major turned and looked at
the private on Balke's right. "All right, soldier."

The private spoke into his radio. "It's on! It's on!"

Fifty men appeared at the base of the hill from the trees at
the edge of the fields and started running toward the ranch
house. Artillery sounded from the far hill. Balke didn't see
anything, but he heard—and felt—the impact of the first
shell. Burp-gun fire came from inside the house. It was
answered immediately by men already lying prone in the
tomato field. Others, well ahead of Balke now, rushed toward
the house. Some were only a hundred yards away.

The front door opened, the light from inside made another
rhomboid swath, this one across the front yard. The man
who had arrived only a few minutes before walked slowly
toward his van.

"Take him out!" the major yelled. "Take him out! Don't let
him reach that van."

Fire was directed at the man. Bullets hit the side of the
van and broke the windows. The man was hit repeatedly, but
he kept moving. He opened the door at the rear of the van and
bent the top of his body inside. He walked out into the open
again.

Balke was now close enough to see his face. He had a bushy
moustache, and he was smiling. A soldier who had made it
to within twenty yards of him, and had his M-16 turned to
what men in Vietnam called rock and roll, fully automatic
fire, turned the spray of his weapon directly at the man's chest.
The man leaned into it, was kept erect by the fire, his body
violated by hundreds of rounds in the seconds he hung there.

Then came the white light so bright it was acid in Balke's
eyes.

On the hill the men who had set up the recoilless rifle were
blinded, too. Some fell to their knees, some flat on their faces,

as if worshiping. Then the fire reached them. The earth shook. The mushroom went up white against a sky turned red by the blast. The shock wave swept past the incinerated men. Heat dissolved the leaves and branches. The trunks were laid flat by the atomic wind.

/ 4 /

"Please come this way, Mr. Pauling." The tall young man spoke English without an accent. It was just after eleven in the morning in Zurich; Sternfeld's employees were all dutifully at their desks in cubicles to either side of a long, fluorescent-lighted corridor.

Pauling was shown through to an office done in teak. Sternfeld was watching a portable television that had been set on the corner of his desk. Robust, in his early sixties, with white muttonchops, he rose and shook Pauling's hand briskly. Obviously he had kept the news from his staff. It was just as obvious that it had shaken him badly. Immediately he turned back to the screen.

"You've heard?" Sternfeld asked.

"Only that there was an atomic explosion. Where was it?"

"We're getting the president's speech now. With the details."

Pauling pulled over a chair, and Sternfeld sat. The tall young man stayed, hovering behind Pauling. When the Swiss announcer had finished repeating that there had been a nuclear explosion in the United States, a picture of the president behind his desk appeared. The president's voice, sad, stern, controlled, was followed immediately by a translation. Pauling listened for the English.

"Ladies and gentlemen, approximately an hour ago, at close to three A.M. Eastern Standard Time, an atomic device exploded fifty miles east of Los Angeles. We don't yet know how many people were killed, but many were soldiers who had been moving against a terrorist camp. We have estimated the pattern and severity of the expected fallout from the detonation site eastward, and I have asked that the army evacuate all civilians from the area. If you are close to the site, local authorities are alerting civilians, evacuation teams are already at work. Help is on the way. Army helicopters equipped with loudspeakers are making circuits of even the most desolate regions affected. The most important thing is to remain calm. The weather is stable, winds over the region are not high. We expect the evacuation efforts to be one hundred percent effective.

"The blast was not part of an attack by a foreign army. We are not being attacked. The bomb was in the possession of terrorists. I repeat, we are not being attacked."

The president leaned back in his chair. He leaned forward again almost immediately to stare into the camera eye. "We knew of the presence of the terrorists in the area, and we moved against them. We don't yet know how the explosion occurred. The terrorists have been wiped out. This is the fourth terrorist-related catastrophe in a week, but in each case the terrorists suffered terribly. Every one of them involved in the attack on Capitol Hill yesterday has been killed or captured."

"Balke," Pauling said softly.

"Excuse me, Thomas?" Sternfeld said.

"My associate. He was there."

"I'm sorry."

"As soon as we have more information, we will make it public," the president said. "Again, the most important thing is to remain calm."

The president paused. He lifted a paper from his desk, looked at it, then faced the camera eye again. "In 1945, the United States Army sent a thousand troops into one of the first atomic-test blasts in Nevada, only minutes after the explosion. To date there has been evidence that some of the men sent in were affected by the radiation they received, but exposure to radiation is not necessarily fatal and does not necessarily result in permanent, physical harm. If you are close to the blast site, remain calm. Help is coming. Stay tuned to your local television and radio stations. They will tell you what to do."

The president replaced the paper on his desk. It was evident that he was greatly moved. He stared from his office at the world. Finally the Swiss announcer's face was flashed on the screen. Pauling didn't try to follow the German. There was mention of the wine crops and a guess at the number of casualties. Sternfeld got up to turn down the volume.

"What is it, Thomas? Why are you in Zurich? It has nothing to do with that?" He pointed at the television.

Pauling nodded.

"I don't believe it!" Sternfeld said. "How can I help you with terrorists? Is it what Miss Gold asked? These two things are connected? This question of investment profits?"

Pauling didn't respond. It had just caught up with him. Balke. The explosion. Marcia. The fear for her life that he had been keeping down welled up out of his stomach. It made him feel as though he was being tilted over the side of a cliff.

"Thomas?"

Pauling nodded. "Connected," he said. "Yes, connected."

/ 5 /

McGraw got a car at the airport and drove toward the city. After he heard about the blast, he left the hospital against doctor's orders and bought his own ticket, flashing his credentials and insisting on preference ahead of other civilians leaving Detroit by air. The young woman at the Hertz counter at New Orleans had been another small source of irritation. Maybe, like almost everyone else in the country, she was frightened; maybe she was taking her fear out on her customers. Whatever, McGraw had to flash his credentials and get tough with her. You do what you have to do. The young woman had to wait on McGraw ahead of everyone else. McGraw had to go find another old friend—acquaintance—Special Agent Alexander Grant.

The office was off Canal Street in a new building. McGraw found it and was allowed to walk in on an action briefing.

About three-dozen men were crammed into a small room watching Grant up front at a blackboard. He'd always looked like a banker, age hadn't lessened the effect. He'd always been slight and bookish. Now his hair was gray, maybe his back was a little straighter. A disc problem perhaps, or just being over sixty.

Silence fell when McGraw came in. Then Grant recognized him, took in the bandage taped over McGraw's cheek, and started where he'd left off.

"All right, like I said, it'll be a Ford. It was chocolate brown when it left Cambridge. If this city is a target, it got in sometime in the last few days and could be anywhere by now, any color. Look for chocolate brown ones and freshly painted ones. You have three years of vans to choose from, all practically the same model. Be sharp. Check garages if you have nothing else to do. The police haven't been told why, so don't you tell them. They're at all major roads into the city in force and at most of the minor roads. What you look for is heavy-duty springs. If you find a Ford van, chocolate brown or freshly painted, heavy-duty springs, you ask no questions. You get it off the road, you get ready for action. Any move from *anyone* toward the rear of that van, you *shoot to kill*. Is that clear?"

No one said a word. It was clear.

"Is that about right, Stub?" Grant asked.

McGraw had put himself against the door behind him. It was too crowded in the room for a man of his bulk to move anywhere else without a fight.

"That's about right," McGraw said.

Grant said, "McGraw's the man who got the first one. We all know what happened to the second. There are three more, including the one we're going to find in this city. Understood?"

Heads bobbed. A few of Grant's men said, "Yes," or "Yes, sir."

McGraw said, "Look, you all might as well know that we think they're into a double stroke, first something like West Depford or Detroit, something big. Then the real kick, those vans. They may want to blackmail the country. But it may also be that the people who supplied the vans and the terrorist groups they work with don't want the same thing. So here are a couple of things to think about. What was the number-one shot for New Orleans? It may still be in the works. Or were the terrorists grouped here responsible for West Depford? More important: the driver of that van is a programmed agent. He or she may appear drugged or hypnotized and will be smiling, constantly smiling."

Someone laughed.

McGraw said, "Go out on the street. How many people out there are happy today? How many people are walking around looking pleased that, after an A-bomb blast in California, police and bureau personnel are searching their city?"

The agents were still looking at him. When Grant spoke, they turned.

"All right. You've got your orders. Don't come back here. Don't sleep. Find that van. And never confirm any suspicions that we're looking for it because there's a bomb in it. If you're pressed, you're after terrorists. Don't confirm the existence of the bomb."

"What if we find it? How do we know it's not set to go off?" someone asked.

"I don't know yet," Grant said. "I'm supposed to hear from Washington about that."

"Yo!" McGraw called.

Everyone turned.

"Listen sharp. You go to the back of the van and find a

removable steel plate on the floor. You lift the plate. You'll be looking at three knobs, like on a safe. If they're not all on fifty-five—five five—you have a problem. Everyone in New Orleans has a problem. If they're on fifty-five, watch the middle one. If the middle one moves, you still have the problem."

McGraw caught his breath, swallowed, and went back to it. "Here's what you do then. Go to the side door of the van. Under the seat, the rear bench seat, is a carpet-covered casing. That's the bomb. Right in front of you, you'll see a carpet-covered steel door held in place by two steel bolts. Twist the bolts, pull them out, open the door. You'll be looking at leather. Pull it out. It'll be empty, an empty shell of a suitcase, the end you weren't looking at sliced off. Throw it away. In the casing under the seat is the charge ready to drop into the mechanism that drives it into the main load. You have to pull out that charge. If you can't pull it out, you have to wedge something, anything, a rifle or a broom, into the mechanism beneath it. If you can slow it down, you can get what they call a fizzle blast. It won't do one hundredth the damage of the real thing. You'll have saved a lot of lives."

No one spoke. Finally Grant said, "All right."

McGraw stepped aside. The men left the office slowly. When they had gone, McGraw took a chair beside Grant's desk. Grant sat too.

"You're a hero," Grant said. "And look at you. You look like hell. Heroes are supposed to shine."

"Thanks," McGraw said.

"You mean it about that smile?"

"I never saw anything like it," McGraw told him. "I kicked one of them where it hurts and he looked at me as though we were in love. The key men in this are intelligence assets who are far beyond caring about pain."

"Whose assets, Stub?"

McGraw shook his head.

"What do you think they'd be up to here?" he asked. "I mean the number-one punch you were talking about."

"I thought about it all the way in," McGraw said. "I think they did West Depford. I know it's closer to the New York group. I still think it was this one. My guess is they're just sitting and waiting."

"For what?"

"Pauling thinks for two days, maybe three. Then they'll let us know they're alive."

"Who's Pauling?"

"Private intelligence. He and I got onto this before . . . we got onto it early. Alex, you might as well know now. I'm surprised you don't already. These assets come from a CIA operation that was turned around."

Grant's eyebrows were white and thick. They went up. "I don't believe it."

"Okay," McGraw said.

"Turned around by whom?"

"We don't know."

Grant snorted. After a moment he said, "So you think they'll just be sitting still."

"No, not all of them. I think the asset, the van driver, will be touring the city."

"What?"

"I think he'll be on a tour bus, or at Antoine's, or The Court of the Three Sisters."

"You're tired," Grant said.

"I told you I've been thinking about it all the way down. You know why I came here, instead of New York or Washington?"

Grant shook his head.

"Because of you, Alex. I hoped you'd trust me."

"I'm flattered," Grant said. ▪

"These assets are a little like children or hippies. They have a peculiar sense of humor. You ought to hear them talk to each other. We have some of it on tape. They're so full of enthusiasm, you'd think they were born yesterday."

"Touring the city?" Grant said after a while. "Why?"

"Because it won't be here soon."

McGraw got to his feet. He touched his fingertips to the bandage on his cheek. He needed another painkiller.

"Want to come?"

"I guess I do," Grant said. "I guess I do."

/ 6 /

The venetian blinds were closed against the afternoon sun, the lights in the small office turned off. Harriman wanted it gloomy; it suited his mood. It was as if that A-bomb had gone off in the back of his own head. He wanted to be alone with the aftereffects. He wanted the shock waves to reach the furthest points of his anatomy, to know in his fingertips that the damn thing was done.

When the knock came on the glass door, and Rita Facett let herself in, he looked at her but said nothing. She closed the door and took the chair in front of his desk. The office had once been used for medical consultations. Harriman was aware of that; he knew Facett was aware of it. It was like him, when he finally spoke, to make a joke of the thing.

"Zo, mine dear, tell us, how long haff you lift in fear from der bomb? Yah?"

Facett didn't answer for some time. Finally she whispered, "You have killed thousands of people."

God, he hated her.

"It might have gone off in a city." He kept his voice even. "Hundreds of thousands might have been killed, tens of thousands might have suffered radiation sickness, their hair falling out, their babies born—"

"Stop it!"

"Talking to you makes me feel good clean through, Dr. Facett. Did you know that? That's why I keep you around. You remind me of what people are really like, that no matter how many times and how hard they are brought face to face with the thing that has kept them down *all their lives,* only a handful ever see it for what it really is."

"I don't know what you're talking about."

He stared her down. When he had won, when her eyes fell to the top of the desk between them and stayed there, he let himself relax. He counted his inhalations and exhalations, until he felt the last of his anger leave him.

"How's Savage?" he finally said.

"She's conscious again. She's ready to be questioned again. I don't know why you care that she's so resistant, that the indicators say she's still lying. If she's not a CIA agent, she's from the government, some agency."

Harriman disregarded that. "How's Harold?"

Facett sighed. "Lawrence took him for a walk in the woods this morning, as you told him to. He's very bad, at times he's catatonic. I sedated him lightly so he could be awakened in time to be at the phones, but he's not going to make it. Soon he'll go into a trance, and he'll never come out of it."

Harriman concentrated on his breathing again, counting his inhalations and exhalations. Shortly, the technique yielded new effects. Not only was his anger gone, but his tension dissipated too, the tension he had built up thinking about the bomb.

"I wasn't in a very good mood, was I?" he said.

It was a rhetorical question, but she had recovered enough to answer. "Your mood was obvious. It still is."

"You don't have to worry. I don't make decisions when I'm in that frame of mind, not without taking it into account."

"I thought you'd be triumphant," Facett said. "Your bomb went off. Instead you're bitter."

"Idiot," Harriman said. "It wasn't supposed to go off."

"Of course not. And the Cubans weren't supposed to destroy—"

"What the hell do you think I wanted? Dead congressmen?" he shouted. His anger was back, fully formed.

She stared at him across the desk and swallowed.

"*Damn you.* I told you I wanted to frighten America, not destroy it. I explained it to you. Frighten America for just long enough."

"You're working for someone," she said softly. "What you want doesn't matter. It's what they want."

"Ah, she's spoken to you. She asked you that, didn't she? She asked you who I was doing it for. She's not only resisted all our techniques, she's still functioning as our enemy!"

Facett looked down at her hands. They were clasped in her lap. She tried to unclasp them and failed. For a long moment she was terribly afraid. The posthypnotic suggestion to be unable to unclasp one's hands was commonplace. For that long moment she thought Harriman had gotten to her too. She thought he had somehow tricked her into hypnosis. Finally, her hands obeyed her; they came apart.

"What's the matter?"

"Nothing."

"I asked you a question. Savage asked you who I was working for, didn't she?"

"She asked me who was behind the subversion of Weldmore. But I don't know, do I? It might be those terrorists."

"But it isn't, is it, Reets?"

"Damn you!"

"*I'm sorry,*" Harriman said quickly. He leaned back. "Look, I'm *sorry,* really *sorry.*"

Facett began to cry.

"*What?*" Harriman asked. "What, *goddamn it!*"

"So many people died last night. So many! And yesterday. And in Detroit. And on that oil tanker. And you apologize for calling me *Reets.*"

Her voice broke, her tears continued. Soon she was sobbing and did nothing to stop it. The sobs wracked her. Then, because she needed air, because her sobbing had interfered with her breathing, a deep throaty sound issued from her mouth.

"Damn! Damn!" she said after awhile.

Harriman got to his feet and walked to the window. He lifted a slat of the venetian blinds to peer out. When he let it go, it snapped back with a sound like a shot.

"I'm sorry," he said softly, "because I promised not to call you that. I never promised not to kill people. *Au contraire, mon frère,* as the comedian says. Now I'm going to my room, Dr. Facett. When you've stopped crying like a child, you come and get me, and we'll talk to Savage again. As you say, there may not be much in it. It may not make the slightest bit of difference who she's working for, what she knows." Harriman's voice had risen, he was speaking more and more quickly. "On the other hand, it's something I don't know. *It's something I'm not aware of.* And I don't like that! *And I don't like her resilience.*"

He had shouted again. He said softly, "Sorry. Sorry."

He leaned against the wall near the window. He stayed there for some few seconds, staring at the floor.

"I'm like a man washed up on a shore," he said. "I was frightened of those bombs. Frightened. They're just bombs. They go boom. BOOM!"

Facett had found a Kleenex in the pocket of her skirt. She blew her nose and wiped her eyes.

"It's almost over, kid," Harriman said. "Stick with me, please. If you don't have any faith in me, GET A LITTLE! Rita, you have no idea what's going to happen. Stick with me, and you'll be a queen. A happy one. Really happy. I'll work like a bastard to see you find what it takes to be happy. I know you've got it, baby. You've got it."

She was shaking her head.

"What?" Harriman asked.

"You're crazy," she said softly. "You're crazy, Mark."

He laughed shortly. "Sure I am. Come on. Tell you what. Instead of questioning Savage, we'll go for a walk. Take her off the drugs, disconnect her from the machines. We'll go for a walk."

Facett looked up at him.

"I mean it. Put her in one of the recovery rooms."

"You'll kill her," Facett said.

"No! Come on. How about it? It's a nice day. Gloomy as hell in here, but nice out there. Let's go someplace where we can forget everything. Into the woods. All right?"

She nodded. Slowly, she stood up.

"You mean it, don't you? You'll come with me? Like when we were lovers. Maybe we'll be lovers again."

She opened the door and went out into the corridor where there was more light, where windows at the ends let the afternoon light pour in.

Chapter Eleven

/ 1 /

The NATO jet touched down, tore across the tarmac, and came to a halt near a long, black limousine. When the cabin door opened, Pauling descended in a light rain.

The temperature was more moderate than when he left for London. Despite the rain, there were stars spotting the black sky. The full moon cast a pale light over the air base.

Pauling walked to the limousine, sank into the rear seat, stared at John Smith, then nodded to Ann Gold on the jump seat in front of him.

Smith said, "Nelson and I talked it over with the president. He's agreed to your request. You got what you wanted. It may work best that way."

"Good."

Gold handed Pauling an automatic pistol in a shoulder holster. As Smith continued, Pauling examined the weapon, removed his suit coat, and put it on.

"While you were in the air, we were able to reconfirm the information you got in Zurich. There's no longer any doubt, assuming your assumptions are right. But you're acting on your own and not just because you want it that way. We want it that way, too. Our people have been instructed to do as little as possible to attract attention. If they have to confront him, they're to show him as few faces as possible and no credentials whatsoever. If you're right, fine. If you're wrong, we don't want him able to prove we were there. It has nothing to do with us or any branch of government."

"That's right," Pauling said. He put his suit coat back on.

"If you're right, you'll be more effective and quicker."

"Yes," Pauling said.

"Were you able to get any rest?"

"Yes. While Sternfeld put his people on it and checked it and rechecked it. And on the flight over."

Smith nodded. He looked at Gold, who leaned over to tap on the thick glass between them and the two men in the front seat. The limousine started moving.

"Can I have an update?" Pauling asked.

Smith grimaced. "The state of emergency began at midnight. When the bureau and the city police in New Orleans, Washington, and New York were unable to find any of the vans, the president decided the best thing was to move in the army. He's decided against evacuating the cities—if we had hard evidence that the vans were actually there, he probably would. The army is ready to begin moving out women and children. The searches have begun. Every street, every garage, every building that could house a van, everything that can be checked will be checked."

"That's being done now?"

"It's being done now. In New Orleans, New York, and DC. Despite assurances from all authorities that the army is looking for terrorists, not for a bomb, people began to leave all three cities shortly after the army arrived. We expected that. It'll make evacuation quicker if the president decides on it later. We'll see the stream from New York as soon as we turn onto the highway."

Pauling grimaced, closed his eyes, and leaned back.

"You don't think the vans will be found, do you?" Gold asked.

"No," Pauling said.

"Neither do I," Smith told him. "You heard about the letter?"

"Just the radio message you sent while I was aboard the plane. I'd like to see it."

Smith reached into his pocket and handed it to him. The limousine had left the hangars and runways behind and was traveling fast down a wide highway.

"Are we sure they're from the right people?" Pauling said.

"A letter was sent to the city editor of the *New York Times* three weeks ago; another, just like it, to his counterpart on the *Washington Post*. Neither man took them seriously or connected them to the terrorists until the blast in California. The letters specified that in the event of an atomic explosion anywhere in the country, they were to look for another letter with the same return address: Quake, 9999 Life Street, U.S.A."

"Cute," Pauling said.

"Yes. What you've got in your hand is a copy of the second letter from Quake."

Pauling unfolded the letter and read it:

Gentlemen:

There are a number of atomic devices secreted in highly populated, sensitive areas across the United States. We had not wished to begin to use them. Our plan was to use more conventional guerrilla and terrorist tactics until you were ready to take us seriously, but you have forced our hand. The situation has escalated. You must now be told that you are at war with Interface, a united left-wing terrorist organization. These are our demands. You will meet each of them, or there will be further devastation with much more serious consequences.

1. The United States will insist and assure that Israel return all lands captured in the 1967 war and that a Palestinian state is formed which will include land on the west bank of the Jordan River.

2. A list of political prisoners now held in U.S. prisons is being compiled. It will be typed on this typewriter and sent to the Department of Justice. These prisoners will be released immediately and flown to Algeria.

3. Shipments of small arms, including 10,000 M-16 and 10,000 AK 47 rifles, 5,000 grenade launchers, and appropriate ammunition, will be sent in good faith to the Irish Republican Army through the port of Algiers.

4. The administration will draw a plan for the nationalization of major industries, including steel production and automobile manufacture; these plans will include reimbursement to minor stockholders only.

5. The administration will draw similar plans for the nationalization of the professions of medicine and the law.

6. The U.S. will confiscate all monies and holdings of citizens of the Republic of South Africa and will seize all holdings of U.S. citizens and institutions in South African enterprises. It will break off all diplomatic ties with South Africa.

It is understood that it will take time to accomplish what we demand, but we have time. We set no immediate deadline. If we feel that the machinery of government is stalling, we will destroy a major city. Our devices are safely secured. You will search for them but you will not find them. You don't know how many we have. You don't know where they are. You must, from this moment on, assume that the government, every official and employee of the government, holds his office or job as a trust from the people, the people as opposed to their employers, the people as opposed to the Capitalist establishment. These demands are obviously only a beginning. We have the bomb. *We* have the bomb. There will be a revolution in American governmental practice. It begins now.

Interface

Pauling handed the letter back to Nelson.

"Somewhere," Pauling said, "whatever else he's doing, Harriman is laughing. It must be Harriman."

"I wonder," Smith said, "if we've all outsmarted ourselves from the first. If it's really been terrorists all along."

Pauling didn't reply. He looked at Gold. "Where's Michael?"

"Still at my place. Brideswell's with him."

"Why so quiet? You sitting on bad news?"

Gold smiled. "No more than the rest of us."

Smith said, "Balke died in the explosion yesterday. You knew that?"

"I surmised it."

Pauling looked out at the night. They had turned onto the highway a few minutes before. As Smith had promised, the lanes on the far side of the meridian were heavy with traffic. Hundreds of headlights dotted the night air. Above, more stars were visible than when Pauling deplaned.

"We're speculating," Smith said, "that since the blast the terrorist groups left in New Orleans and New York may have been abandoned by their Mark II's."

"Maybe," Pauling said.

"It doesn't get us very far."

"No."

"Do you want to talk about how you're going to proceed?"

"No," Pauling said.

"We've got someone with him of course, and his home surrounded. Don't think for an instant he's the wrong man. If your theory is correct, he's the only one possible. People at the Securities and Exchange Commission were at this up until a few hours ago. There just isn't anyone else whose companies have put themselves in that kind of position. If there's panic, he stands to make almost a hundred million on the way down. Maybe more. If he holds at the bottom and the markets recover, he could do even better on the way up. He could make over a billion or more. He'd be one of the richest men in the world."

"And if Thomas isn't right?" Gold asked softly.

No one answered.

The limousine moved steadily against the flow from the opposite direction. Ahead, finally, Pauling saw the dark outline of the New York skyline against the night.

"Apparently he was planning to take a vacation. He was leaving for the Caribbean in the morning," Smith said.

"He'll have to cancel," Pauling told him.

/ 2 /

The only light in the room came from the ten-watt bulb over the call buzzer, just enough for Facett to negotiate to the bedside, find the chair she knew was there, and put herself in it. She touched Savage on the arm and put her hand over her mouth.

"Whisper," she said. "It's me. It's all right. Whisper, please."

Marcia pulled herself up onto one elbow and sank back immediately. She hadn't strength enough even for that.

"It's all right," Facett said. "You're all right. As soon as you eat something, you'll begin to get your strength back."

"What—"

"Listen, please. I want you to know, I've done everything I could for you."

"Why?"

"What?"

"Why do you want me to know?"

Facett leaned forward. "I just wanted to . . . to talk to you."

"All right," Marcia whispered.

"There isn't anyone else here I can talk to. There hasn't been anyone in ages. He's . . . he's got everyone drugged or hypnotized except his . . . creations."

"How many are here?"

"Three. He has his personal bodyguard, you know, they go with him . . . almost always . . . and he has Lawrence."

"The one who was on the tanker?"

"Yes."

"Where are they?"

"Stop trying to get up," Facett said. "You can't. You're too weak. You haven't had any solid food since you were brought here. The drugs you've been given are meant to weaken you. Lie back down, please."

Marcia had been trying again to right herself. She let Facett put her back against the bedclothes.

"You couldn't get out of here anyway. You're not even strong enough to get out of bed. Even if you were, you couldn't get below this floor without setting off an alarm. The doors are locked, the windows are barred. Lawrence or one of the bodyguards is always in the lobby."

"They're human beings. They can be beaten."

"Please keep your voice down. The doctor and his wife are asleep just down the hall. And . . . and he's finally asleep. I never knew him to do it, but he drank tonight."

"You were with him?"

Facett knew what she meant. "Yes," she said. "Yes."

"You want to get out too, don't you?"

"Yes. I can't. I want to, but I can't. You don't understand. It's all changed. It's not just my son anymore."

"What do you mean?"

"Out there. The army tried to stop him in California. One of the vans was there."

"What?"

"There were five vans. Each one is an A-bomb. An A-bomb," she repeated.

"*What?* What did you say? California?"

"Near San Bernardino," Facett told her. "Last night."

"*Oh my God!*"

"If he gives them the word, they'll detonate the others.

They'd even sit on top of them and detonate the others. They think Berger is God. Literally. Literally!"

Marcia's eyes opened wide, her palms became cold, and she found it difficult to breathe. "We've got to do something."

"We can't. There's no way."

"Can you get a message out of here?"

"No. Of course not. Even if I could, don't you see what he'd do? He'd blow up all the cities he could. That's what he wants . . . I think. I think that's what he wants. He says he doesn't, but I don't believe him."

"Berger?"

"No! Harriman. Harriman."

"But it's Berger who's—"

"No! Berger is in trance. I told you. You can't believe it till you see it. He started him slowly, just a few minutes a day. Now he's drugged and under hypnosis always."

"But you said—"

"The agents think he's Berger's man, but it's the other way around. It's Harriman. You don't believe me? Don't try to get up. Please."

"I believe you. But I thought you said Berger."

"Harriman. His people. He calls them Mark II's."

"Mark II's, Mark Harriman."

"He's like that," Facett explained. "He makes jokes of things people can't accept as jokes. He's insane. Of course he's insane. I see that now. But he had my son, and now he has the bombs."

Marcia made still another effort to get up. "Help me, please."

Finally Facett took her by the shoulders to help her.

"If I could just sit up," Marcia said.

Facett propped her pillows behind her. "Is that better?"

Marcia nodded. "My head."

"It's the hunger. I'll get you something to eat."

"No, wait. Don't leave."

Marcia felt her forehead. "But you said they think Berger is . . ."

Facett tried a smile.

"Were many people killed?" Marcia asked.

"Yes. There was Detroit too. They say over a thousand died there. Did you know about Detroit?"

"No. Another bomb? Not another—"

"No, not that bad. A small war. He caused a small war."

"How?"

"Distributing weapons, automatic weapons. During a black-out. In Washington yesterday he attacked Congress. They stopped him, they were ready for him."

Marcia's mind was racing. First she thought Facett was telling the truth. Then she decided all this was being said to make her talk. In the end she believed it all. She sensed something in Facett had snapped or was about to.

"You have to hold yourself together," Marcia said.

"Yes! And you! If you will, I will. I'm all alone here except for you. It was all right. I mean I could keep my sanity until . . ."

Facett leaned forward. Marcia found herself holding her.

Facett pulled back. "I'll be all right. I'll get you something from the kitchen."

"You've got to get a message out. If they're all asleep . . ."

"No. The phones all go through the computer. There's always someone there. The machine operator or one of his men. You know, they'll never find us. The government. Whoever you work for."

"Rita, when we drove up, I saw woods. We're not far from Cambridge, we didn't come that far."

"We're in Wellesley." Facett laughed ironically. "I went to school here."

Marcia touched her hand. "If we could get as far as the woods . . ."

"No chance," Facett said. "Lie back down. I'll make you some soup."

Facett blinked several times, stood up, and put Marcia's pillows back flat on the bed. She eased Marcia down.

Marcia smiled. "Look, could you get me a gun? My gun was in my bag. Or any gun."

Facett shook her head. "He doesn't trust me. Why should he trust me?" She almost started crying again. "He has my child. He has the bombs. He has me . . . my body. Why should he trust me?"

She went out. For a few moments, Marcia could hear her footsteps in the corridor.

With considerable effort Marcia finally managed to sit up by herself. Taking great gulps of air, as if the stuff had nutritive value, she struggled to put her feet on the floor and, at last, to stand. She walked. She walked, always in danger of falling, to the window. She drew back the curtains and lifted a single slat of the venetian blinds.

The windows were barred. It was twenty feet to the ground below. The woods began about seventy yards away. She could make out a low, broad frame building near the far edge of the woods. Finally convinced that Facett was right, that she hadn't the strength to escape, she staggered back to the bed to wait for some food.

/ 3 /

When the troops arrived in New Orleans at midnight, some people feared the worst and left their homes; a stream of private cars began to leave the city, just as in New York and Washington. But most residents accepted assurances of the authorities, repeated over television and radio stations and confirmed by police operators, that the troops were searching for the terrorists who destroyed the refinery at West Depford.

It was different in the French Quarter. While small squads of First Cavalry troops—their shoulder patches were black horses' heads on a field of yellow—searched garages and warehouses, the rumor that a bomb was the real object of the search spread so fast among the musicians, B-girls, strippers, waitresses, and bartenders, it might have been free cocaine.

The atmosphere in the Quarter quickly became desperate. Nevertheless, people hung on. Their attitude seemed to be that it just wasn't going to happen—even if there were a bomb, it wasn't going to go off. Most of them stayed.

McGraw and Grant arrived there late that afternoon. They had gone from bar to bar, working their way up from the Esplanade. They fingered pralines in souvenir shops and stared at people in the horse-drawn carriages. During the evening hours they visited over two dozen restaurants. At midnight when the troops arrived, they were going from bar to bar again.

Then the faces of the people in the Quarter became a lesson in psychology, even for McGraw who had been investigating people for almost forty years.

Some of the faces were set, determined. Those people didn't want to know why the army was out there. They didn't want to think too much about what had happened in San Bernardino. They were like poker players running a high-stakes bluff they knew no one was buying. They weren't going to give anything away. Down deep they knew they weren't going to win either.

Other faces showed fear so clearly that McGraw smelled the rank odor of cold sweat until he thought it was impossible. He couldn't be smelling it. The sensation went away.

Still other faces were like the faces of salesmen at a convention, hounded men with only one night a year away from their wives, tonight; except that some of those faces belonged to women. They were lusty, they were laughing and crying.

It was like that at a place called Maxie's when McGraw and Grant walked in at close to two o'clock in the morning. McGraw's cheek hurt, but he was off the painkillers. They made him drowsy. An occasional beer seemed to help. He ordered one, took a sip, and set it down.

Three strippers on the stage, two brunettes and a blond star, had just turned to show the audience their backs. The star whirled to face the audience again, put her hands under her breasts, lifting them up and out, and began to bump. She cocked her hips back and threw them forward. She let the crowd have it so hard, one of the salesman types seated near the stage let the energy of her saccharine lust knock him backward.

"There," McGraw said.

"What?"

"The woman with the frizzy hair. Over there."

Grant turned and saw Caroline at a table against the wall. She was alone, sipping from a tall drink. When she set the drink down, she smiled like an angel.

"She's not laughing, she's not crying, she's not scared," McGraw said. "She's pleased with the world. Look at her, Alex."

"I don't know," Grant said, but his tone suggested he agreed. He took down two inches of beer and stared across the top of his glass.

"I thought it'd be a man," McGraw said.

"Maybe she's stoned."

"No," McGraw said. "Look at her eyes. She's alert. Get a team, for the love of God."

Grant put his beer down. He walked over to the bartender. He asked for the phone and was directed to a flight of stairs to the right of the stage.

At the table against the wall, Caroline stood up, put some bills down and started across the floor. Behind her the strippers, all facing front again, had fallen to their knees. The music had slowed, and the strippers had started to grind, their thighs wide, their heads bent back so their hair fell behind them. The audience was applauding.

The man who had let himself be whipped back before stood up and shouted, "Oh! Honey! Move that thing around! Oh! Honey!"

Caroline made it across the club and was walking toward the door to the street. McGraw took a forlorn look toward the stairs over his glass. He put it down and started after her.

/ 4 /

There was a better view of the Manhattan skyline from the road below the estate than there had been from the highway. Up the hill, beyond the six-foot cement wall, the moon illuminated the shapes of carefully manicured bushes, gravel paths running among them, and what were flower or rock gardens on terrace after terrace to the level place where the house stood.

"He could land a helicopter in there; it's big enough," Pauling said. "Have we got air support?"

"Yes. Nothing flies tonight that isn't ours, not for very long." Smith, like Pauling, Gold, and the two men in the front seat, was staring up at the mansion on the top of the terraced hill.

Gold had to strain to get a good view. "If New York goes up, he'll be able to watch it from there."

"He won't enjoy it very much if the wind blows this way across the river," Pauling said.

"That may be why he was about to leave for the Caribbean," Smith conjectured.

Pauling gritted his teeth and waited. Thirty yards ahead, caught in the headlights of the parked limousine, were two automobiles, one to either side of an iron gate set in the cement wall. A man was walking along the shoulder of the road toward them, having just stepped out of the passenger side of one of the cars. When the man got close, Smith hit the electric switch for the window on his side, lowering it.

"I'm Mason, sir," the man said, leaning down.

"Hello, Mason. Come in."

Smith opened the door; Gold moved over to the jump seat in front of Pauling so Mason could take hers. Mason nodded to Pauling and Gold and closed the door, leaving them in the dark again. He had a round, pleasant face; he was about Pauling's height and age.

Smith closed the window. "How many men around the perimeter?"

"Almost a hundred, sir. No one's going to get out of that place tonight unless they tunnel out. You said to be as inconspicuous as possible, so we moved the transport vans down the road a few hundred yards."

"Good," Smith said. "It could happen that we were never here. We don't want to attract the attention of neighbors or people on the road."

"Yes, sir. I understand. But we've had contact."

"What's happened?"

"A little while after we cut off their phones and blocked their gates, a car came to the front gate. I walked over. A man let down the window of the driver's side and stuck his head out. About forty, graying temples, dark, Florida tan, I'd say, over a pitted complexion. I couldn't make out his eye color but I'd say that was him, sir."

"Yes."

"I told him, politely, that there was a state of emergency, that I had orders to send a man back with him to the house, that no one was going to leave for a while. When he got angry, I suggested he might blast his way past me and past the cars at the gate if he really wanted to, but he would get no farther than that. I didn't tell him why not. He seemed to believe me. He asked for credentials. I refused his request, and he backed up."

"Then?" Smith asked.

"He tried the rear gate and got the same response. Once he knew we were here, we sent a team up to make sure he couldn't do himself any harm. They met him on his way back from the rear gate. The senior agent is Feldman. We're in touch with him by walkie-talkie. He says the subject is behaving. His wife is upset, but the subject himself is calm."

"Our information is that his wife has no hand in his business affairs. Tell Feldman to just keep her to the side."

"Yes, sir."

"Feldman's not letting him out of his sight?"

"Not for a minute, sir. What happens next?"

"I'm what happens next," Pauling said.

Smith said nothing. Mason just looked at him for a moment.

"How are you, Thomas?" Mason said.

"Fine, Lenny. Been a long time."

"Yes."

"Would you like to go up there with me?"

Mason looked at Smith.

"I don't want any agency people there when you actually question him."

"He's already seen Mason's face," Pauling told him. "It's a big house. I'll need not to be disturbed. I know Mason and trust him to keep everyone out of the way."

"Like that," Mason said.

"That's right."

"All right, I'd like to go. Sir?"

"All right," Smith said.

Pauling got out on his side of the limousine, Mason on the other. They met on the shoulder of the road and walked in the beams from the headlights toward the gate.

"How much do you know?" Pauling asked.

"There are three more bombs somewhere in the country. New York, Washington, and New Orleans are the probable targets. That's about all, except that the guy up there may have something to do with it."

"Do you remember my wife?"

"Yes. She wasn't your wife when I knew her, and you weren't riding around in the back seat of a limousine with one of the top people in the agency."

"They've got her."

Mason didn't reply for a moment. When he did, he said, "I see. I'm glad I'm coming along. What do you want me to do?"

"Just see I'm not disturbed, no matter what happens when I'm alone with him."

Mason nodded. They had stopped at the car Mason had been in when they arrived. While Mason stuck his head in to say something, Pauling looked beyond the gate to the house at the top of the hill.

There was a door in the cement wall next to the stanchion that held the wrought-iron gate.

"Do we go in that way?" Pauling asked Mason.

Mason nodded.

"Let's go."

They walked to the door—it wasn't locked—and started up the drive past the gardens Pauling had seen from the limousine. The moon and stars above them were held like ice sculptures in a frozen universe, but it was hot on the ground. Once outside Smith's air-conditioned limousine, Pauling had begun to sweat. There were both flower and rock gardens on the terraces. Fake Japanese, Pauling thought.

They arrived at a long flight of wide stone stairs with risers of only four or five inches. They went up quickly toward a wide patio and a porch beyond. While they were crossing the patio, they were distinct shapes in the moonlight. They went across the porch to a wide oak door. Pauling put his finger on the bell.

Immediately, the door was opened. Light poured onto the porch, onto the patio, and down the stone steps, throwing the shadows of the men back the way they had come.

The woman standing there was about thirty and too thin. She looked pretty but unhealthy. "I demand to know what is going on?" she said. "Who are you people? Why won't you let my husband leave his own home?"

"Mrs. Reese?" Pauling said.

An agent Pauling had never seen before was standing behind the woman holding a squawk box. He was staring at Mason.

"That's right," the woman said. "I asked you a question! I want to know who you are, and why you won't let my husband leave. Are you CIA?"

"No. Where is your husband, Mrs. Reese?"

"I insist on seeing your credentials."

Pauling said, "We'll show them to your husband, Mrs. Reese."

"You'll show them to me."

Pauling walked past her into the house and up to the man with the squawk box. Mason followed.

"Where's Reese?" Pauling asked the man.

"Now look here!" Mrs. Reese said.

The man nodded toward a flight of stairs.

"He's not alone?"

"No, sir."

The flight of stairs curved to a landing on the second story. A door opened on the landing. The man Mason had described to Smith came out to stare down at them. A bulky man, Feldman, came out right behind him.

"Reese!" Pauling said.

"Yes! Who are you?"

"Pauling. Thomas Pauling. Where can we talk?"

"What about?"

"This is outrageous!" Mrs. Reese said.

"Where?" Pauling asked again.

"Go to hell!" Reese said. He went back into the room above the landing and almost slammed the door before Feldman stopped him from doing it and followed.

Pauling turned to Mrs. Reese. "Are there servants?"

She didn't answer.

Pauling looked at the man with the squawk box.

"There are servants asleep, maybe, in an apartment over

the garage. There's a man keeping them there. No one else. No kids at home."

"Where do you think you're going?" Mrs. Reese said.

Pauling, Mason close behind him, had started toward the stairs. Mrs. Reese ran after them. "I want to see your credentials!"

They went up the stairs in a line—Pauling, Mason, and Mrs. Reese—and at the top of the stairs, Mason turned and held her back.

"Goddamn it!" she said in a hoarse whisper. When Pauling turned to look at her, she was close to tears.

"Go away," Pauling said. "Go somewhere where you won't be tempted to interfere. Your husband may or may not have a connection to the nuclear detonation in California last night."

"What!?"

"Go away, Mrs. Reese."

"You're insane!"

"No, I'm not, Mrs. Reese."

The woman took a step back.

"Go away," Pauling told her again. "I'm sorry."

She turned and started down the stairs. She looked back only once. Then she went all the way down. They watched her cross the front room and disappear into a sunken living room, followed by the man with the squawk box.

Pauling said, "Give me five minutes. Then I want to hear one shot." He was speaking very quietly. "After the shot, I don't want to hear anything."

Mason nodded.

Pauling went to the door behind which Reese had disappeared. He knocked on it.

"Come in," someone said; not Reese, Pauling guessed.

Pauling let himself in. A moment later Feldman let himself out, closed the door behind him, and went to stand outside on the patio under the moon and stars.

/ 5 /

For a long while Pauling just took him in. He looked a less likely villain than he would have imagined. Pauling wanted time to bring his intelligence to bear against the man's face and form, the stuff of his self and consciousness; he wanted to be able to remain implacable later to whatever the man would use to keep the extent of his greed even from himself. There wasn't going to be any safe place to back into once this started. And Pauling wanted to take in the setting: a well-stocked library, walnut paneling, leather-bound books, a long teak desk. He came back to the man himself. Yes, his complexion was pitted, but not as badly as Pauling had assumed when Mason described him.

"It'll make things less complicated," Pauling said, "if you cooperate. You're beaten, Reese. So is Harriman. You've gambled and lost."

Pauling had taken a seat in front of the desk; Reese was seated behind it. There was a large globe near Reese and statuary—authentic pieces no doubt—mostly Chinese, mostly on the shelves of the bookcases immediately behind Reese's head. There was a horse Grace Argent would have liked.

"Who the hell are you?" Reese said very softly. "And what do you want?"

"I think what will happen now is that the less intelligent you are, the longer you'll hold out," Pauling said. "A man's wife is a help in times like these. It's easier to see your guilt in her eyes than in yours. But there wasn't any need to confirm it."

"What guilt?" Reese asked. He clenched his teeth. "What have I done, exactly? All I can guess I've done, my friend, is make money."

"That's right. About ten million so far, in various markets, through various brokers and corporate fronts. It's estimated you could make as much as two billion if the markets break.

There's a strong feeling they'll do just that if there's any more trouble, another bomb, another Detroit."

"I should have known it was too much," Reese said. "I got *too* lucky."

Pauling didn't even smile. He said, "This is the way things are going to go now, Mr. Reese. I have no doubt, even less than your wife has, that you knew the stock market, the dollar market, every American stock and bond would crack. You knew it because someone—probably Mark Harriman—told you just how it was going to be made to happen. Harriman isn't a market analyst, he's a psychiatrist; so you may have even helped him work out the details. How much to destroy, how far to go, how to space the occurrences."

"Absurd," Reese said.

"Of course. But I believe it. That's what counts, and that's what's going to count for the rest of your natural life. Mr. Reese, the operation I'm referring to has probably been financed by a foreign power. I realize no money of yours may actually have gone to Harriman. Funding was also available from an international terrorist group run by someone we call Field Marshal—you've heard of Field Marshal?"

Reese did not reply.

"But that doesn't matter," Pauling said. "What matters is you're part of it, part of a conspiracy. It's already killed thousands. It possesses at least three more atomic devices that could kill millions within the next weeks, days, hours, or minutes. And here's a personal note, Reese; my wife has been captured, or killed, by your people."

"You're insane!" Reese said. "I don't have any people!"

"Of course," Pauling replied. "But in the face of that number of possible deaths—add to that my desire to find my wife if she is alive, or my own disgust for you if she is not—this is what we get: you're now going to talk to me. You're going to tell me everything there is to tell. You're going to begin by telling me where the operation is now headquartered. *Now,* Reese, or I'm going to kill you, slowly and painfully."

"Insane!" Reese shouted. "You're called! Go on! You're called!"

"Very slowly," Pauling said. "Very damn slowly."

"I said you're called!"

Pauling stood up and removed the automatic from the holster under his suit coat. He moved to Reese's side of the desk.

"Well," Reese said.

Pauling liked Reese's pants. They were a lightweight glen plaid. He liked his shirt too. He hadn't seen a button-down with that long and sharp a collar in some time. Reese probably had shirts made especially for him.

"How much did you go short with, Reese? About a million?"

"Yes, about a million. I thought I was being smart."

"Nice try," Pauling said. "Who did he say had bought the plan, the Shah? The Saudis? The director of the CIA favors the Chinese. Or did he give you the terrorist line too?"

Reese licked his lips. Pauling's automatic was pointing between his thighs.

When the shot came Reese jumped back so hard his chair rammed the bookshelves. A jade statue of a Chinese monk fell over and cracked. They both heard it crack. But the shot had come from downstairs, not from Pauling's weapon.

"Christ!" Reese said.

"Did you really think you were going to get out of this with your statues intact?"

"What was that shot?"

"We gave your wife a chance to get out of it gracefully."

Reese was sweating, but he laughed. He looked into Pauling's eyes and laughed at him.

"You're called," Reese said again.

"Too bad," Pauling said.

He shot Reese in the right thigh. The sound was terrific in the closed room. He must have hit a vein, because a spout of blood appeared immediately, rose a half a foot, and subsided.

Reese's face went white. His mouth hung slack. It wouldn't take any time for the pain to become intense.

"Did you think the Bill of Rights was going to help you? There are millions of lives at stake! You're the one who's insane, Reese. Did you know about the bombs?"

Reese's eyes had opened to about twice the size they had been before Pauling shot. He said nothing.

"Listen carefully. This is a .45-caliber machine. They won't ever be able to put your hand back. It won't ever work again."

Pauling pulled the trigger for the second time. The shot went through the base of Reese's left hand. Reese had been gripping his chair. This time there was less blood. It formed a pool immediately where the bullet had torn through a large chunk of flesh and bone.

"What do you say, Reese?" Pauling said. "The other hand? Or the right foot? Or the left one? An Achilles tendon? A hamstring?"

"Oh no," Reese said. "They won't let you . . . they'll come now and stop you. They don't know you're doing this. I have friends. Someone will—"

A surge of pain must have reached him. His face, white before, went even paler. He gasped for air. Pauling raised his weapon for a third time, pointing it at Reese's shoulder bone.

"Where are they, Reese?" Pauling asked.

"All right! For the love of God! All right," Reese said. "They're in a private clinic in Wellesley. I bought it for them a year ago. It's called the Avery Clinic. Is my wife all right?"

Pauling nodded. "She's all right."

"Get me to a doctor!"

Pauling stepped back. "Is *my* wife all right, Reese?"

"I don't know! I don't know! I have no connection with them, none. All I do is put a call through every day, so they know I'm all right. Then I wait for word."

"Word of what? The bottom?"

"Yes! *Get me to a doctor!* I'm losing blood!"

"Of course," Pauling said. He walked to the door, took the stairs down to the first floor and went outside. He found Feldman on the first terrace looking across at Manhattan. Feldman had his walkie-talkie out, and Pauling took it from him.

"John?"

"Yes. Thomas? Is that you?"

"Yes. You can have a medical team sent in."

"You were right?"

"Yes."

There was a long pause, then Smith said, "Where do we go now?"

"Drop a chopper down here and come on up and meet me."

Pauling switched off the walkie-talkie. He handed it back to Feldman. Before he was back inside the house, he could hear the chopper beating the air far overhead. It must have been waiting for some time.

/ 6 /

The chopper lifted off the patio, flattening flowers and shrubbery. Within seconds it was moving at high speed toward the sky north of Manhattan. Smith was strapped in beside the pilot and was shouting into the radio. Gold and Pauling were strapped in just behind.

"Wellesley . . . That's right . . . Find a place called the Avery Clinic, set up at least a mile away . . . Surveille it from as far away as you can . . . Radio back your position . . . A-V-E-R-Y . . . Yes!"

Pauling watched and waited. He stared at his hands and wondered why they weren't shaking. He looked at Gold in the seat next to him and tried to be encouraged by her smile.

It was over an hour before the pilot brought his aircraft down into the field where the task-force Cherokee had landed. Pinpoint lights had been set, directed toward the sky. There were seven new Ford sedans in the dark on the shoulder of the road and Special Forces soldiers near each. The cars had been commandeered from the local Hertz garage by the police and driven to the rendezvous a half hour before.

Pauling was out of the helicopter first. He hurried to the Cherokee where a Special Forces colonel and a man in civilian clothes were peering at a map. Smith was right behind him.

"I'm Pauling. This is Smith."

"Yes, sir," the colonel said. "I'm Cabot. This is Police Chief Decker. If you'll look here, gentlemen." The colonel held a flash on the map spread against the side of the Cherokee. "We're here, on this dirt road. The clinic is on the highway on the far side of these woods, here."

Smith said, "Pauling will be with your assault unit. We don't expect heavy resistance. There may be prisoners in there. No one is to be shot who isn't armed."

"Yes, sir," the colonel said. "That's understood."

"All right," Smith said, "it's your ball game, Thomas."

Pauling nodded. "My wife may be in there, Colonel. I'll be in the first car."

A lieutenant appeared at the colonel's side. "Sir!"

"Yes?"

"Sir, a light plane is taxiing across the field behind the clinic. It was in a hangar near the woods."

Pauling spun on the colonel. "You cut their communications?"

"No!"

"Damn it! He tried to get through to Reese, failed, and he's running."

"What do you want us to do to that plane, Mr. Pauling."

"Let it take off," Pauling said. "Don't destroy it. You can stay with it in that chopper no matter where it goes, can't you?"

"Yes, sir," the colonel said. "Lieutenant."

The lieutenant ran to give the chopper pilot his orders. As

the chopper lifted off the ground, the lieutenant, the police chief, Smith, and the colonel backed away. Pauling ran toward the first of the cars.

"Let's go!" the colonel yelled.

The troops were climbing into the commandeered cars. Pauling got into the front of the first one and turned to the driver.

"All right, son, let's go."

The driver took off down the dirt road.

"A right when you find the highway," Pauling said.

"Yes, sir."

They spun onto the highway and went speeding down a clear road between trees in heavy foliage. Pauling turned and saw the other cars behind them. He could hear the sound of the Cherokee overhead. The two soldiers in the back seat looked like children, he thought. Both were armed with M-16's.

"Shoot at no one who isn't armed," Pauling said.

"Yes, sir," the driver answered.

Pauling was watching the road again.

"All right, that's it!" he shouted. "Jump the shoulder, soldier, and go right for the front entrance."

"Yes, *sir!*"

The trees on their side of the road had given way to the lawn where the clinic was set. The driver turned onto the lawn. He was heading for the front of the building and the double glass doors.

"Right through those doors, soldier!"

"Yes, sir!"

A helicopter, the one Pauling had come in, was descending at the back of the clinic. Pauling's Ford bounced up the single cement step toward the glass doors. The Ford crashed into the lobby. Pauling had the automatic out. He opened the car door and rolled onto the ground as an armed man—one of Harriman's bodyguards—came through double doors on his right. Pauling shot him through the temple.

Pauling rose to see his driver fall to the car floor to avoid a burst of automatic fire from a corridor to the left. The fire was answered by the soldiers in the rear seat. While other soldiers ran into the building through the demolished doors, Pauling found a stairway and raced up.

He heard the lieutenant shout. "You two stay on the entrance. You come with me. You down that way, that's right."

Pauling ran along a corridor, looking into each room as he had at 400 Brattle. A door opened, and she was standing there with light behind her, in a hospital gown, pale.

"Thomas!"

"Holy God, you're all right!"

"Yes!"

He grabbed her and lifted her into his arms. He carried her into the room, put her down, and went to the window to pull back the blinds.

Soldiers had taken up positions in the field and were turning portable lights against the building. The colonel rushed into the room.

"Is this your wife?"

"Yes, Colonel." Pauling was beaming.

"The place is secured, Mr. Pauling."

"Good. Marcia?"

"It's Harriman," Marcia said. "There's a computer in the basement that uses Berger's voice, but it's Harriman. Facett helped me as much as she could. She's all right. They've got Berger drugged."

Pauling nodded.

The lieutenant came into the room and said, "Colonel, two men with automatic weapons have been killed. Three other people taken captive. We took no casualties, but there's something down the hall you should see."

"Facett!" Marcia said. She started for the door. The lieutenant led them to a room, and they went in.

"Christ," the colonel said.

Rita Facett was hanging from a man's belt she had rigged over a closet door. Her body was limp, her face swollen, her lips and tongue greatly exaggerated. Pauling found a note on the bureau beside her bed.

Berger and I blackmailed Harriman into helping us. For Field Marshal and Interface.

As Pauling handed the note to Marcia, another soldier rushed into the room and stopped at the sight of Facett's body.

"What is it?" the colonel asked.

"The plane, sir. It's heading toward Boston. It won't respond to the helicopter's orders, sir."

"Tell the chopper pilot to stay with it," the colonel said.

"She did it for her son," Marcia said. She was still staring at the note. "So Harriman wouldn't kill her son. She felt so unnecessarily guilty having abandoned him."

In the basement they found the doctor, his wife, and Levine. All three were being held at gunpoint near the computer. Smith was there with Gold. The doctor looked pale and confused. When Pauling appeared, he appealed to him immediately.

"My wife and I know nothing about what this man and Dr. Harriman have been doing. Nothing!"

Levine was smiling stupidly. "They'll go crazy now, of course," he said softly. "When they can't get in touch with Harold, they'll go berserk."

Pauling pushed him hard against one of the machines. "Where are the vans?"

Levine laughed. "What vans? Everything is in the machine, somewhere, but it's all coded."

"Easy, Thomas," Smith said. "It's the same code they used at Four Hundred Brattle, on the tapes you saved, it has to be. We broke it days ago. There's a computer team flying in."

Pauling let out a vast amount of air. "You've checked for a bomb?"

"Yes. They had to leave too quickly."

"They?"

"Dr. Harriman, Dr. Berger, and Lawrence Douglas," the doctor said.

Pauling bit his lower lip. Something bothered him. He put it aside and took Marcia the hell out of there.

/ 7 /

The raids hit simultaneously, shortly before dawn. Special Forces troops came in both entrances at once, moving away the front door with a small charge, destroying the back door with a grenade. They knew it was the right house; it was the address yielded by the computer in Wellesley to the CIA personnel flown in from Washington. Army Intelligence had double-checked by verifying the descriptions of the occupants with groggy neighbors.

Carl heard the explosions, jumped naked out of a cot in the small middle upstairs bedroom, grabbed an automatic pistol from the floor, leaped down the stairs to a landing three steps above the dining room. He wanted to get out the rearmost window of the downstairs and to the garage to set off the van. He got a shower of slugs in his abdomen from an M-16. He doubled over and fell on his face.

Stephen grabbed his flack jacket. Wearing it and nothing else, he launched himself to the sill of the second-story rear bedroom window and through the wood and glass. Perhaps he thought his ability to disregard pain, to reach high levels of consciousness, would prevent his legs from breaking when he lighted on the cement fifteen feet below, that he would be able to make it to the garage, set the three dials, and blow Brooklyn into the stratosphere. He never got off the sill.

He was caught full in the window by a high-intensity spotlight and by the same kind of rifle fire that killed Carl. Stephen was hurled back into the room by the hail of bullets against his flack jacket, back against the inside wall; blood spurted from his face and neck and groin. His smile, permanent this time, the rictus of death.

In the garage, a team of experts from Nevada raised the camouflage curtain, found the brown van. The man who removed the charge was dressed in a white suit, white two-inch-thick asbestos gloves, and a glass helmet. When he finished, he smiled as broadly as Stephen in the upstairs bedroom. Sweat was pouring off the man's face so fast he might have stepped out from under a waterfall. He placed the charge into a lead-lined box, closed it, and took off his helmet. He walked to the middle of the small backyard. He removed his gloves. After considerable difficulty with his white suit, he relieved himself on the lawn.

In Washington John and Jean Harcourt's door offered less resistance than had the one in Brooklyn. It blew into the living room of the small apartment like a playing card. In poured five Special Forces soldiers. They hit the Harcourts with automatic fire aimed at their heads as the couple appeared, armed, in the doorway of their bedroom. The Harcourts were dead within seconds. They never had a chance to display their abilities or their dedication to the man for whom they did everything: Harold Berger.

Their van too was disarmed. It had been hidden inside a Mayflower truck like the one the Cubans used to hide their recoilless rifles. The charge was lifted out like the rib out of Adam.

But New Orleans presented a problem. At precisely the same moment the explosive charges were going off in Brooklyn and Washington, blowing away the doors between the Special Forces troops and Carl, Stephen, and the Harcourts, a New Orleans SWAT unit was breaking into an apartment on the Esplanade. According to Harriman's computer, Caroline should have been inside it, but when the SWAT team rushed in off a balcony into a series of connecting rooms that had once been slave quarters, no one was home.

Worse, the white-suited expert from Nevada whose job it was to disarm Caroline's van found himself staring at thousands of cartons containing tins of chicory. There was no van in the warehouse where, according to the decoded tapes, Caroline was supposed to have hidden it.

Smith and Pauling decided New Orleans would be lost. From the helicopter returning them to Washington, five minutes after the raids against the remaining Mark II's, Smith radioed the White House to recommend that New Orleans be evacuated.

/ 8 /

McGraw knew nothing of the proposed evacuation or of Pauling's success in Wellesley. He was standing at a third-story hotel window, his hand in his sport-coat pocket, staring across Royal Street. There was an unpleasant odor in the room, like that of stale tobacco and cabbage, but McGraw didn't mind. He was just where he wanted to be.

Caroline had not made it difficult for him to follow her after she left Maxie's. She had gone right from the strip joint to a hotel just across the street, and she hadn't yet come out. Maybe he was getting lucky.

Grant was stretched out on the bed behind him. He was supposed to be sleeping, but he was staring at the ceiling.

"What time is it?" he asked McGraw.

"Five twenty."

The small squawk box clipped to Grant's belt sputtered. He struggled, got it loose, lifted it to his face. "Yeah?"

"We just got word, Chief. A SWAT unit broke into an apartment on the Esplanade and into a warehouse out along Canal. The apartment was empty. The warehouse was full of chicory."

"No van?"

"No van."

"All right. Cowell, you there? You still watching the back? Everything calm?"

"Yes, Chief."

"All right. Keep your eyes open."

Grant put the squawk box back on his belt.

"She's gone maverick on them," McGraw said.

"What?"

"She's not following orders from her control. Something must have made her suspicious. Maybe something they did. Maybe she's going to blow up the town."

"Let's go in and get her."

McGraw was still looking out the window. "Then we'll never find the van," he said. "You want to leave it sitting out there?"

"Okay. Okay."

The sky over the buildings across the street was beginning to give way to dawn. There were fewer cars moving through the streets than there had been immediately after the army arrived, but there were some; people were still leaving town. At least there had been no panic; at least a few thousand were safely away.

McGraw's face hurt. He was bone tired. He could have gone along with Grant. He could have agreed to pick up the suspect. Then he could have taken a shower and gone to bed.

Grant's walkie-talkie squawked again. The voice McGraw had learned was Cowell's said, "Frizzy hair, about forty, maybe thirty-five, stocky . . . smiling."

"That's her."

"She came out the back door. Here she comes."

"Right. Here we come, too."

McGraw was already at the door. They ran out, down the stairs, past a sleeping desk clerk, and down another steep flight into the street. They hurried to the corner.

Grant's squawk box said, "She's gone past, heading toward the markets."

"Stay back. Stay way back," Grant said.

"Let's go," McGraw said.

They jogged to the corner, turned it, and had her in sight. She was passing an eight-foot wall, then a tall iron fence that separated the narrow sidewalk from an overgrown garden. She crossed to the other side where the houses were built flush with the sidewalk. McGraw and Grant ducked back around the corner.

"She's going toward the markets, all right," Grant said into his box.

"Got it," someone answered.

"You mean to the river," McGraw said. "The levee could be the target; maybe it's been the target all along. If the blast is close enough to the levee, the river might do as much damage as the explosion."

McGraw stuck his head out. When he caught sight of Caroline turning another corner, he started to run after her again. Grant stayed with him. McGraw got to the corner in time to see her turn into an alley.

"I'll take her," McGraw said. "You stay here and set up your men. Don't be long coming after me."

McGraw didn't wait for an answer. He went into the alley with no more hesitation than he had gone into the alley in Detroit before it all started.

It was no more than five feet wide. There were no lights, not even a glow from a bulb over an exit. On either side the warehouses stood like stone giants. McGraw thought of David and Martin and how you don't stop these people easily. You shoot at them. You keep shooting until you hit them in the head.

He started down the alley, listening carefully, his senses reaching out and coming up with nothing but dark and a feeling that the warehouses, the alley, had been there for cen-

turies. Then he saw a light pass swiftly across a high window
on his right, and he knew where she was.

He found a door and pushed against it. It was locked. She
was more careful than David had been. He got out his pick,
cleared his throat, and went to work. It seemed to take forever.
Finally he got it open and went inside. He left the door open
for Grant to find.

She had to have enough time to set the charge and get out.
It didn't figure that she was a suicide, not unless she thought
she was cornered. If she did, he had bought it, and so had
a lot of other people.

He used his pen flash and found he was in a small office
with a chair, a desk, and a bulletin board cluttered with *Play-
boy* centerfolds. There was a door behind the desk. He turned
off the flash and went through it.

He found the stairs Caroline must have used. He went up.
The steps creaked. He figured Grant would come after him
in a minute. He could stall her for just a little while, talk to
her about David maybe or Martin.

He got to the top of the stairs and pushed in on a fire door.
It was as dark as it had been downstairs, but this time he
didn't use the flash. He stepped into an enormous room with
a tiny red light about forty yards away. The light gave it an
eerie glow, the foyer to hell. He took a step forward.

Caroline hit him from behind with a length of two-by-four
that had been used to prop open the fire door. She hit him so
solidly on the neck and head, his head rang and kept ringing.
It felt as though his tongue had been launched out of his body.
He reeled, fell, and lay on the dusty floor.

She knelt over him, found his gun, and ripped it out of his
holster. With one hand, she turned him over.

He stared up wide-eyed, unable to close his mouth, his
head vibrating as if it had been a tuning fork all these years
and he had only just found out. Pain came like the cannon
in the *1812 Overture*. She stared right back at him.

His eyes were still wide, glazed, and teared. She smiled.

Goddamn, if only she hadn't smiled. She took his gun and aimed it at his forehead.

"You're pretty damn strong," McGraw said. "I'm not that light."

Her expression didn't change.

"Listen, honey, Harold says . . ."

She smashed him on the temple with the barrel. She hit him so hard, it set up a new and contrary set of vibrations from the vibrations caused by the two-by-four. For a full second he felt nothing, nothing at all. The one pain canceled the other. Then the pain doubled over what it had been at first. Blood streamed into his right eye.

"Don't shoot him," Caroline said aloud. "Too much noise."

It was as if she were giving herself orders. She raised the revolver to strike him again.

He closed his eyes, let his head roll, let out his air, and lay limp.

She didn't hit him. She got up and moved away. He opened his eyes to watch. Only the left one worked. He saw her dark form go toward the red light and disappear where shadows reached the roof. He rolled over and crawled after her.

For what felt like a long while, he was unable to lift his head at all. He kept going anyway. Soon he found himself pressed against a forklift. He had once driven a forklift. Struggling against the pain, he hauled himself into a standing position. Grabbing hold of the machine, he got one foot up on it. He hoisted himself into the seat.

When his head cleared, he found he was staring, one-eyed, at ten-foot stacks of burlap sacks on wooden pallets. Feed, probably. Since that was the way Caroline had gone, he guessed the van was in there. It had to be. It must have been brought up on a freight elevator and hidden behind the burlap sacks.

He started the forklift and headed for the stack in front of him. He dropped the forks, slid them into the pallet, lifted them six inches, and backed up. His head was still rocking with pain. The blood had not stopped pouring into his right eye. When he had pulled the stack back a few feet, he went right so he could get a look without turning his head.

Caroline was there. She had the van door open. She was playing with the knobs. He couldn't see her face, but he knew she was smiling. He dropped the forks, backed free of the pile, spun the machine, and went for her.

McGraw almost got her with the machine before she side-stepped. He swerved it at her and jumped. She had to move to avoid the lift. She turned the gun on him and fired. The bullet hit him high in the back, but he kept going anyway. He reached the back of the van. He found the knobs. He stared at them with his left eye and turned the one on the right where it had to go. She fired again. There was a tearing pain in his left arm. He got the other knob right. There was another shot and another tearing pain, this one in his lungs, like someone had put in a red-hot poker and twisted it. He never heard the next shot. He lost consciousness and fell.

Caroline was no longer smiling. She had allowed herself to become angry, but she knew what she had to do. She put herself into a higher trance state—total—so that she could accomplish what she set out to accomplish no matter what. McGraw had prevented the charge from entering the chamber with the bulk of the fissionable material. She had to remove the charge, put it back in the case, place the case back in in reverse, and reset the knobs.

What Caroline didn't know was that McGraw had stopped the charge from entering the cavity and completing the critical mass only after the bomb door had opened. The charge was turning red hot. If left there a few moments longer, it would yield a fizzle blast—a blast which would level the warehouse at least, and probably let the river into New Orleans.

She went to the side of the van, opened the door, opened the compartment under the seat, and withdrew the suitcase. The side of the case that had been closest to the bomb cavity was open; the case was empty. She placed it on the warehouse floor. She reached in for the charge.

She withdrew the charge and bent to replace it in the case. In all probability her actions were futile, the bomb would no longer function, but Caroline willed herself to try. She kicked the heavy case until the open side faced her. She knelt to put in the charge. As she knelt, she noticed that her fingers were giving off smoke. She dropped the charge.

Her palms and the tips of her fingers were entirely burned away. She was staring at blood, raw flesh, and bone.

Shocked, Caroline came out of total. She screamed. She screamed very loudly. She screamed again.

She wanted to kill herself. She looked for McGraw's gun. It was on the floor. She reached for it, but her fingers would not close around it. Men were coming at her across the warehouse floor. She saw them as her salvation. She charged at them, screaming: *"I'll kill you!"*

Kneeling to take aim, Grant put a bullet into her right eye. She spun and fell. The pain stopped.

/ 9 /

The Paulings had once watched the president give a fireside chat from the room where they were seated on one of a pair of long white couches. White curtains were drawn back across tall windows on the far side of the room. The director, Nelson, was standing before them in the morning sun, delivering his report. The president was standing before the fireplace. John Smith was seated in the chair the president had occupied when the cameras were in the room.

"The emergency is over. There are no Mark II's left alive. The terrorists in New York were rounded up over an hour ago. The explosive devices they installed in the World Trade Center —in the uptown one—are being dealt with now. The New Orleans terrorists were captured in a small town called Bayou LaForge. They were responsible for West Depford, and we have them all. The Mark II's corresponded in number to those on the agency files—Harriman wanted to take no unnecessary chance that we would find a discrepancy between his reports and what he was actually doing until he was ready to act—so we have them all accounted for too."

"Are you absolutely sure about the number of Mark II's?" the president asked.

In his seat beside Marcia on the couch, Pauling took out a blue pack of Gauloises he had bought in Zurich the day before, took out the last cigarette, looked at it, then threw it and the pack into a leather wastebasket near an end table.

"We're sure," Nelson said. "We have verification from the tapes that we found at the clinic, from the tapes Pauling rescued from Four Hundred Brattle Street, from captured personnel, especially from the man Levine."

"Levine?" the president said.

"Yes, sir. Levine was the computer operator Harriman used exclusively once he'd gone into action against us. Levine tried to become a Weldmore agent and failed. A large number failed. But he responded well to narcosynthesis, to Facett's techniques. His background included work for IBM at Poughkeepsie, so Harriman used him in that capacity."

"He was not a Mark II."

"No, we were able to bring him down just by withholding his drugs. He broke and he's still talking to our people. He's able to remember almost everything."

"And the head of the project?"

"Berger is dead. One of the corpses in the wreck of the private plane that escaped from Wellesley was his."

"Whose were the others?"

"There was only one other. Lawrence Douglas. The plane took off just as we were moving against the clinic. The pilot, Douglas, would not respond when we tried to force him down or when we threatened to shoot him down. In the end we had to destroy them to prevent him from becoming a kamikaze. He was heading for Boston."

The president grimaced.

"Of course," Pauling said.

The president turned to look at him.

"The plane was only a diversion! He fooled us. He walked away through the woods. He must have had a car parked on some back road or at a house."

"Of course," Smith echoed.

The president said, "You're referring to Harriman?"

Pauling nodded.

"Go on." The president was looking at Nelson again.

"I was saying Berger was dead. Facett was the third executive-level personnel. She hanged herself, I guess to save her son. She took the blame on herself and Berger to conciliate Harriman. She was under great pressure. But it was a useless death. We've got the boy."

The president was not cheered by this news either.

Nelson went on. "Grace Argent was told about the boy by Mrs. Pauling. His adoptive parents are in her constituency. She is on her way to Albany, New York, right now, to help look after him and to deliver him personally to his parents. She had him taken to Albany after he was rescued from a farm in Colrain, Massachusetts. The people who were holding him have all been arrested."

"Sometimes I wish someone would do the same for Argent," the president said.

Pauling laughed.

"Nelson, is there no possibility that Facett was telling the truth in her suicide note?" the president asked.

"No, sir. Berger was heavily drugged. His voice was recorded for a sophisticated, computerized response system that answered the agent's phone calls. Harriman set Berger up as a godhead for the Mark II's. We don't have all the details of their programming, but Harriman obviously found it easier or more practicable, maybe both, to set someone else up as head man and remain a kind of prime minister."

The president nodded. "The vans, Nelson?"

"There were five. Forensic techniques, which were used all night at the farm where the bombs were manufactured, verify that number. So does a bill of sale from a Ford dealer in New York City where the vans were purchased. Five, sir, as Thomas's people said from the beginning. All five are accounted for."

Pauling spoke again, "McGraw almost died accounting for the last of them. He was shot four times. He's in critical condition at Charity Hospital in New Orleans."

The president came over to sit down on the couch opposite the Paulings.

"You look tired, Thomas," the president said.

Pauling laughed again.

"I'm glad as hell you've got her back."

Marcia smiled.

The president was still somber. "What about Harriman, Thomas?"

Nelson answered. "We'll pick him up. The FBI, police across the country, are alerted."

Marcia said, "There's nothing Harriman can do now except go to ground. Instead of picking him up, why not let him leave the country?"

Everyone stared at her.

Finally Pauling said, "Marcia's right. Only Harriman knows who financed him—what country. There wasn't enough terrorist money to set all that up and still leave enough for him. He'd want a great deal. He would have wanted a great deal before he began. The Reese angle, the market angle, was his largest but not his only line of profit. From the beginning we've known we were at war with someone. We need to know who."

Nelson made a face as if he wasn't quite happy with Pauling, but he said, "Yes. I agree."

"It doesn't make sense any other way," Pauling said. "It wasn't Carlos to whom Harriman had his first loyalty, or even his second loyalty. No gains were made by the terrorists. The demands came late and were only meant as a ploy to help panic the country and set up his market hopes. Just as we conjectured, those bombs weren't necessarily meant to go off, not all of them certainly. Harriman's interest in the American economy was too great. He wanted to drive the markets well below the real strength of the country, and when Reese had taken his short profits and established a bullish position and bought up as much depressed stock and as many dollars as possible, he'd have created a bottom by giving up the remaining terrorists and the remaining bombs. Panic was what Harriman wanted, but it probably wasn't what the country behind him wanted. They probably wanted to come to the assistance of a weakened America, just as we once came to the assistance of most of Europe."

"Panic." The president threw that word back at Pauling as John Smith might have done.

Smith said, "Thomas, why are you so sure Harriman wanted extreme wealth?"

"Because he programmed those Mark II's by using insights gained from mysticism. I've read of such things and men have talked to me about them, men I met when I was in Vietnam. If Harriman was, is, an adept himself, in Zen or Yoga or Sufi or Tantra, no idealistic cause would move him. Even a perverted mysticism wouldn't hold with the value of ideas. That left compassion, ascetic inversion of a kind I don't really understand—sitting in a cave I mean—sensuality, or . . . a game. I think Harriman was playing the biggest game he could find. He would know he'd won only if he made a great deal of money."

No one interrupted him, so he continued. "He allowed himself to be bought, or offered himself for sale, to a foreign power. He seduced Field Marshal through his Mark II. Finally he went to his old friend Reese and told him what was about to happen. That's when he greatly multiplied his possible profit. No foreign power would be interested in a short-term gain on the various markets, so room was left for Harriman to make a personal fortune. Two billion means nothing to the Japanese or to the Saudis or even to the Shah, but that's what Reese's companies might have made, according to people in Zurich."

"Two billion," the president said.

"With an initial investment of only a million," John Smith told him. "Consolidating and expanding his position as the market went down. Turning about-face just before Harriman surrendered his people or gave up the bombs."

"Where is Reese now?" the president asked.

"In a hospital in New York City," Nelson said, "both he and his wife."

"Incommunicado?"

"Yes."

"Perhaps Harriman will try to reach him."

"Doubtful," Nelson said.

The president looked at Marcia and then at Pauling. "I'm sorry about your agents in Boston. I hope McGraw pulls through. There was another of your friends, Thomas . . ."

"Balke," Pauling said. "Yes. He died in California."

The president pounded his right fist into his left hand. "Thomas, I want you to know I'm not crazy about your analysis of Harriman's motives, but your overall view brought us success, so it deserves another look."

Pauling said nothing.

"What it comes to is this," the president said. "I absolutely must know whom we were fighting. I want to know who bought Harriman, to whom he sold himself."

Nelson said, "If you want a guess, I'd say—"

"I don't want a guess. I want to know! I want proof."

Nelson nodded. "We'll find out, sir."

Pauling was shaking his head. "Harriman would have been careful to leave a false trail, maybe several. Those trails will be hard to find, but not impossible. The real one may be."

The president stared at him.

"Harriman didn't make a single mistake. He fooled the CIA, turned an entire program against us. Brilliance, nothing less, enabled him to succeed. We may never find the country he worked for."

"Thomas, I'd like you to help with that."

"I'll have to consider it," Pauling said.

He got a nod from the president and stood up. Finally the president got to his feet too and shook hands, first with Smith, who had also risen, then with Nelson. When he took Marcia's hand, he held it for several moments. Then he took Pauling's.

"Will you both come to dinner next week. Tuesday?" Around seven? And you have . . . a son?"

Pauling nodded.

Marcia said, "Thomas has three sons by a former marriage. Only one is living with us now. He's seventeen."

"Bring him! Bring him! And we'll have the Nelsons and . . ." He turned to Smith.

"Certainly," Smith said.

Nelson nodded. "Fine, sir."

"Sir?" Pauling said.

The president stepped back. "Yes, Thomas."

"I've had extraordinary expenses. There's a pension for Balke's wife, for the families of the men I lost in Boston. Mc-Graw's hospital costs will be large. Then there's my usual fee for—"

"Of course!" the president said.

"I'm going to send the country a bill," Pauling said. "It won't be small."

"Of course! Of course!"

Pauling laughed, and so did Marcia. Nelson and Smith laughed, and so did the chief executive. But the Paulings laughed all the way home.